# JUST A KISS

## CARRIE ELKS

**Just A Kiss by Carrie Elks**

**Copyright © 2019 by Carrie Elks**

**2210193**

**All rights reserved.**

This book is a work of fiction. The characters, events, and places portrayed in this book are products of the author's imagination. Any similarity to persons living or dead is purely coincidental.

# JOIN ME!

I would love you to join me on my exclusive mailing list, where you'll be the first to hear about new releases, sales, and other book-related news. Even better, by signing up you'll receive an EXCLUSIVE novelette, not available anywhere else.

To download your book and sign up for my mailing list GO HERE https://dl.bookfunnel.com/j9zzdveqiw

Thanks for reading! Carrie xx

recken Miller stomped the dust from his black leather construction boots and pushed open the door to Déjà Brew. Almost immediately the aroma of coffee and pastries spilled out, mixing in with the salty ozone rising up from the Atlantic Ocean. It wasn't even eight in the morning but the coffee shop was already busy – full of commuters and tourists inhaling their first caffeine shots of the morning.

Behind the counter, Ally Sutton raised her hand in greeting. He waved in return, a grin curling his lips. He'd been back in the small beach town of Angel Sands for almost six months now, but he was still getting used to everybody knowing who he was. He shouldn't have been so shocked that everybody remembered him from when he was a kid, but he'd been living in Boston for most of his adult life. Yet as soon as he'd stepped foot back in Angel Sands, thirteen years since he'd last been here, he'd found himself surrounded by old friends.

As he joined the six-person line for coffee, Breck stared out of the huge picture window facing the beach. Water was lapping against the sand like a lazy cat, the waves big enough to attract the early morning surfers out on their boards, but not so choppy they provided much of a challenge.

"A latte and a coffee donut, please," the man in front of him ordered. Breck leaned on the counter and idly sorted through the leaflets different companies had placed there. A new car cleaning service that offered the first wash for free, a magician who guaranteed to set any party alight – literally. And a printed piece of paper asking for volunteers to help out at the official Angel Sands Christmas light switch on.

"You interested?" a voice from behind him asked.

Breck turned around to see Frank Megassey standing there. As well as running the local hardware store, Frank was well reknowned for being the unofficial Angel Sands organizer. If it needed volunteers, Frank was always at the front of the line.

"It's only October," Breck said, hastily putting the leaflet back down where he found it. He tried to find the right word to say *no*, he really *wasn't* interested. But all he could come up with was, "It's a long time until Christmas."

"Not if you're organizing an event like this," Frank told him. "We have to apply for permits, make a start on fundraising for the electricity, and of course there's the entertainment to organize. We could use a strong man like you to help us out. What do you say?"

"I...ah..." Breck raked his hand through his hair. "I go away every Christmas. I probably won't be here."

"Frank, are you press-ganging my customers again?" Ally asked, grinning at him. "Can't you let them have some coffee in peace?" She turned to Breck and gave him a sympathetic look. "Your coffees are all ready. We're bagging up the donuts now and I'll have someone carry them to the car for you."

"Thanks, I appreciate it." Breck handed her his credit card. It was Friday, which meant it was his turn to buy breakfast for the team he had working for him at the Silver Sands construction site. Six cartons of coffee and a hundred donuts for his hungry workers was a small price to pay for the dedication and hard labor they'd put in over the past few months, bringing the old 1920s derelict resort back into its resplendent glory. There were still six more months of work ahead of them, and he'd learned from experience that keeping his workers happy was an important part of coordinating a project like this.

"Add Frank's order to my bill," Breck said to Ally. "Whatever he wants is on me."

Ally raised an eyebrow. "Guilt coffee?"

Breck grinned. "Something like that."

A couple of minutes later he was back outside, opening his truck up and loading the coffee and pastries inside. Like the rest of the vehicles that regularly parked outside the Silver Sands construction site, it was covered with dust that never seemed to disappear no matter how often he cleaned it. Even through the sandy particles you could see the name of his family's company, Miller & Sons Construction, proudly emblazoned on the side. He was proud to be part of it, and to be running their Californian operations, while his dad ran the company over on the East Coast.

"Hey man!" Lucas Russell called from across the parking lot. "You still on for tonight?" He was carrying a surfboard, his hair and shorts wet from a morning out on the water, and from the grin on his face it had been a successful one. Leaning his board up against his own truck, he crossed the blacktop to where Breck was standing, reaching his hand out for their own version of a handshake.

Lucas was one of Breck's oldest friends, and yet the two of them had only recently reconnected. That had been Breck's fault. When he'd left town at the age of seventeen, he hadn't wanted to talk to any of his old friends. Hadn't wanted to think about the way his mom had died, or how he and his brother had to leave town to join their father in Boston.

But now he was back in the town he grew up in, spending time with friends who didn't give a damn he'd disappeared for years. It gave him a little buzz to be so readily accepted back into the fold.

"I'm up for tonight," Breck told him. "Do you need me to bring anything?"

"Nope. Just yourself. We'll have some drinks and some food, and some dancing. Ember's got it all covered. I know it's an engagement party, but we want everybody to have fun."

"I can't believe you're getting married," Breck said, grinning. "Surely we're not old enough."

"We're thirty," Lucas pointed out. "A good time to settle down. Speaking of which, Ember's friend was asking about you."

"What friend?" Breck frowned.

"Rachel. She's another teacher at the school. You remember her, right? She was at our place a couple of weeks ago when we had the cookout."

Breck blinked, trying to place her. But whenever Lucas and Ember hosted parties, their little cottage and the beach beyond was always full of their friends and coworkers. They had a way of drawing people in, and they always wanted to make sure their friends were taken care of. That was one of the things Breck liked about them both.

"Rachel?" Breck said. "Is she the dark haired one?"

"Nope. She's blonde."

Not that her hair color mattered. Breck wasn't looking for a relationship. He'd been burnt too many times. No woman wanted to be with a guy who wouldn't let her in. Whatever way he tried to cut it, they always tried to get under his skin, exactly where he didn't want them.

"Blonde?" Breck said, wrinkling his nose. "Nah, I really

can't remember her. And anyway, I'm too busy for that kind of thing. I'll leave the romance to you." He leaned against his truck, grinning. "By the way, did you set a date for the wedding?"

"Yeah, we did. The twenty-third of December."

Breck blinked. "At Christmas?"

"Yep."

"This year?"

"That's right." Lucas raised his eyebrows. "The way I see it, the sooner the better."

"Sounds like a good plan. You don't want somebody to snatch her out of your grasp." Breck laughed, trying to hide his dismay. Another reason relationships never worked for him. Try telling a girl you didn't want to celebrate Christmas. In fact, you'd prefer to hide away for the whole festive season and pretend it didn't exist.

He hadn't met a woman yet who didn't try to make him change his mind.

"Like Beyoncé says, I gotta put a ring on it." Lucas grinned. "But don't tell Ember I said that." He cleared his throat. "So, I was wondering if you'd be one of my grooms-men, along with Griff and Jack. Only if you feel up to it, I know it's not everybody's cup of tea."

Breck felt his chest tighten. "I'd be honored," he said, ignoring the growing unease in his chest. "But you don't have to ask me to be kind. I know you've got a lot of friends who'll want to help."

"You're family, man," Lucas said. "You and Griff and Jack are the only three people I want up there beside me. We grew up together, and in a world like this it means a lot to know you'll be there for me."

A wave of emotion crashed over Breck. "It would mean a lot to me, too."

"Excellent, that's agreed." Lucas slapped his back. "Now

we only need to persuade Caitie to help us organize the wedding."

"Caitie?" Breck asked. "As in your sister?"

"Yeah. She's flying in today for the engagement party. All the way from New York." Lucas shrugged. "It'll be good to see her."

"I bet she's changed a bit."

"She's twenty-eight now." Lucas widened his eyes. "Can you believe it?"

"No." Breck shook his head. "The last time I saw her she was a kid. I can't imagine her any older."

"Yeah, well she's all grown up." Lucas didn't look happy about it.

"Like Daniel," Breck murmured. His own brother was twenty-four, old enough to be finishing up his master's degree at Harvard. Growing up, the two of them had spent a lot of time at the Russell house. Lucas's parents – Deenie and Wallace – had been like second parents to Breck and Daniel. Feeding them when their mom was working her ass off to keep a roof over their heads, and helping them with homework when school was threatening them with detentions.

And of course, there was the year their mom died, and Deenie and Wallace had taken them in for Christmas. Breck swallowed hard at the memory. He'd been seventeen and Daniel had been eleven, and both of them had been bereft. Their father had long since divorced their mom and had relocated to Boston where he still lived now. Thanks to the holidays it had taken him two days to fly to California to pick up his sons.

Two long, painful days that Breck tried not to think about too often. The same way he tried not to think about his mom. And yet he couldn't forget the kindness the Russells had shown to him and Daniel, nor the way fifteen-year-old

Caitie had tried everything she could to make Daniel smile. She had such a soft voice and caring eyes.

"I need to head off," Lucas said, giving Breck's back a final slap. "Ember has a to-do list as long as my arm. I'll see you at the Beach Club later, okay?"

"Sure." Breck grinned. "I should head off, too. Before my workers refuse to work over the lack of coffee. I'll see you tonight."

As Lucas crossed the parking lot to his truck, Breck climbed into his own, turning on the engine and backing out of his space.

So Caitie was coming back. That was interesting. He couldn't help but wonder what kind of woman she'd grown up to be.

———

The moment Caitie Russell stepped out of the airport and onto the sidewalk she could feel the warmth of the Californian sun beating down on her. Though she'd left good weather behind in New York, somehow this heat felt different. The rays looked brighter as they bounced off the windows of the airport buildings surrounding her. It felt different, too. Not the muggy heat every New Yorker complained about in the summer. But a lighter, clearer happy-kind-of-heat that made people smile as they passed her to get to the taxi line.

Even though she'd grown up here, it had been years since she'd been to California, thanks to attending an out-of-state college, and then setting up her business in New York. Life had become so busy she never found the time to visit home.

But now she was here, and it felt strange. No, that wasn't right. It was *her* who felt strange. As though she was trying on old clothes that no longer fit, stretching them out until they were threadbare and worn.

She picked up the rental car her assistant had booked for her, and slung her luggage in the trunk, grabbing her phone to see if she'd missed any messages between the arrival gate and the rental office. There was only one message – from her best friend, Harper. Caitie read it with a resigned grin.

*Remember what I said. You're the sister of the groom, you get first dibs on all the hot guys.*

*There are no hot guys,* Caitie quickly typed back. *And even if there were, I'd probably be related to them.*

She climbed into the car and threw her phone into the cup holder right as it buzzed in reply. Harper would have to wait until she got to Angel Sands. Right now she had to concentrate on the road.

Caitie steered the car out of the lot and headed toward the highway, ignoring the way her phone kept vibrating in the cup holder. Harper must have given up on messaging and was trying to call. Caitie grinned at the thought of how impatient her best friend could be.

She'd first met Harper Hayes at school. They'd been assigned as roommates at the private arts college they'd both attended. Caitie had been a Fine Arts major, Harper had studied Fashion Design and Dressmaking. The day they'd first met, Caitie'd walked into their shared bedroom to find Harper curled up in a ball, sobbing dramatically about the boy she'd left behind, proclaiming she'd never find love again.

Later that night, Harper had dragged Caitie out to some drunken dorm party, and proceeded to kiss at least twenty boys, in an attempt – so she told Caitie – to forget Mr. Hometown.

That was Harper. Emotional, dramatic, always looking for love. She was the yin to Caitie's calm and organized yang. No wonder when they'd both relocated to New York after college, they did it together, moving first into a dingy apartment in Williamsburg, before working their way up. She stopped Caitie from taking herself too seriously, and in return, Caitie gave her the steadfast support she'd never had growing up. Together they worked.

As her traveling progressed and she joined the Pacific Coastal Highway, Caitie felt her pulse rise up at the sight of the ocean. It unnerved her, being so close to the deep blue water and crashing waves. The smell of the salty ozone made her stomach do a flip-flop, and she tried to push down the anxiety that rose every time the road curved toward the shore.

She switched the air conditioning to circulate and took a deep breath, keeping her eyes on the blacktop ahead. It was fine. She was fine. She wasn't a kid anymore. The ocean wasn't something to be afraid of.

It had been years since she had a panic attack. The last one she could remember was when she'd gone to stay with a client in Michigan, near the waterfront. They'd asked her to join them on their boat, suggesting dinner moored up in the water. Once aboard, she'd felt the familiar rush of fear and adrenaline shooting through her veins. She didn't have to feign her headache that night. She'd lost the contract, too. Another reason to avoid relocating to California. She wasn't sure her business would survive it.

Her heart rate calmed as the road curved inland, and the coastline became a pinpoint in her rearview mirror. She could do this, she really could. Just two days and she'd be on a plane back to New York. Back in the concrete jungle and far away from the Pacific coast.

It was late afternoon when she pulled off the highway and onto the small road leading toward Angel Sands. To her left were the familiar hills, which led to her hometown. The abandoned brick buildings of Fort Bradley stood proudly at the top, guarding the town like an old soldier. On the other side – in contrast – were the shiny glass towers of Newton Pharmaceuticals. Caitie knew those towers well. Her father had worked there for most of his life, before he retired. Newton Pharmaceuticals was the biggest employer in Angel Sands, and half of her graduating year had gone on to work there.

Her parents – Deenie and Wallace – lived in a sprawling bungalow a half mile inland from the bay. Caitie steered the car onto the blacktop driveway, turning off the engine when she came to a stop. Letting her head fall against the headrest, she inhaled a final lungful of stale air, before closing her eyes, and letting the oxygen seep into her bloodstream. It wasn't hard to imagine she was seventeen again, climbing into her mom's old Honda to make the journey to L.A. then onward to New England, her heart full of hope at the fresh start she was about to make.

"Caitie!"

She opened her eyes to see her mom running down the steps of their Spanish bungalow. Her white hair was streaming behind, revealing her still-youthful face and broad smile. Caitie climbed out of the car and ran toward her, letting her mother wrap her in her warm, strong arms.

Deenie Russell wasn't like other moms. Caitie had worked that out at a young age. A hippie at heart, and a free spirit to her soul, she'd embraced parenthood the same way she embraced everything else in her life. Coming at it from a different angle, being laid-back to the point of being horizontal. All of Caitie's friends had been jealous of her since she had such a chilled-out mom.

Plus she ran the town's bookstore, which was super cool when you were a kid. Caitie's friends used to love hanging out there with her.

"How was your trip? I told you we could've come and picked you up. You didn't need to rent a car." Deenie wrapped an arm around Caitie's waist, leading her up the steps to the bungalow.

"In that old hunk of junk?" Caitie teased, turning her head to the eighteen-year-old Toyota. "Is it even legal to drive that on the highway?"

Deenie shook her head, grinning. "It's more reliable than the tin cans they make nowadays. I've never had a problem with it. Now come inside, you must be exhausted. Would you like a cup of chai tea?"

"Do you have coffee?"

Deenie shook her head. "I don't, but I'll pick some up in the morning. We've stopped drinking it. Your father's blood pressure was way too high at his last checkup. They wanted to put him on diuretics. He told them no thank you, he can control this with diet and lifestyle. So no more caffeine for your dad."

Caitie tried to suppress her smile. There was something ironic about a man who'd spent his life researching pharmaceuticals refusing them when faced with illness. "Is it helping?"

"Absolutely. It's already dropped quite a bit."

Caitie sat down on a stool behind the breakfast bar while her mom made their drinks. It all felt so strange yet familiar. She could have easily just gotten home from school and thrown her books onto the counter while her mom was asking her about her day.

"And how are things going with Lucas and Ember? Are they all ready for the party?" Caitie couldn't help but smile. Her big brother was finally settling down. For a while they'd thought he was married to his job as a firefighter. Until he'd met Ember Kennedy, the one woman who made him think about something other than the service. Now they were engaged, and she was here for their party. Caitie couldn't help but feel delighted for them both.

"I think so. Ember's arranged most of it. Everybody in town is going to be there. It should be a good night." Deenie cleared her throat. "Actually, they wanted to ask you something while you're here."

Caitie blinked. "Ember already asked me to be in the bridal party. I said yes."

"She did? How lovely." Deenie smiled. "But that's not what I'm talking about. They want your help organizing the wedding. They're both so out of their depth."

"They want my help?" Caitie repeated, frowning. "But I don't know a thing about organizing a wedding."

"You run events. That's the same thing, isn't it?" Deenie pointed out, pouring out their drinks.

"I don't plan events, Mom, I consult on them." Caitie bit her lip. She consulted on way too many of them, in fact. She was running herself ragged. "I could probably point them in the direction of some good event planners, but unless they want a winter wonderland I'm not going to be able to help them too much."

Caitie's business was always the cause of interest in the Russell family. When she'd first told her parents she was going to be a Holiday Consultant, they'd been confused. Her father had asked her what she planned on doing for the other eleven months of the year.

*"It's a year-round job, Dad," she'd told him. "It's not just businesses and retailers, there's the movie and TV industry, too. They all need consultants to help them plan their holiday themes. It can take months to get everything done."*

*"People think about Christmas in February?" He sounded skeptical. "Isn't that a little weird?"*

*"It's normal. It's not like you can make a movie in a month. And TV series are taped months ahead. Plus, the retail industry has long order times. I promise it's a real thing."*

As it turned out, she was right. And her father had been

the first to congratulate her when her business started to grow. She was lucky to have such supportive parents, even if she didn't see them very often.

"I think your brother and Ember will take whatever help you can give them," her mom said, sliding her cup of chai in front of her. "Neither of them has organized something like this before. They need you, Caitlin."

A little voice in Caitie's head told her to run right now. She was way too busy with her work to organize a wedding.

But he was her big brother. She couldn't let him down.

"Of course I'll help them," she said, taking a sip of chai. "What else are sisters for?"

## 2

"Are you sure you don't want to ride with us, honey?" Deenie asked, poking her head around the door to Caitie's childhood bedroom. Caitie was set up at her laptop, replying to a raft of urgent emails her assistant had forwarded to her. One of the worst parts of being your own boss – it was almost impossible to take time off without some kind of crisis occurring.

"It's okay, I'll drive myself over once I've finished this," Caitie replied, smiling at her mom. Her eyes widened. "Oh my goodness, you look gorgeous." She stood to admire her mom's outfit. A long silver dress and purple scarf which brought out the platinum strands in Deenie's hair. With her youthful skin and sun kissed smile, Deenie didn't look anywhere near her sixty years. Was it wrong to hope she'd inherited those same genes?

Caitie leaned forward to kiss her mother, pressing her lips against Deenie's cheek. Her mom smelled of apple blossoms and roses, a scent that sparked an olfactory memory. The Christmas, back when Caitie was fifteen, she'd given her mom a gift set from the local beauty store. It was the same

Christmas when Lucas's friend, Breck and his brother, had stayed with them, right before her heart had broken for the first time.

"We sit down to dinner at nine," her mom told her. "Make sure you're there before we do."

Caitie glanced at her watch. It was a bit past seven. "I'll jump in the shower as soon as I finish this. I promise not to be late." Knowing when to stop and put her laptop away was one of the hardest parts of being the boss. Her work was never done. When she wasn't working on a project she was writing proposals for the next. And because her work took her all over the country, the different time zones meant she was getting emails twenty-four-seven.

But an hour later, she managed to pull into the parking lot of the Angel Sands Beach Club looking far more put together than she felt. Her dark hair was freshly washed and dried, her red strapless dress was zipped up tight around her chest, and she'd even remembered to move her wallet and phone into a silver clutch Harper had loaned her.

She eased her car into a space about a hundred yards away from the Beach Club. Through the open car windows she could smell the sulfur coming up from the sea, and hear the gentle sound of the waves as they hit the beach. She took a deep breath and held it for a moment longer than necessary.

She could do this. She really could.

When her brother had told her his engagement party was taking place at the Beach Club, Caitie had felt her heart drop. Not because of anything to do with him or his wife-to-be, but because the beach always brought out this reaction in her. She hated the way it could bring her to her knees. There was nothing logical in the way it made her feel like a child again. The child who was pulled under the surface of the ocean by a riptide, and almost drowned.

She swallowed hard. She wasn't a child any more. She was

an adult, and she could do this. It was her brother's engagement party, and she wasn't going to miss it for the world.

As she stepped inside the door, a waiter offered her a glass of champagne from a silver tray. Caitie shook her head, grabbing a tumbler of water instead, downing it in one long gulp. She could feel the liquid filling her stomach, ice cold against her body heat, but still it wasn't enough. Her entire body felt on fire. She pressed the glass to her cheek, but it was no help.

"You made it. Lucas has been looking everywhere for you. My god, you look gorgeous. That dress is to die for." Her sister-in-law to-be, Ember, was standing in the doorway, welcoming guests to the party. She grabbed Caitie's hand, pulling her in for a hug.

"Congratulations," Caitie said, hugging her back. "I'm so happy for you both."

Ember gave her a happy grin. She looked beautiful, her tanned skin set off by the palest of yellow dresses. The spaghetti straps were intricately woven with gemstones, the bodice tight across her chest. Her dark hair was twisted into a low bun, tendrils spilling out onto her smooth neck. "Thank you for traveling to be with us. Lucas is so excited to see you."

"I wouldn't have missed it for the world. I know I'm not around much. I'm so sorry..." Caitie had always liked Ember Kennedy. They were the same age and had attended Angel Sands High at the same time as each other. Though they'd not hung around in the same group, Caitie'd always had time for the studious brunette with the kind heart.

Ember released her from her hug. "It's our fault, too. We keep talking about visiting you in New York, but life gets so busy. I'd love to get to know you again now that we'll be sisters."

"I'd like that a lot." Caitie's voice was thick. "Maybe once the wedding is over we can agree on a date. I'd love to show you around the big city."

Ember grinned. "That would be great. Lucas keeps telling me about your business and how well it's going. I'd love to see what you're working on. You have my dream job. I can't imagine anything better than working on Christmas all year round."

"You'd be surprised how many people think it's a terrible job," Caitie confessed. "I get a lot of people telling me they can't stand Christmas."

Ember's mouth dropped open. "Who are these people?" she asked. "Christmas is my favorite time of year."

"Mine too," Caitie said, grinning. "And of course I'll show you where I work. Though it's not much to look at. Most of the things I do are at clients' locations." She licked her lips, remembering the conversation she'd had with her mom earlier. Now would probably be a good time to bring it up. "Mom told me you might need a little help with your wedding?"

"She did?" Ember's shoulders dropped with relief. "Oh thank goodness. I wasn't sure whether to ask you. I know how busy you are..."

"I'm never too busy for family," Caitie said firmly. She'd find the time, somehow. "So what do you need?"

Ember grimaced. "Everything. We've agreed on a date but that's all. We have just over two months to arrange the rest."

"Two months?" Caitie tried to keep the panic from her voice.

"I know. It's crazy." Ember shook her head. "But if we don't get married in December, we won't get another chance until next summer. I don't get much time off between Christmas and June."

"The pitfalls of being a teacher," Caitie commiserated.

"We really don't want to wait until next June. Plus I love the idea of a Christmas wedding."

"Have you chosen a venue?" Caitie asked her. "I'm

guessing a lot of places are already booked up for the holidays."

"We haven't found anywhere yet," Ember confessed. "Even this place is booked up for Christmas parties, not that it's my first choice. I really want to get married somewhere a little different. Out of town, but not so far that people can't travel for the day. I just can't find the right location."

Caitie could sense Ember beginning to panic. She reached out and took her hand, squeezing it tight. "Why don't we get together tomorrow to discuss it?" she said, trying to keep her voice as positive as possible. "I'm sure we can work something out. And in the meantime, forget about it and enjoy your night."

Ember let out a mouthful of air. "Thank you so much. I can't tell you how relieved I am to know you can help. And we'll pay you, of course."

"You'll do no such thing." Caitie shook her head. "You're family. This one's on me."

Four women around their age walked out of the ballroom and into the entrance where the two of them were standing. "Ember," one of them called. "Your mom is looking for you. She wanted to talk to you about the seating arrangements."

Ember's eyes flickered over to Caitie's. "I should go," she said, giving her a big smile. "But before I do, let me introduce you to my friends. This is Brooke and Ally, you might remember them from school?"

Caitie shook their hands. She thought she recognized the two of them, but that was par for the course in Angel Sands. It was that kind of town.

"Hi," she said, smiling. "It's great to meet you."

"This is my sister, Chelsea," she said. Caitie grinned at the petite brunette. She looked like a younger version of Ember.

Ember turned to the final girl, standing on her left. "And

this is Rachel. We work together. Everybody, this is Caitie, Lucas's sister. You'll all be my bridesmaids together."

After greeting them, Caitie excused herself to find her parents and let them know she'd finally made it. Grabbing another glass – this time filled with orange juice – she made her way into the main dining room. It was full of people milling around, some holding glasses of champagne, others grabbing appetizers from the trays as waiters weaved their way through the throng. A band was setting up on the raised stage in the corner, testing their instruments before setting them carefully out for later. One side of the room was open where the glass doors had been pulled back, and guests spilled out onto the wooden deck. Beyond were the tennis courts and swimming pools, which led to the private club beach.

So many of Caitie's friends had summer jobs here when they were growing up, wearing the requisite purple shorts and white polo shirts, the club logo printed on the left. But never her. Despite her parents' urging, she'd claimed she was too busy studying, reading, and doing anything else to avoid working there. Eventually she'd found a weekend job at a small home goods boutique in the mall, far, *far* away from the beach and surf. That was where she'd started to get an eye for design, a passion that grew into her degree, and finally her business.

"You made it." Deenie waved at her from the crowd. She was surrounded by neighbors Caitie had known since she was a kid. The next few minutes passed in a flurry of hellos, of telling them how she liked living in New York, of explaining the role of a Holiday Consultant, and reassuring them it really was a paying job.

Caitie was in mid conversation with Frank Megassey, her parents' old friend, when a shout of laughter cut through her words. She looked over, flashing Mr. Megassey a smile of apology, to see her brother and his friends doubled over in amusement.

"Lucas seems to be enjoying himself," Mr. Megassey said. "I remember when you guys were kids; he was always playing tricks on everybody. I'll never forget the time when he put food dye in my swimming pool. Boy was your father mad."

"He grounded him for a week and made him come and scrub all the tiles with a toothbrush." Caitie grinned, remembering the way her brother had complained about being covered in blue dye for days.

"He's grown up to be a good man," Frank said, nodding approvingly. "Everybody at the fire station raves about him. And of course your parents are very proud." Frank raised his eyebrows at her. "They're proud of you, too. They talk about you non-stop."

"It's all thanks to them." Caitie shrugged. "And don't forget to email me about the Christmas decorations you need for the town this year. I've found a few places that will provide them for free in return for the sponsorship."

"That's wonderful." Frank grinned. "We're always very grateful for your support."

Caitie glanced over to the bar again. Lucas was talking rapidly to his friend, Griff, while his other friend, Jack, handed each a bottle of beer. A fourth man was standing in their circle, his broad muscular back facing her. She frowned, trying to figure out who it was. Lucas's group of friends had been tight for as long as she could remember. He, Griff, and Jack were practically glued together all through school.

"Who's that?" she murmured, leaning across to her mom.

Deenie turned around, smiling at Lucas's antics. "Oh that's..."

But she didn't need to say anything more, because at that moment, he turned, his dark-blond hair catching the light from the chandeliers. Caitie took in his profile; his strong nose, his razor-sharp jawline, and those lips she'd never forgotten.

Her hand shook, juice almost sloshing over the rim. She stilled it with her other hand, feeling herself flush with embarrassment at her reaction.

"Is that Brecken?" she asked, her voice thin. "Brecken Miller?" She turned to look at her mom for confirmation.

"Yes." Deenie nodded. "He moved back to town a few months ago. Lucas was over the moon when he found out he was back."

Caitie hadn't laid eyes on Brecken Miller for almost half of her life. Not since the Christmas thirteen years ago when he'd arrived at their house with his brother, both of them grieving their mother's death from cancer. For nearly three days they'd stayed with the Russell family, waiting for their father to fly across the country to pick them up. When he'd left for Boston, he promised to keep in touch.

But she'd never seen either of them again.

"What's he doing here?" She was thinking out loud, not realizing she'd said anything until her mom answered her.

"He works with his father. Miller Construction is renovating the old Silver Sands Resort. Isn't it wonderful to see him? I spent so many sleepless nights worrying about that boy after he left, wondering how he was doing. It's great to see him so successful."

Caitie allowed herself to glance over at him again. Somehow the gesture felt furtive, as if she was a child peeking out from behind the sofa, hoping nobody could see her. "He hasn't changed much."

Deenie smiled. "He was a good looking boy, and he's an even better looking man. Devastating you might say."

Yes, devastating was definitely the right word. Caitie felt the full effects of it all over her body. A flush had broken out on her chest, staining her pale skin a strawberry pink. It was in danger of spreading up her neck and face.

Caitie had spent just as many sleepless nights as her mom after Brecken and his brother left. Their father – David – had picked them up the day after Christmas, once he was able to make the trek after hearing of his ex-wife's passing. After the funeral, he'd flown them back to his home in Boston, thousands of miles away from Angel Sands and their friends. Caitie closed her eyes, remembering the lost expression in both boy's eyes, and how desperate she'd been to bring some happiness to them that Christmas.

"You should go say hi," Deenie suggested. "I'm sure he'd be pleased to see you."

"He won't remember me." She took another sip of her juice.

"Of course he does. He was asking about you. Told me he still remembers how kind you were to him and Daniel when they stayed with us. I'm sure he'd love to catch up with you."

The thought of talking to him was paralyzing. Of all Lucas's friends, Breck had been the one who had drawn her in. While Griff and Jack were merrily joining in with whatever scheme Lucas thought up to torture his little sister, Breck was the one who would check if she was okay. He would offer to protect her and she'd developed a little crush on him.

Okay, so it wasn't *that* little.

He turned around again. This time his body twisted toward Caitie until his gaze locked on her face. Her skin started to fizz, as though somebody had thrown soda all over her.

*Devastating.* Somehow the word didn't seem enough now that they were face to face. How could she have thought he hadn't changed? Everything about him screamed masculinity, from the sharp angles of his face to the scruff across his jaw.

When she was fifteen years old, Brecken Miller had left Angel Sands, and it had felt as though her world had left with him.

Now he was back, all grown up, and Caitie couldn't form a single lucid thought in her brain.

## 3

As a child, Breck hadn't spent a whole lot of time at the Beach Club. Though his mom earned a fair wage working as an admin at Newton Pharmaceuticals, it hadn't been enough for luxuries like club memberships. The three of them had lived a frugal life. Even buying his first surfboard had been a huge investment, paid for by working the whole summer in Frank Megassey's hardware store.

He wondered what his mom would think of him now. Coming back into town as a grown man, his business going from strength to strength. Would she be glad he'd mended bridges with his father, or would she be angry that he'd grown to love the man who had been a stranger to them before she passed?

"You want another beer?" Jack asked, inclining his head toward the bar.

"I'm good, thanks." Breck shook his still-full bottle at him.

"Hey, do you remember the time we all drank Jack's mom's whiskey?" Griff asked, grinning. "I swear I lost about thirty-six hours of my life after that. No sixteen year old should feel that much pain."

They launched into another round of reminiscences, joshing about the kids they once were. Breck couldn't help but laugh at Griffin's impression of him stumbling around before being sick in his mom's leather purse.

"As I remember, you vomited on her dog," Breck pointed out. "She was a lot more upset about that."

The back of his neck began to tingle, the same way it did when he had a shave at the barber. He reached up to touch it but the sensation remained. He rubbed the skin with his fingers, frowning.

Griff was saying something to Jack about being a lightweight, but Breck couldn't quite hear the words. He was too busy turning around to look at the group of people behind him. They were older, a collection of Lucas's family and neighbors. Brecken smiled when he saw Lucas's mom, resplendent in a silver dress. When the light caught the thread it looked almost luminous.

A second later, his eyes locked onto a brunette standing with the group. A shock ran through him as he realized she was staring back. As much as he knew he should, he couldn't pull himself away from those melted chocolate eyes.

He wasn't sure what about her grabbed his attention. Maybe it was the dark brown hair that cascaded in waves down her back. Or her pale-as-alabaster skin. The only evidence she'd ever been touched by the sun was a line of freckles smattered across the bridge of her nose.

The back of his neck tingled again.

"Oh hey, Caitie's here." Lucas had followed Breck's gaze over to the crowd beside them.

*That* was Caitie? The gorgeous brunette with curves to kill for was the girl they used to tease and rib mercilessly? His mind was still trying to wrap around the idea when she started to walk toward them, her hips swaying effortlessly as she crossed the distance. When the hell did she grow up?

"Hey, Vampira, you okay?" Griffin asked her. Breck had forgotten about Caitie's childhood nickname. She used to avoid the sun, always refusing to sit out in it or come down to the beach. They'd been such douches to her in those days.

"Caitie, how are you?" Breck's voice was soft, as he reached out to take her hand in his. The way her skin felt was electric.

A smile broke across her lips. "Breck," she said, her voice full of warmth. "My mom said you were here. I can't believe you came back. I thought you'd be gone forever."

He grimaced. "Yeah, I wasn't the best at keeping in touch, was I?" He kept the rest of his sentence to himself. No need to tell her how depressed he was after leaving Angel Sands. How it was a miracle that he even got up every morning after heading east. Back then, he didn't have the capacity to keep in touch with the friends he'd left behind. It was all too painful and raw.

Old history, he told himself. That was then, and this was now.

But he was still holding her hand.

"Well, we missed you. I'm glad you're here. Lucas must be ecstatic the gang is back together." She was staring up at him with those doe eyes. He could easily get lost in them.

"Lucas is standing right here," her brother said. "And yes, he's very happy."

Her brother's interruption was like a bucket of ice. She pulled her hand from Breck's, breaking their connection. "Shut up, Lucas. And stop talking about yourself in the third person."

"Lucas will be happy to do that."

Griffin started to laugh. It really was like old times, with

Lucas and his friends teasing the younger girl. Except she wasn't a girl anymore, was she?

"It really is good to see you," Breck said. "How have you been doing?"

There was her smile again. All goofy and lopsided the way he'd remembered it. He wondered if her lips were as soft as they looked. "I'm really good, thanks. I've been living in New York. This is the first time I've been home in ages."

He fought the urge to reach out and touch her again. "Yeah, Lucas told me you have your own business. That's pretty cool for somebody so young."

"I'm not *that* young," she pointed out.

"Tell that to the thirty year old."

She laughed. "Well in that case, old man..."

"Hey, less of the old." Their easy conversation relaxed him. "So what exactly do you do?"

"I'm a Holiday Consultant."

"A what?" he asked, perplexed.

She laughed at his expression. "I work with businesses on Christmas themes and events. I consult on future trends, past trends, and help source festive items and decor. Basically, if it has anything to do with Christmas, I do it."

"That's a thing?" His lips were dry. He lifted the bottle of beer to wet them. The mention of Christmas made him want to down his drink in one.

"It really is." She shrugged. "It's a pretty lucrative thing, too."

"Sounds as though you're doing really well."

"I'm getting there. I'm working on a big contract with a company in L.A.. If I can close it, things will really go to the next level."

"No wonder Lucas is so proud of you."

"He is?" Her surprise made him wince.

"Yeah, of course he is."

She smiled at his revelation. "Talking of brothers, how is Daniel? He must be twenty-three by now."

"Twenty-four last week. And he's doing great. He graduated from Harvard a couple of years ago, and is doing research. You wouldn't recognize him if you saw him. He's about ten feet tall and all muscled up, nothing like he was as a kid."

"I'd recognize him if he looks anything like you." Her tongue peeked out to lick her lips. They looked as dry as his felt. "Say hi for me the next time you speak to him, okay? He was like my little brother back in the day."

"I definitely will."

A loud bell rang from the corner of the room, right as the MC stepped up to the microphone. "Ladies and gentlemen, please take your seats. Dinner is about to be served."

"I guess that's our cue. What table are you at? I've got table ten." He pointed over to the far corner.

"I'm at the family table." She inclined her head at table one. "I'll catch you later?" Was it his imagination, or did she look disappointed?

He shot her a wink. "It was really good to see you."

"And you." She nodded. "So good."

---

Table ten turned out to be the raucous one. Griffin and Jack sat to Breck's left, pouring wine out as if a drought was about to kick in. On the other side of the table were Ember's friends, Ally and Brooke, plus their partners, Nate and Aiden. Breck knew Aiden very well. He was one of the directors of Carter Leisure, the huge hotel company that owned the Silver Sands Resort. That made Aiden Breck's boss, and the two of them were friends from the start.

On Breck's right was Rachel Foss – Ember's friend from

school that Lucas had mentioned. Breck still couldn't remember meeting her before, in spite of talking with her for the last five minutes.

"So you grew up with Lucas?" Rachel asked, resting her chin on her hand. "That must have been fun. What made you leave town?"

"My mom died when I was seventeen, so I moved to Boston with my dad."

"I'm so sorry to hear that." Rachel's face dropped.

"It's okay. It happened a long time ago." He smiled at her to take the sting away.

"So are you back for good now?" She leaned forward, her eyes soft. As she spoke, Breck found himself sneaking a glance at table one. Caitie was talking to her mom, her face turned away from him.

"I don't know how long I'm here for. We're due to finish the reconstruction at the Silver Sands Resort next year. After that we're hoping for another contract nearby." He'd already discussed staying in California for a while with his dad, so they'd begun placing bids on contracts which would keep him close. He liked the area, liked having some autonomy. Luckily, his father was in agreement.

"That's really interesting." Rachel tipped her head to the side. "I drive past there every day. I keep wondering what is happening behind all those fences. Are you having to demolish a lot of it?"

He shook his head. "No, we're mostly restoring. There's a lot of history in those buildings. It was here before the town really grew. It would be a crime to knock it down." From the corner of his eye, he saw Aiden nod in agreement.

"I'd love to see it sometime," Rachel said, looking at him expectantly.

Breck took a sip of his drink. "Once we reach the next

stage of construction, we'll start having open days for the town. Maybe you could come along."

Rachel grinned. "Oh, yes please." She leaned forward. "So, do you surf like Lucas does?"

"When I get a chance," he replied. "How about you?"

"No, but I love to watch. I go down sometimes before school and sit on the beach for a while. When do you surf?"

"Mostly on the weekends." He shrugged. "When I'm not working."

"Maybe I'll come and watch you some time," she suggested. "We could grab coffee or something afterward." She was leaning so close his personal space was non-existent. It made him want to shuffle his chair back.

"Um, yeah. Sure." From the corner of his eye he noticed Griff grinning. "I'm pretty busy though."

"It's fine. Let me give you my number." She grabbed a pad and pen from her purse, and scribbled her digits down, tearing out the sheet of paper and pressing it into his hand. "Call me next time you're free."

Breck slid the piece of paper in his pocket. He had no intention of calling her. Not that she wasn't a nice girl – if she was friends with Ember, he had no doubt she was. But she wasn't his type. And he wasn't in the market for a relationship.

Strange how his eyes were drawn to the front table again. To the woman he hadn't seen for the past thirteen years. He swallowed hard as he took in her dark, lustrous hair, pulled over one shoulder to reveal her pale, slender neck.

As though she could feel the heat of his stare, she turned around and her eyes caught his. Breck felt like he'd been hit by a freight train. What the hell was wrong with him?

You didn't go near a friend's sister. That was part of the bro-code he'd grown up with, and as far as he was concerned it still applied now. So why was his heart racing like it was trying to win the Kentucky Derby?

Maybe it was shock. The last time he'd seen her, Breck had been in a bad place. Seeing her again, all these years later, was bound to stir up memories. The Russells had been the one chink of light in the darkness that was his life in those days. No wonder seeing her felt strange.

*Yeah*, the little voice in his head said. *Keep thinking that if you want. But tell me, why didn't you have the same reaction the first time you saw Lucas again?*

## 4

Deenie looked up as soon as Caitie walked into the kitchen the next morning. The sun was shining through the window leading out to the yard, its yellow glow lighting up the marble countertop where Deenie was laying out breakfast. The coffee her mom bought especially for her was already brewing, the pot spitting and sizzling as it filled up, the aroma rich in the room.

"Hey sweetheart. Did you sleep well?" Deenie asked.

Caitie smiled at her mom. "I think my body's still on New York time. I woke up before five."

Deenie sighed sympathetically. Neither one of them were great sleepers. Caitie couldn't remember either of her parents sleeping in, not even on weekends. They were always up with the roosters.

"Where's Dad?" Caitie asked, noticing his absence.

"Playing golf. He was out the door at six."

"I didn't hear him leave." She looked around, as if she were checking for him. "Is he always that sneaky?"

Deenie coughed out a laugh. "Your dad, sneaky? Oh, boy, he'd like that description. He couldn't sneak around to save his life. Do you remember when I turned fifty and he tried to surprise me with a birthday party? I had to practice my shocked expression for weeks."

"Oh I remember. He was so proud, too." Caitie poured herself a cup of coffee and sat at the breakfast bar, taking a sip of the earthy brew. Her parents were like night and day. She'd always marveled at how they'd made their relationship work for so many years. On paper, they were such a mismatch, yet together they worked. They set a high bar for Caitie and Lucas – one her brother had managed to scale. But for her the climb seemed almost impossible.

"How's he enjoying retirement?" Caitie asked.

Deenie joined her at the breakfast bar, pulling up a stool and setting her mug of green tea on the counter. "Ah, he's getting there. The first few months were difficult. He didn't know what to do with himself. After he ran out of all those little repairs you put off for a rainy day, he started getting under my feet. He was like a lost puppy following me around."

Caitlin grinned. Her mom would never have the patience for that. "Did he drive you crazy?"

"You better believe it. I even thought about breaking things to give him something to repair. When he began interfering at the bookshop, I knew something had to change." Deenie took a sip of her tea. "That's when he started booking regular slots at the golf club. He's made some new friends there, and gotten reacquainted with old ones. It's made everybody's life easier."

Caitie tipped her head to the side. She'd always been fascinated by her parents' relationship. "So what's your secret?"

"Our secret?" Her mom looked confused.

"You're so different from each other. How do you keep things going? You were never the kind of wife who bowed to her husband. Look at Dad's job. You've always been against big pharmaceuticals and how they push their own agenda, but never once have I heard you tell Dad you don't agree with his job."

Deenie rubbed her chin, giving Caitie a speculative look. "I've never thought relationships change who you are. And I *definitely* don't think they mean you have to agree on everything. Look at the way your father and I met. From the first moment we laid eyes on each other, we knew how different we were. I guess the secret is seeing that everybody has their own point of view, and they have the right to that." Her lips curled into a smile. "Love doesn't mean having to agree on everything, but it does mean respecting each other's choices. If you love somebody and want to spend your life with them, you have to love every part of them. Even the bits you don't quite understand."

The front door slammed, and Lucas's greeting echoed down the hallway. Caitie turned around to see her brother walking into the kitchen, followed by Ember. Both of them looked exhausted.

"The coffee's just finished brewing," Caitie told them, inclining her head at the pot.

"Mom has coffee in the house?" Lucas asked, his eyes wide. "This must be some kind of miracle." He pulled two mugs from the cupboard and poured coffee into them, adding milk before stirring them. Passing the first to Ember, he took a big mouthful of his own, sighing deeply.

"I'm so tired," Ember said, pulling out the stool next to Caitie's. "I can't imagine what you must be feeling like. Did you get any sleep."

Caitie grinned at her. "I got some." She took another mouthful of coffee. "And this is making up for the rest." She put her mug down and grabbed the notebook she'd been scribbling in since she woke up. "Oh, and I started writing down some ideas for your wedding. We should get started on making some plans." She glanced over at Lucas. "And if you've had enough coffee."

"We decided Lucas should probably go surfing," Ember said, winking. "Organizing weddings isn't really his thing."

Caitie turned to her brother. He shrugged at the question in her eyes. "I'm good with that," he said. "As long as you guys don't mind."

"Whatever works for you." Caitie shrugged. "I assume you've agreed on a budget?"

"Yep." Lucas nodded. "And if you have any questions, I'm only a phone call away."

"No problem. You can go." Caitie grinned. "Let the adults get on with organizing things."

"Okay, little sister." He winked at her, walking over to give her a hug. "Thanks for everything. Seriously. You've made two people very happy."

"We'll see," Caitie said. She still wasn't sure she could pull this off. Organizing a wedding in a little over two months was no small feat. Doing it mostly from the other side of the country was going to take a miracle. "Enjoy the surf." She stood to pour herself another cup of coffee. "You want a top off?" she asked Ember. "I think we're both going to need a major caffeine injection."

---

After Ember left later that morning, Caitie spent the day researching locations and calling to make enquiries about hosting a Christmas wedding at their venues. By the time evening came around, the exhaustion she'd woken up with was making every muscle in her body ache. And she didn't want to think about all the business emails piling up in her inbox.

There was only one thing she could do to manage this

all. She'd have to extend her stay. It made sense to work from Angel Sands for the next week until she found Ember and Lucas a venue. After that, she could return to New York and help them organize things remotely. But until they had somewhere to hold the wedding, nothing else could happen.

"You're staying until next weekend?" Harper inquired when Caitie called to tell her she wouldn't be returning to New York the next day. "Well that's one for the books. I thought you couldn't wait to get out of California. Are you thinking of moving back? Should I call some contacts in L.A.?"

Harper often talked about them both moving to California. As a costume designer, it was a choice between working at theaters in New York, or costume departments in Hollywood studios.

Caitie flicked the phone to speaker and laid it on the table, lifting her hands to rub her tired eyes. "I have a meeting in L.A. on Thursday, so I would have been flying back here, anyway. I decided it would be easier to work from Angel Sands rather than New York for the rest of the week. Don't start packing our bags yet."

"Spoilsport," Harper said cheerfully. "I guess I'll be wearing the same old winter clothes. Back to the drab blacks and greys."

"You never wear black. And anyway, it's hardly winter in New York. It's been pretty warm for October."

"It'll be cold soon enough. And then you'll have to listen to me moan every night."

"Nothing new there. I've been listening to you complain about the weather for the past eight years."

"So do us both a favor and let's move to California. I promise not to complain about the beautiful, year-round sun and alarming lack of rain."

Caitie laughed. "You'll find something else to moan about."

"Of course I will. But for once it won't be about the New York winters."

"You know, there's nothing stopping you from moving to L.A. without me." Caitie's tone was teasing, but saying those words made her stomach feel weird. As though she'd gone for days without eating.

There was a pause, followed by a full-on Harper sigh. "I can't believe you said that. We're the two musketeers, dude. I'm not moving to L.A. without you. If you insist on living in this miserable, cold, wet city for the rest of your life, that's where I'm staying. You need me to make sure you don't work too hard and nag you to get some rest."

Even though her abdomen still felt tight, Caitie smiled. Was she being selfish wanting to stay in New York, far away from the sea and sand of California? They'd probably both be better off work wise if they moved here. Especially if she got the new contract in L.A.. "Well, since you're not here, it looks like I'm going to be working all night. I've got meetings to move and a submission to get in. Not to mention the small problem of finding a wedding venue on short notice."

"Well, good luck with that, honey. I'll be putting my feet up and binge watching some TV. And because I know you're so sorry for making me stay in New York, I'll also be helping myself to your secret stash of chocolate."

"You don't know where I hide it." Caitie grinned.

"Of course I do. I know all your secrets, sweetie. But like all the others, I'll take this one to the grave."

"If you eat all my chocolate, you'll be going there sooner than you think," Caitie warned. "Just keep your hands off the Swiss stuff."

"I'll do my best. But remember, I'm drowning my sorrows because I have to live in this frozen hellhole of a city forever.

So you may have to buy me chocolate for the rest of my life so I can cope with the misery." Another dramatic sigh. "Especially the Swiss stuff."

"Goodbye, Harper." Caitie's voice was firm. "I'll talk to you later, okay?"

"You'd better. Otherwise I'll eat the Belgian stuff, too."

It was an hour later when Lucas stopped back at their parents' house, his hair wet from hours spent in the surf. He smelled of saltwater and sunscreen. His skin was warm and brown from an afternoon at the beach, and he was grinning from ear to ear.

"Hey, Ember tells me you're staying for a while." He attempted to grab Caitie and pull her close. When she dodged his grasp, he shook his wet hair at her, the same annoying way he used to when they were kids.

"Just for the week. We need to agree on a venue before next Saturday, otherwise we won't be able to get everything organized in time." Caitie gave him a serious look. "So you'll need to be ready to look at places, okay? Even if it means rearranging things."

"Of course. We're beyond grateful for your help, and whatever you need from us, you've got it. Seriously, sis, you're a lifesaver. Ember's over the moon you're going to help organize things. Are you sure we can't pay you?"

"No." She shook her head firmly. "It's a pleasure to be able to help, it really is. Just remember, I'm *not* a wedding planner. I'll probably need to find someone to help with things. But I do work with venues all the time, so securing one that works is exactly what I can do."

"You're amazing, you know that?" He reached for her again. This time, Caitie let him envelop her in his arms. He was still wet and warm, and smelled of the damned sea. "Oh, and Breck says hi. He wanted to come over, but he got a phone call and disappeared." He pulled back, wiggling his eyebrows at her.

Caitie tried to keep her tone innocent, ignoring the way her heart sped at his name. "You were surfing with Breck?"

"All the guys were there." Lucas shrugged. "Weekends are made for surfing."

"Yeah, sure."

"Oh, and Griff wanted to talk with you, too. He's scared you're going to dress the whole wedding party in Santa suits. He wants to point out he doesn't need a fake beard since he already has a real one."

"That sounds like Griff." She grinned. "And he would look great in red."

"It's his favorite color." Lucas paused, running his tongue along his bottom lip. "You're not going to dress us in Santa suits, are you?"

Caitie laughed. "Of course I'm not going to dress you in Santa suits. Unless you want me to, in which case I'll argue with you, but agree to, because it's your wedding."

"Ember would kill me. And you."

"I think we should both kill Griffin for thinking of the idea."

Lucas nodded. "Yeah, we definitely should. Except he's my best man. I kind of need him alive for now."

"Okay, okay, I won't kill him. But if he mentions Santa suits again, I may maim him. Or at least kick him in the groin, okay?"

Lucas smiled. "You could do it tonight. Everybody's coming over this evening. I was hoping you'd join us since you aren't leaving."

"At your beach cottage?" she asked. Lucas and Ember lived in the old cottage that used to belong to their grandparents. Caitie and Lucas had jointly owned it, but she'd happily sold her interest to him a while back. She had no desire to live anywhere near the ocean.

"Yeah. I can't wait for you to see what we've done with the place. You won't recognize it."

She took a deep breath. This was where she should finally confess her fear of the water. Explain how much she hated the sea, the beach, and everything it represented. But the thought alone made her chest tighten.

At first, maybe it had been self-preservation which caused her to keep her mouth shut. Back in those days, admitting to fear was like inviting Lucas and his friends to taunt her. But she was embarrassed, too. What California girl would admit to having a phobia about the beach? She wouldn't have been able to survive the ridicule.

And now it didn't matter. She lived in New York. No point in having a heart to heart about something that wasn't even an issue for most of the year.

"I have to work tonight," she said, wrinkling her nose. "I've got so much to catch up on before tomorrow."

"No way. Come on, Caitie. Everybody wants to see you. Breck and Jack, jeez even Griff. It won't be the same without you."

She swallowed hard. "I have too much to do. I need to rearrange a dozen meetings, plus I have to research venues for the wedding. I want to be all ready tomorrow when they open up for business."

"You sure?" Lucas looked genuinely disappointed.

If she was a stronger woman she'd head back with him. Hang out on the beach with Ember and her friends, splash in the surf with Griff and Jack.

See Brecken, the way her body wanted her to.

But she wasn't strong. It had been enough of a struggle last night at the beach club, but at least there'd been a distance between herself and the water. But she knew how close Lucas's cottage was to the shoreline. And the thought of being anywhere near there made her hands shake.

"I'm certain," she said, her voice full of apologies. "But tell them I'll catch up with them before I bail for New York, okay?"

Lucas shrugged and ruffled her hair. "Okay, little sis. It's your call."

She'd made the only one she could right now. She was only here for a week, and was determined to make it as painless as possible. Even if that meant missing out on seeing Brecken Miller again.

## 5

"Hey, Breck. Over here!"

Breck turned to see Lucas and their friends gathered down the beach from Lucas and Ember's cottage. They were sitting in a circle around an old fire pit, drinks in hand. The sun was slowly falling below the horizon, casting an orange hue across the surface. The light caught the faces of everybody looking toward the ocean, making them glow like there was a fire already lit in the pit.

"Hey." Breck put the six-pack of soda he'd brought into the cooler, keeping one for himself. "No fire tonight?"

Ember looked up at him. "Nope. We don't light fires if we don't need to."

"Not when the captain's around," Griff added, inclining his head at Lucas.

It was strange to think that Lucas was a fire captain now. He ran the Angel Sands station, having worked at the bigger White City station for the previous ten years. Breck admired him for it, knowing how hard his friend worked and all the terrible things he had to deal with.

"Makes sense," Breck said, shrugging. "And better for the environment, too."

"Right?" Ember's friend, Ally agreed. "I hate the way the beach looks all scorched after somebody's lit a fire. It can't be good for the ocean."

"It's not good for my heart rate either." Lucas grinned. "I have to deal with fires all day at my job. I'd rather not have them raging near my house."

Breck looked at them all. Everything about his friends felt familiar. There was something comforting about it. For the longest time after he'd left Angel Sands, he'd tried to imagine life going on here without him. It had hurt, knowing they'd still be happy even with him gone. But then again, everything had hurt in those days.

Now though, the pain was only a memory. Sometimes he'd poke at it, like a kid playing with a scab, trying to see if it still hurt. He'd picture his mom helping him build a sandcastle, or teaching Daniel to swim. Now they were echoes, instead of knives to his heart.

"Who's coming tonight?" he asked Lucas, looking around. There was Griff and Jack, of course, plus Ember and her friends, along with a few faces he recognized from the fire station where Lucas worked.

But there was one person who was missing. And it made his stomach feel tight.

"Pretty much everyone's here," Lucas told him.

"And one of them is very happy to see you," Griff said, taking a seat next to him, as he tried to get music to stream through the Bluetooth speakers.

"What?" Breck frowned, tipping his head to look at his friend. "Who?"

Griff gestured across the pit to where Ember and her friends were sitting. "Rachel Foss. She's been asking when you're going to get here for the last half hour. Man, that girl can talk."

Breck's mouth turned dry. He hadn't been expecting that at all. "Oh, yeah. She seems ... um... nice." It was the second time he'd seen her in as many days, and her interest was making him uncomfortable. In Boston, he would have told her he wasn't interested and never saw her again. But in a small town like this it wasn't so easy. Wherever he went, she'd be there. Plus she's Ember's friend. Better to let things fade out.

"She likes you, my friend," Griff said. "She told me at least ten times."

Breck grimaced. He had no idea what to say. So he took another mouthful of soda, swallowing it down.

"Is Caitie coming tonight?" he asked Lucas. The need to change the subject imperative.

Lucas shook his head. "Nah. I invited her, but she's too busy working. Said she had a lot to catch up on."

"Is that what she said?" Breck asked.

"Yeah." Lucas gave him a funny look. "Why?"

"I thought maybe it was because of the ocean. I'd hoped she might've been over that by now."

"Over what?" Lucas frowned, putting his can in the sand in front of him.

"Her fear..." Breck trailed off, his words swallowed up by the music that Griff finally managed to stream. The deep bass pumped through the evening air, keeping time with the pulse in his ear.

"What fear?" Lucas had to come closer to be heard. His face wrinkled in confusion.

So she'd never told him. And now Breck was revealing secrets that weren't his to tell. His stomach fell. Why the hell couldn't he keep his mouth shut? "Oh nothing."

"Come on. What are you talking about? Is my sister afraid of something?"

His lips felt as dry as the sand surrounding them. He took another mouthful of soda to moisten them. "Not that I know of. I haven't seen her for years."

Lucas wasn't letting go of it. He was like a dog with a bone. "But you said she *was*. Come on, man, what are you talking about?"

"I was kidding. You know, the way we used to call her Vampira? I was making a joke, a stupid one. Pretending she was afraid of the daylight."

"But it's not even light. The sun's going down." Lucas looked more confused than ever.

"That's why it was a stupid joke." Breck was a moment away from slapping himself. Why the hell did he start this? Only the worst kind of asshole spilled secrets about their friends. He could only hope his lame-ass explanation kept Lucas happy. Otherwise he was going to have some explaining to do.

---

"Honey, we're going out for an evening walk," Deenie called to Caitie. "We'll lock the door behind us. Try not to work too hard."

"I won't. Have a good walk," Caitie called out, turning back to her laptop. She was sitting on her bed, her MacBook balanced on her bare thighs. She'd changed into her pajamas after her shower; plaid shorts and a tank that revealed her pale skin in all its glory. Her wet hair was pulled back into a ponytail, and her reading glasses were balanced on her nose. Harper always called this her 'Clark Kent' look. She wasn't sure it was a compliment.

Caitie had already bookmarked twelve venues to call in the morning. Her plan was to find at least three she could take Lucas and Ember to look at. They'd told her they wanted a luxury hotel, one big enough to hold all the guests. Somewhere they could decorate with the holiday theme Ember loved. Of course the decorating would be easy – it *was* Caitie's niche – but unless she found somewhere to decorate, they'd be out of luck.

The sharp shrill of the doorbell made her jump. Caitie moved her laptop to the bed, securing it among the folds of the duvet, and ran to the hallway, assuming her mom had forgotten her key.

She pulled the door wide, her mouth open, ready to tease her mother. But standing there, beneath the glow of the lamp, was Brecken Miller, not her mom. He was leaning against the doorway, his golden hair ruffled by the breeze blowing in from the ocean.

"Breck?"

"Hey." He was smiling at her, that familiar, Brecken smile. All warm and full of sun. "Am I disturbing you?"

Hell yes he was disturbing her, but not in the way he'd meant. Her chest fluttered as he glanced down at her legs, taking in their bareness. "No," she said, smiling at him. "You're not disturbing me at all. Would you like to come in?"

He hesitated for a moment, looking at her with those warm eyes.

"You don't have to," she added quickly. "Mom and Dad are out if that's who you're looking for. They've gone for an evening walk. It's only me here. Or are you looking for Lucas?" Why wouldn't she shut up? Caitie tried to bite her tongue to make the agony stop.

"I know Lucas isn't here. I just left him at the beach."

"You were at the cottage?"

"Yeah, at their party. I was surprised not to see you there."

"He asked me, but I'm too busy." She gave him a tight

smile. "I have a wedding to organize and an inbox three feet deep."

"I have something to tell you. I think I really messed up," Breck told her with a quiet voice.

"Messed up how?" Her brows knitted together.

He cleared his throat. "I said something about you being afraid of the water."

"*Afraid?*" She wrapped her arms around her torso. "You said that?" Her breath caught in her throat.

"Yeah. I know you used to be when we were kids. Do you remember the time Lucas and Griff tried to drag you down there? You ran away and I found you crying. It only occurred to me when you didn't turn up tonight that you might still feel the same way. Somehow I started blabbering about it to your brother. I don't think he heard me though."

A shiver wracked through her. "Oh."

"Are you cold?" he asked, noticing the way her body shook. "I'm sorry, I shouldn't have come."

"Of course you should've. Come in," she said, stepping to the side to give him room to pass. "I'll make us both some coffee."

A strange expression passed over his face. "Sure, okay. I'll come in." He took a deep breath. "Man, it's been years since I walked through this door."

Caitie covered her mouth with her hand. He hadn't been here since *that* Christmas? "Oh, God, I hadn't thought. The last time you were here..."

"Was the Christmas my mom died." He blew out a mouthful of air. "I haven't been in this house since my dad picked us up all those years ago."

"That was such a bad time." Her eyes met his. "You don't have to come in. We can talk on the porch. You can stay here, I'll grab a sweater."

He shook his head. "No, I want to come in. It's just bricks

and mortar, right? Can't hurt me anymore. Anyway, some of my happiest childhood memories were in this house. The good definitely outweighs the bad."

"Only if you're comfortable."

He gave the faintest of smiles. "It'll be fine." As he brushed past her to make his way inside she felt the whisper of his jeans against her thighs.

Her bare thighs.

"Why don't you go to the kitchen?" she suggested, her face heating up at the thought of how exposed she was. "You remember the way, right? I'll grab my sweater."

She ran down the hallway to her bedroom. Pulling the door shut behind her, she leaned her back against the wall. Taking her glasses off, she closed her eyes and pressed her palms to her face, feeling the heat from her flushed cheeks. Why did she have to be wearing so few clothes and these ugly glasses? He must think she was such a mess. Way to show she was all grown up, looking like a teenage girl, with a wet pony-tail and all.

Mortified, she grabbed a hoody from her closet. Once she pulled it over her head, she readjusted her hair. Refusing to glance in the mirror – she wasn't *that* much of a masochist – she pulled her door open, and went to join him in the kitchen.

"Regular coffee okay?" she asked him. He looked up and nodded with a half smile. "That's good," she said, desperate to cheer him up. "So many people prefer decaf in the evenings. I think they're missing the whole point."

"Decaf's for wimps," he said gruffly.

She grinned. "My sentiments exactly."

He was sitting at the breakfast bar, his elbows propped on the counter. As she filled the coffee filter with granules, she scrutinized him out of the corner of her eye. Though his jaw was still set tight, the color had returned to his face. She hoped the memories weren't tearing him up.

"So, how was the party?" she asked. "Apart from spilling all my secrets, of course." She kept her tone light.

"I'm so sorry. I think I managed to cover it up. I didn't realize Lucas didn't know. I thought after all these years you would have told him. Or maybe you'd gotten over it."

"I thought I'd be over it, too." It was awkward as hell, discussing this with Breck.

"But you're not?"

She wrinkled her nose and grabbed the milk from the refrigerator. "No, I'm not. But it doesn't matter."

"Of course it matters. Why didn't you tell him? Does your mom know?"

She grabbed two mugs from the cupboard. It felt so much better to be doing something than looking at Breck. "No. I haven't really told anybody, apart from you and Harper."

"Harper?"

"My best friend. I live with her in New York. We went to college together."

"Why would you tell her and not your mom?" He sounded genuinely interested. "You've always gotten along with your folks, haven't you?"

"Yeah, of course. But the longer I didn't tell them, the worse it got. Now I'm older, and it really doesn't matter. I hardly spend any time here, so the beach isn't an issue any more. And they don't need to spend their time worrying about me."

"It's an issue if you can't go visit your brother at his cottage," Breck pointed out. "If it stops you from doing what you want to, then it's a problem, isn't it?"

She rubbed the back of her neck. "I didn't go to the party because I have work to do."

"Seriously?" He cocked his head, squinting his eyes.

"Yes," Caitie lied. "There was nothing more sinister than that. I've spent most of the night trying to find a location for their wedding." She shrugged and poured out their coffees. "How'd you take it?"

"Milk, no sugar please. And I'm sorry if I upset you."

"I'm sorry, too. I didn't mean to snap at you."

He smiled. "I shouldn't have been so intrusive. What kind of friend turns up after being away for all these years and starts making you feel bad?"

"The sort of friend sitting opposite me." She grinned back at him. "And I know you're trying to be nice. The water's a stupid thing to be afraid of, even I know that."

"Phobia's aren't stupid. They're reactions to traumatic events." He swallowed hard, his eyes never leaving hers. "After what happened to you, it's completely understandable you'd be afraid of the ocean. But there are people out there who can help."

"Like therapists?" she asked. "I tried a couple of them. One of them wanted me to jump in the ocean and get over it." She frowned, looking down at her mug. "I figure it's not worth dealing with. Not when it's not a phobia that affects me everyday."

When she looked up from her coffee, Breck was still staring at her. She couldn't read his expression at all. But whatever he was thinking, there was something so glorious about him that it made her feel like she was fifteen years old again, mooning after her brother's best friend. Wishing he'd think of her as more than an annoying kid.

Yeah, well he didn't back then, and he clearly didn't now. He'd come here to check on her and make sure she was okay, not because he was attracted to her. And though it was sweet of him, it made her heart hurt.

Because there was a part of her that wished he felt the same way she did.

## 6

Breck never had any problem sleeping, or at least he hadn't until tonight. When he was a kid, his mom used to say a bandit could sneak into his bedroom, carry him out and smuggle him across the border, and he'd just mumble and turn over.

So why was he finding it impossible to sleep now?

He turned in his bed, the sheets tangling over him as he reached for his phone and checked the time. One-forty. Only five hours before he had to get up and head over to the resort, and be in charge of fifty men and god knows how many pieces of expensive, heavy machinery.

He needed to get back to sleep, dammit.

Another fruitless minute of twisting and turning passed before he dragged his ass out of bed. He was wearing nothing more than a pair of sleep shorts, thanks to the California weather. Even in October, the night temperatures didn't dip too low. As he walked into his kitchen, he circled his head, trying to loosen the knots of muscles in his neck and shoulders.

He grabbed the carton of orange juice from the fridge and

poured it into a glass, drinking the sweet liquid in one mouthful. His lips twitched as he remembered the way he used to drink from the carton to annoy his mom. She'd shake her head at him as he walked past, but there was always a twinkle in her eye.

God, what wouldn't he do to see her twinkle again? She'd have loved the fact he'd come back to Angel Sands. Even though she was constantly busy, working to keep a roof over their heads, she always had time for talking about school and his friends.

He leaned on the counter, looking out of the big glass doors leading down to the beach. He'd chosen this cottage for the view. Within twenty minutes of seeing this place he'd signed a year long rental contract, determined to enjoy being within close proximity to the beach for the first time in almost fifteen years.

Though it was too dark to make out the sea, he could hear it. The rhythmic lapping of the waves against the shore managed to sneak in through the gaps in the windows, syncing with his heartbeat as he softly breathed in.

What would it be like to hate that sound so much it made you want to leave town? He thought of the way Caitie frowned when he'd mentioned her fear of the water. How she tried to change the subject. And those two little lines that appeared in between her brows, that he'd itched to smooth away.

He swallowed hard, the taste of orange juice lingering on his tongue. Her skin was as smooth as porcelain. Somehow in the years since he left, she'd grown up to become a stunning woman. The type of woman that people stopped and stared at, just because she had a presence wherever she went. With her dark hair, pale face, and warm brown eyes that seemed to be as big as saucers, she was impossible to ignore.

*Yeah, she's also your best friend's sister,* the little voice in his head reminded him. You didn't go there. As a kid that kind of thing was verboten. Nowadays, it was asking for trouble. He'd only recently come back into town and reconnected with friends he hadn't realized he'd missed. He wasn't ready to mess that up because his skin tingled whenever a certain woman was around.

She'd be leaving soon, and maybe that was a good thing. He didn't like complications, and he definitely wasn't looking for a relationship. He ran the pad of his thumb along his jaw, feeling the growth of hair that had happened since he last shaved, his eyes fixed on a faraway spot in the darkness of the outside.

It was better to be single. Less messy and so much easier. Seeing his parents break up when he was a kid was bad enough. Losing his mom when he was a teenager made it worse. Love hurt like hell no matter which way you looked at it. He'd spent a lifetime watching people leave; he didn't need to put himself through that again.

He'd be okay. He was a grown man in charge of his feelings. Just because something was itching, didn't mean he needed to scratch it. Best to push it deep down inside, where all his emotions were locked up, and carry on being laid back and carefree.

Pulling the dishwasher open, he put his empty glass on the rack and headed back to his bedroom, determined this time he'd fall asleep. And tomorrow? Well, maybe then he could get the pretty brunette out of his mind.

---

Caitie paused outside the bridal store in the mall, looking at the dresses modeled on the mannequins; the display was stunning. There were dresses of every shade of white, some strapless, some with fur stoles wrapped around the cloth shoulders. Hanging from the ceiling were giant cut out snowflakes, and scattered across the floor were wrapped gifts in shades of gold.

*Everything You Need For Your Winter Wedding*, the sign proclaimed. Caitie bit her lip as she wondered if they could provide a venue, too.

She'd agreed to meet Ember here for a dress fitting right before four. All the bridal party was due to be here, apart from Ember's sister, who was back in Sacramento where she was studying. Her fitting would be last minute, when she was back for winter break. Ember had been breathless when she'd told Caitie she'd seen the exact dresses she'd always dreamed of, and wanted her opinion. That's how she found herself walking along the tiled floor of the mall that afternoon.

"Caitie, over here." Ember waved as she walked into the shop. She was surrounded by her friends, sitting on the luxurious leather sofas, frosted glasses of champagne in their hands. "Would you like a glass?"

"No thank you. I'm driving." Caitie smiled in greeting at Ember's friends. She remembered Brooke and Ally from the engagement party. They'd made her feel so welcome, reminding her that they knew her from school, talking about mutual friends. And then there was Ember's work friend, Rachel. She was quieter than the others, but seemed nice. Caitie said hello to her, and Rachel waved back.

"Okay ladies," the saleswoman said, coming over to top up their glasses. "Who wants to go first? Should we start with the bride?"

"Do we have to?" Ember's face was pink, as though she didn't like the limelight.

"Yes," Ally said, grinning at her friend's discomfort. "We definitely do."

As Ember was fitted for her dress, Caitie took her seat,

and sipped a glass of cool spring water. Her muscles were aching from too little sleep and too much midnight thinking.

"How's the search for a venue going?" Brooke asked, her eyes full of sympathy. Caitie guessed Ember had shared their futile search with her friends already.

"Not great," Caitie admitted. "We tried twenty different places today. I can't find anywhere available within driving distance of Angel Sands."

"It's such a shame the Beach Club's fully booked," Ally said. "That would have been perfect."

"Or Delmonico's on the pier," Brooke added, referring to the town's favorite restaurant. "That would have worked if it was a little bigger."

"I'm scared we're going to have to change the date," Caitie confessed. "And I know it'll break Ember's heart. She seems so set on a Christmas wedding."

"I think she just wants to be married to your brother as soon as possible," Rachel said, shrugging. "And who can blame her. He's hot as hell. He needs to be off the market right now."

"Yuck," Caitie said, wrinkling her nose. "That's my brother you're talking about."

"I thought you preferred Breck," Ally said, grinning.

For a moment, Caitie thought Ally was talking to her. But she realized her eyes were on Rachel, and Caitie's stomach dropped.

"I do," Rachel said, her voice low. "He's gorgeous. Have you seen him when he's surfing? He has muscles in places they have no right to be."

Caitie took another sip, her pulse drumming against her ears. So what if there was something going on between Rachel and Breck? It had nothing to do with her; she didn't even live here. They were grown ups, what they did with their private life was up to them.

And yet she couldn't ignore the way her heart ached a little. She was being stupid, she knew, and yet it hurt to think of Breck and Rachel together.

"How are things going with you two, anyway?" Brooke asked Rachel.

"I'd say they're going well. I saw him at Ember's place last night and we talked about going surfing together. He just seems really shy."

Breck shy? That's not how she'd describe him. Caitie put her empty glass down on the table and picked up one of the magazines displayed there. She leafed through it, trying not to listen as Rachel, Brooke, and Ally talked about Breck. A glance at her watch told her it was only quarter past four. With four more of them to fit, it was going to be a long afternoon.

"Oh!" Brooke gasped. Caitie looked up from the magazine she'd been staring at to see Ember slowly walking out of the dressing room. The sales assistant was behind her, holding the back of the ivory dress out. But it wasn't the dress that drew Caitie's eye, it was the way Ember was beaming at them all.

"What do you think?" she asked.

It was made of warm ivory satin that contrasted with Ember's dark hair. The bodice fit her tiny frame perfectly, the Bardot-style neckline revealing her tan shoulders and delicate arms. It was cinched in at the waist before flaring into a full skirt covered with a layer of lace. The way it cascaded down to the floor made it look like a frozen waterfall.

"You look amazing," Brooke said.

"Like a princess," Rachel breathed.

"It's perfect," Caitie said, her voice thick. "Lucas is a lucky guy."

"He really is," Rachel agreed. "I can't wait to see his face when you walk down the aisle."

"Do you really think he'll like it?" Ember said, turning her eyes on Caitie.

"He'll love it," Caitie told her, nodding firmly.

"Can I go next?" Rachel asked, as the sales assistant led Ember back to the dressing room. "I want to see the bridesmaid dresses."

"Yes, of course." Ember smiled warmly at her friend. "Let's go and try them on."

Rachel clapped her hands together, looking a little giddy. "Oh I love weddings. They're the only time we get to look like princesses. I can't wait for Breck to see my dress."

It was another hour before Caitie was standing in front of the floor length mirror, wearing her bra and panties as the sales assistant lifted the dress over her head. Her arms were pointing at the ceiling as the assistant had directed, and Caitie stood as still as she could while the woman zipped up the strapless dress.

"Oh, this color is amazing," the assistant said. "It looked great on the others, but it's like it was made for you. You have the most perfect skin."

"Thank you," Caitie said. She looked at herself in the mirror, taking in the rich burgundy satin and the way it clung to her upper body.

"It's not often we see skin like yours in California. Let me guess, you're from out of town."

Caitie couldn't help but chuckle at that. "Kind of," she admitted. "I was born and raised here, but I left for college when I was eighteen."

"You grew up here and have skin like this? What did you do, wear sunblock from the moment you were born?"

Caitie shrugged. "I've never been much of a sun-worshipper. I preferred reading in the shade when I was younger."

"Well it looks good on you. It's weird how you can buy

fake tan, but you can't buy fake pale. I'd pay good money to have your skin."

"Thank you." She wasn't sure what else to say.

"Okay, you can go on out. Let your friends see how good you look." The assistant stepped back so Caitie could turn around. She fussed with the pinned hemline for a moment, lifting it so Caitie could walk in the bridal shoes they'd loaned her. "Remember, when you're wearing a dress like this you're never in a rush to get anywhere."

As soon as she stepped into the main shop she heard Ember's gasp. All four of them stood and walked over to her, telling her how beautiful she looked, how the color was perfect on her.

"It's perfect," Ember whispered to her, giving her a hug. "I'm so happy it suits you. I want everybody to have a great time at the wedding, you included. Or especially you, since you're working so hard on it."

Caitie felt her chest flutter. She was trying her best, but right now it wasn't good enough. Without a venue, buying these dresses was pointless. She couldn't help but feel like she was letting her brother and Ember down. They'd asked her for help, but they were no further forward.

Ember was still smiling at her, and Caitie did her best to smile back. Even if she had to build a damn venue, brick by brick, one way or another, she was determined to make this wedding work.

## 7

"Hey, you planning on riding the waves on Saturday?" Lucas's voice echoed through the phone speaker. Holding his phone in one hand, Breck opened the refrigerator with his other, pulling out a can of soda and popping the tab.

"Sounds good to me," he said, lifting the can to his lips. "I have to do some work in the afternoon, but as long as we go out early, I'm up for it."

"I've gotta make it early, too," Lucas agreed. "I'm on shift on Sunday, and Ember has a list of things to do as long as your arm. It's a good thing she's no bridezilla."

Whenever Lucas talked about his fiancée there was a warmth in his voice that made Breck smile. "How's the wedding planning going?" he asked.

"Kind of so-so. We still havn't found a venue. Ember's panicking and Caitie keeps apologizing, even though it's not her fault. The poor kid's doing her best, you know?"

The mention of her name made Breck's breath catch in his throat. God, he thought he was over that. Since the other night he'd deliberately put her out of his mind.

He sat on the deck of his beachside bungalow and propped his feet on the table in front of him. He'd gone for a run earlier that evening, and his hair was still damp from the shower he'd taken afterward. But his body still felt full of energy.

"You know, if you wait another year you could have the wedding at the Silver Sands Resort. We should be up and running long before next Christmas."

"Yeah, well we can't wait that long. It'd kill Ember to have to postpone the wedding." Lucas cleared his throat. "She was engaged to another guy before, and he ran off before they got married. There's no way I'm breaking her heart by suggesting we don't go through with it. We're getting married *this* December, even if we have to do it in a shed."

"You're a nice guy, did you know that?"

Lucas laughed. "Ah, I have my moments. But really, I'm a lucky guy. I know when I have a good thing, and I want to make her mine forever."

When they were kids, they would have laughed at anybody being so openly emotional. And yet Lucas's honesty touched Breck in a way that wasn't funny at all. You only had to see Lucas and Ember together to know how much in love they were.

And yeah, maybe it felt weird to see so many people in love when he was single. But that was okay. He liked being his own man, making his own decisions. Being single was simple, and he preferred things that way.

"You'll find somewhere," Breck said. "Or Caitie will. She's always been the kind of girl you can depend on."

"Yeah. She's a diamond. I just wish she didn't have to spend all this time trying to help us out. With her business she's constantly busy. I feel like we've added to her burdens. She should be in New York right now, and instead she's here trying to save her big brother's wedding."

"She loves you, man."

"Yeah." Lucas's voice was thick. "Makes me feel bad for the way I treated her when we were kids."

"You weren't so bad. No worse than any other big brother. She knew at the end of the day you had her back. Heck, we all had her back. It must have been like having four big brothers when we were around."

Lucas laughed. "And yet she's still talking to me. Okay, I'd better go. Ember just walked through the door."

"She been working late?"

"Yeah. At some school event," Lucas told him. "I'll see you on Saturday."

"Not if I see you first." Funny how that always came out, the same way it had when they were kids.

After hanging up, Breck grabbed his can and slid his shoes on, walking down the steps leading to the beach. The sun was setting over the horizon, sliding down into the sea, leaving a trail of orange and purple behind. He sat down on the sand and gazed out at the ocean.

There was something so peaceful about the beach at this time of night. Though the waves were still crashing, they were gentler somehow. The wide expanse of silver sand was empty; all the families and tourists had long since left. Now it was only the residents whose feet left impressions in the grains.

He'd missed this feeling. The smell of the sea, the sound of the waves, the sensation of the gentle breeze on his face. He'd grown up with it, having spent his happiest times on the beach. It was hard to be upset when faced with such beauty.

Unless you were Caitlin Russell. Funny how his thoughts always slid to her whenever he was out here. He wondered what she'd say if he showed her around his bungalow. Whether she'd start to shake the way she always used to whenever she was within sight of the shoreline. More than once he'd seen her become physically sick at the thought of being dragged down to the beach.

*Yeah, well everybody has fears, dumbass. Even you.*

He rolled his eyes at his own thoughts. There was no way he was going to listen to them. So much better to think about Caitie and let his knight-in-shining armor instincts win out.

He grabbed his phone and pulled up his contacts, pressing on a number to connect a call. Even if his own problems were unsolvable, he knew Caitie's – or at least one of them – wasn't impossible to fix.

---

It was an hour and several phone calls later when he finally dialed Caitie's number, having texted Lucas for it. He was still sitting on the deck, but this time he had a notepad in front of him, an address scrawled across it in his terrible handwriting. His soda had long since been replaced by a beer.

"Hello?" She sounded breathless. Or maybe breathy. Either way, he liked it.

"Caitie?"

"This is she. Who am I speaking to?"

He felt a weird sense of disappointment that she didn't recognize him right away. "It's Breck."

"Breck?" Her voice softened, as though she was relieved. "Oh, I'm sorry, I didn't recognize your voice. I thought it might be a business call."

"At this time of night?" He raised an eyebrow.

"I get calls at all kinds of crazy hours. Especially when I'm consulting for a movie. The director wakes up in the middle of the night and wants to know whether Christmas trees had angels or stars on them in the seventeen hundreds." There was a trace of laughter in her voice.

"What's the answer?" he asked, intrigued.

"Neither. The Christmas tree didn't make it over here until the 1850s. There wasn't one in the White House until 1853." She let out a deep breath. "Sorry, this must be boring as hell for you. I get all kinds of geeky about stuff like this."

"You don't need to be sorry. It's interesting. You really love your job, don't you?"

"Yeah, I do. I'm a Christmas freak; everybody thinks I'm crazy. Good thing it pays well."

"I bet your mom doesn't think you're crazy." He tried to imagine Deenie's indignation if she heard anybody insulting Caitie like that.

"No she doesn't. She's my biggest cheerleader, thank goodness. She was really supportive when I started up the business, even if everybody else told me it would never work."

"I bet she was. Your mom's amazing."

"She is." Her voice was soft. "I'm lucky to have her."

"I owe your folks a lot. They really took care of Daniel and me." He blinked, staring out at the ocean. "You did, too."

"You both deserved to be looked after." Her voice cracked. "After all you'd been through."

It felt like she was tugging at a zipper on his skin, trying to open him up. But he couldn't expose himself – not even to the girl with a heart of gold. He took a deep breath. "Anyway, there was a point in my phone call," he said, deftly changing the subject.

"Do tell."

"I was talking to Lucas and he said you haven't found a wedding venue yet."

"He's right, I haven't." She sighed, her breath gentle down the phone line. "I've tried everywhere but it's too short notice. They're all fully booked. I hate to say it, but I'm thinking of invading the Beach Club and refusing to leave until the two of them are married."

"Well, I might have found somewhere for you."

"You have?" she asked, her voice rising up with surprise. "Where?"

Breck leaned his head back on the bungalow behind him. "I called an old friend up in Golden Hills. We worked on their hotel a few years back. They've had an event canceled on the twenty-third of December. If you want to book it, it's yours."

Her voice rose with excitement. "That sounds too good to be true."

"It's for real. They said they could hold the date open until Friday. After that, they'll have to release it to the market. Juan – he's the owner – said you can go over and take a look whenever you like. If you're free tomorrow I can take you up there. I've got some business to do over that way."

"Brecken Miller, you're a miracle worker." The silkiness of her voice made his skin heat up. "And Golden Hills really isn't that far. What is it, a couple of hours?"

"Yeah, and there's plenty of accommodation if people want to stay the night. Plus it's miles away from the ocean."

Caitie laughed. "In that case, I'm sold. But honestly, you might've just saved my life. And Lucas's. Quite possibly Ember's, too. Are you really okay to take me over there tomorrow? Otherwise I can drive myself."

He bit his lip, trying not to think about the meetings he was supposed to have at the Silver Sands Resort the next day. His foreman could take care of those.

"It would be my pleasure. I'll pick you up right after nine."

"That would be great. Thank you so much, Breck. I owe you big time."

For some reason, he liked the sound of that.

---

Le Chateau Des Tournesols stood proudly at the top of a

steep hill, the castle towering over the valley below. The slopes surrounding it were carved with terraces housing bungalows and swimming pools, as well as the beautiful sunflowers the hotel was named after, which were reaching the end of their growth. Built in a French-renaissance style, with a grey-stone façade and rounded turrets so typical of that era, it looked as though a tiny piece of the Loire Valley had been transported into the Californian hills. Caitie stared at it again, narrowing her eyes as she took in the majesty of the estate. Picturing her brother's wedding here didn't take much effort at all.

"It's perfect." Caitie turned to look at Breck, her eyes glowing. "Are you sure it's in their price range? They're already stretched as it is."

Breck gave her a half-smile. "Juan promised he'll keep the cost as low as he can. With the deposit the cancel event paid, they should still turn a healthy profit."

She hesitated. In her line of work people were always doing favors for each other. She'd practically worked for free during her first year of business, determined to build up her client base as quickly as possible. But she also knew business was business and people had to make a profit.

"As long as it doesn't cause him any problems, this could be the answer to all our dreams."

"It won't," Breck assured her. "And anyway, I did him a few favors in the past. This is just payback." His eyes were soft as he looked at her. "And if you need something to swing it for you, Juan has a wedding coordinator on the staff. She's agreed to assist you while you're back in New York."

"Oh my god, that's fantastic." Caitie's smile softened her lips. She hoped he knew how grateful she was. "I'll need Ember and Lucas to take a look before I can confirm. I've taken as many photos as I can, but there's no way I can agree to anything without them seeing it for themselves. But I'm definitely sold."

"Agreed. While you were on the tour with Juan, I texted Lucas and told him to get up here by Friday. As long as we put the deposit down by Saturday, Juan's happy to give you the date."

She rolled her lip between her teeth, feeling herself relax for the first time in days. Maybe she could pull this wedding off after all.

They sat at a white-painted cast iron table on the lowest terrace. Though the sun was beating down, the clouds were hanging low in the sky, their wispy forms turning greyer by the minute. The air around them felt heavy.

"I won't be able to be here. I have to be in L.A. for a meeting Thursday," she told him. "And then I am flying home." She felt a knot forming in her belly at the thought.

Breck nodded. "Lucas and Ember can come on their own. I'm pretty sure Juan will provide them with lunch. Maybe you can persuade them to stay the night. To see everything the place has to offer. Hopefully the weather will be a bit better." He gestured at the darkening sky. "They could even go for a swim in the Greek-themed pool.

"That's some pool," she said, remembering the cerulean mirror of water, surrounded by Grecian columns and marble statues.

"You didn't like it much, did you?" Breck said, scrutinizing her expression.

"No I did. It was nice," she told him, nodding her head to emphasize her answer. "Beautifully styled. They did a good job on it."

"Thanks." He raised an eyebrow.

"Did you build it?" she asked, blinking with surprise.

"Yep." His brows knitted together as he stared at her, hesitation deepening his voice. "Are you scared of swimming pools as well?" he asked. He sounded genuinely concerned. Seeing her blanch at his question, he hurriedly added, "You don't have to answer. If I'm getting too personal, please tell me."

She looked at him, taking in the dark blond hair, brushed back from his brow, and the light blue shirt, tieless, open at the collar. He did business casual as effortlessly as he did surfer-cool. "You're not being too personal," she told him. "I know how stupid it sounds. I've never had any terrible experiences in a swimming pool, but if I go near one I feel weird. It's not the same as going near the ocean, nowhere near. But I still avoid them when I can."

"Do you take baths?"

She busted out laughing. "Now *that's* getting personal. Do I smell or something?"

"I'm trying to figure out how far this phobia goes. Is it all water, or just bodies of water? Do you hate showers? Hate getting your face wet?" He pointed up at the sky. "If it starts to rain, am I going to have to carry you inside like some asshole out of a movie? I can if you want me to. I go to the gym, I work out. I just need to know how far you want me to go here."

She pursed her lips, trying not to laugh. "I'm not scared of rain."

"Showers?"

"I take one every day."

"And baths?" he asked again.

Caitie sighed. "We don't have a tub in our apartment in New York. Just a stall. But I'm not really a bath kind of girl. I don't find it relaxing like some people do. So maybe there's a little bit of fear there. And for the record, I'm not scared of rain, unless it starts a flood, in which case all bets are off."

He leaned forward, refilling her glass from the water carafe Juan had left them. Their plates of cheese and fresh

French bread had long since been emptied. "If it floods, I think we'll be okay. We're on a hilltop, there's no safer place to be. And if the worst comes to the worst, I've always fancied myself as a knight in shining armor. I'll save you."

"I bet you would." She was trying to stop an inane smile from breaking out on her lips. Spending time with him was like looking into the sun. Dazzling and bright, yet oh-so-warming. She wanted to bask in him.

"Have you ever thought about going back to therapy? Giving it a try again?"

She blinked. "That's even more personal than asking me about my bathing habits."

Breck shrugged. "There's nothing embarrassing about therapy. Or there shouldn't be. I went for a couple of years after Mom died."

"Did it help?" She took a sip of water. Her mouth felt dryer than ever. Maybe she shouldn't have eaten so much bread.

"As much as it could help anybody. I was a teenage boy, remember? I wasn't keen on talking about myself. Plus I went with Daniel, so half the time I felt like the protective older brother. I just wanted him to cry it all out."

"He was so young. You both were. It must have been a hell of a shock having to move east with your dad."

Breck leaned back on his chair, crossing his arms in front of his chest. He was staring right past her – at the hotel, she guessed – a frown played at his lips and brow. "It was..." he trailed off, as though he couldn't find the words. "It was devastating, I guess. I don't remember everything. I think the mind blocks a lot of the trauma out. But having lived with Mom for the first seventeen years of my life, it was like moving in with a stranger. We hadn't seen a whole lot of our dad until then. And if I'm being honest, I really resented him. Where was he when Mom was going through treatment, through chemo? Where was he when she was throwing up in the bathroom every day?"

"It was a lot for a kid to take on," Caitie said, her heart clenching. "Plus you had Daniel to look after. I don't know how you did it." She reached out for his hand, pulling it from his chest. He slid his fingers through hers, folding them so the tips almost covered her skin.

"I did it because I had no choice. And if you ask my dad he'll tell you I made him pay for it, too. I was an asshole to him for the first year we were there. I challenged his authority at every turn. If he got into a fight with me or Daniel I'd been there with my fists, telling him he wasn't a real father.."

"Did he hit you?" She leaned closer. The thought of anybody hurting a teenage Breck made her want to be sick.

"Never. Nor Daniel. I was the punk back then, not him. It took me a lot of time to finally trust him. Much longer than it took Daniel. But Dad had the patience of a saint. He was willing to wait as long as it took for me to believe in him."

"He sounds like a good man." Her neck felt tight. As though the lining inside her throat was swelling, restricting her airways. It made her words sound deep and thick.

"He's a great guy, more of a friend than a parental figure now. Plus he's technically my boss, so I kind of have to be nice to him." He grinned. "He's over this way often. Maybe you can meet him the next time he comes."

"Oh." She looked down at their intertwined hands. "I'm not in California very much. This is my first visit to Angel Sands in years." Looking up, she gave him a small smile. "I don't suppose you have a lot of work in New York?"

Breck laughed, his chest rising and falling as he chuckled. Her eyes were drawn to his neckline again, to his strong throat, and his light brown chest hair. He hadn't bothered shaving that morning, and his jaw was peppered with stubble.

And though his eyes were covered with aviator sunglasses, she knew behind them his irises were a vivid blue.

"Nah, we've never cracked into New York. New England and California, that's pretty much as far as the Miller Empire extends." He screwed up his nose. "I don't think I could stand to work in New York. It's always so crazy and busy. Noisy, too. I'm getting palpitations just thinking about it. And God only knows what the zoning laws are like."

"New York's not that bad."

A large drop of rain fell into her water glass, another following close behind. She looked up to the sky, watching as the clouds overhead turned even darker. A third raindrop splashed her face. "I think the sky's about to empty," she told Breck, wiping her cheek with the back of her hand. They stood up, gathering her things, stuffing folders, papers, and pens into Caitie's bag.

"You know the offer's still open," Breck said, sliding his sunglasses over his brow. She'd never get tired of staring at those eyes.

"What offer?"

"I can carry you in. It'll be as romantic as hell. At least until I pull a muscle in my back."

"Osteopathy's always sexy," she agreed, lifting her bag up to cover her head. The rain began coming down fast, fat droplets splashed against the stones beneath them. "Thanks, but I'll be okay. I can save myself."

"I bet you can."

The way he was looking at her took her breath away. All narrow eyed and strong, sharp jawed. She swallowed hard, feeling her dress as it started to cling to her skin, her hair falling in wet tendrils in spite of the shelter her bag provided.

Yes, she could save herself. She'd been doing it for years. But she couldn't help but wonder what it would be like to let somebody else do it for a change.

## ❧ 8 ❧

"Come on. I'm not taking 'no' for an answer." Harper grabbed at Caitie's arm, urging her out of the dining chair she'd been holed up in for the past nine hours. "Seriously, girl, it's almost eight on a Friday night. You're twenty-eight, not ninety-five. Come out and have some fun."

Caitie had been back in New York for over a week, but she hadn't settled into her usual breakneck speed. Maybe it was something to do with the fact she wasn't sleeping well. She'd blame it on the wedding planning, but thanks to Breck, that was actually going well – they'd secured the hotel, and now she was working on the little details.

Of course, she was swamped with work as usual. More so, since she was preparing for a big pitch after Thanksgiving, hoping to win a five-year contract at the Hollywood Hills Theme Park as their Holiday Coordinator. If she got it, she'd be spending a lot more time in California. The thought of it made her skin fizz.

Then there was Brecken Miller. She hadn't heard from him since she'd flown back from LAX, but that hadn't stopped her from thinking about him every night as she tossed and turned in her bed. It was stupid. He was being his usual kind self, helping her out with the hotel and talking to her about her fears. Yes, she still found him crazily attractive, but there was nothing she could do about that. They lived across the country from each other, and even if they didn't he didn't see her as anything more than a friend.

She'd have to get used to it.

"You look amazing," Caitie said, looking at Harper. "I love that dress. Is it new?"

"I made it myself," Harper told her, tucking a lock of her blonde-and-pink hair behind her ear. She gave Caitie a little twirl, her broderie anglais skirt fanning out as she turned. "I found this material in a thrift store downtown. Somebody had donated a whole roll of it. I'll make you something out of it if you like."

"I'd love that." Caitie grinned. To supplement her income as a costume designer on Broadway, Harper made one-off designs and sold them on eBay and Etsy, as well as in markets around New York. For a while she'd considered giving up her day job altogether and concentrating on her dressmaking, but in the end the lure of a regular wage was too strong.

Still, their apartment was filled with racks of one-off dresses, along with the boxes of decorations and samples Caitie regularly brought home from work. When people walked in they always did a double take, wondering if they were in a private residence or a downtown boutique.

"Okay, I'll make you a dress. But only if you come out tonight. Come on, I *need* to spend some time with my friend." Harper gave her an impish grin. "Pretty please?"

"Maybe..." Caitie vacillated. "If I can just get this board finished off."

"What are you doing?" Harper asked, putting her hand on Caitie's shoulder as she looked at her laptop screen.

"I'm making a mood board for Ember and Lucas's

wedding. We need to get everything ordered by next week, and I want to make sure they're happy with the designs." She leaned back to let Harper see.

The mood board was a screen full of photographic ideas. On the left was a picture of the venue at Christmas, the exterior decorated with snow tipped garlands and surrounded by fir trees all lit up with stars on top. The second photograph showed the interior, with its sweeping staircase that Ember would walk down. Caitie had done a mock up to show how the Christmas tree would coordinate with the colors Ember had chosen, with thick silken ribbons of burgundy and ivory swathed around the branches. Then there were the chair decorations and the table settings, along with suggestions for the invitations and the placement cards. Everything was painstakingly chosen to be festive yet elegant. Caitie hoped to hell Ember and Lucas would like it when she sent the link to them tonight.

"That's amazing," Harper breathed. "You're so talented."

"Says the girl who makes beautiful clothes."

"I swear we need to go into business together," Harper said, still staring open mouthed at the screen. "We could make everybody's dreams come true."

"You can make the bride's dress and be the wedding singer, I'll do the rest," Caitie grinned.

"Wouldn't it be a blast? Let's give up our jobs and run away together." Harper looped her arms around Caitie's shoulders and hugged her. "You know you want to."

"I haven't got time to run away," Caitie said ruefully. "I need to organize this wedding. And I haven't even booked our plane tickets for Thanksgiving. They're bound to have gone up by two hundred dollars since I last looked."

"Eek!" Harper tipped her head to the side. "You want me to get them? I can take a look tomorrow?"

Caitie shook her head. "Don't worry. I said I'd do it, and

it's my own fault I haven't. And I'm kidding about the cost. It'll be fine."

Caitie's mom had invited Harper to join them for Thanksgiving, and Harper had jumped at the chance to fly to California. Especially now that the temperatures had plummeted in New York.

"I bet you feel like you're living on airplanes at the moment," Harper said, giving her a soft smile. "It feels like you've only just come back from Angel Sands."

"I've been back for a week. Although with the amount of work I've had to catch up on it feels like longer." Caitie grimaced.

Harper shook her head, her black hair swinging out behind her. "You work too hard. I've been telling you this for years. That's why you need to come out tonight. I've only got a few weeks off before I start the next production, and after that I won't be going out on Friday nights at all. So do your friend a favor and come out and have some fun. I miss you. New York misses you."

"Okay, okay!" Caitie put her hands up in submission. "Let me email this to my brother and I'll go and get ready."

Harper did a fist pump. "Yes! I knew you'd give in eventually. And while you're making yourself pretty, I'll make us both a cocktail. It's Friday night and it's time to feel good."

---

An hour later, they were walking into the Dead Rabbit Bar, their hair sprinkled with rain, which began to fall as they scrambled out of their cab. The bar – a converted warehouse in the meatpacking district – was packed, and it took them a while to make their way to the corner where their friend Kristi and her workmates had gathered at a booth.

"Hey, stranger!" Kristi stood up and grabbed Caitie,

pulling her close. They'd been friends ever since they'd all moved to New York, having shared an apartment until Kristi moved in with her boyfriend, and Harper and Caitie had upgraded. "I haven't seen you for months. Where've you been holed up?"

"Work." Caitie screwed her nose up. "And I should have called you, I'm sorry. How's Trent?"

"He's good. Just got a promotion. We're hoping we'll be able to save enough money to get married next year."

"That's wonderful. I guess it's still too early to say congratulations?"

"It's never too soon," Kristi said, grinning.

"How about Trent?" Caitie asked her. "Is he excited?"

"He's over there." Kristi gestured at the bar. "You should say hi later. He brought Damon with him."

Against her better judgment, Caitie looked over at the bar. Trent was there, leaning on the counter, chatting to the bartender. She saw Damon right away. He was standing next to Trent, holding a bottle of beer, his hip resting against the bar. She felt her mouth go dry. Their friends had been trying to matchmake them for forever. He really was a nice guy, but he wasn't...

...the one she wanted. Ugh.

"Oh, Damon's here?" She tried to rearrange her features into something less awkward. Why did she agree to come out tonight?

"Don't sound so innocent. We both know he's got a thing for you. As soon as Trent told him we were coming to see you guys, he found an excuse to join us."

Carrying two glasses of wine, Harper walked back to the group. "Hey, did you see Damon's here?"

Kristi inclined her head to the bar. "Oh yes."

"Ooh, he's looking fine. Here's your chance, Caitie. You need to have some fun and we all know Damon's up for the job." Harper wiggled her eyebrows. "If you'd ever actually give the guy a chance. Remember how you called off that date at the last minute?"

Caitie buried her face in her hands. "Oh, God, don't remind me. I felt terrible about letting him down. But I had a last minute job I couldn't get out of."

"Wait... What... You guys almost got together?" Kristi tipped her head to the side, scrutinizing Caitie. "Why didn't I know about this?"

"You didn't?" Harper frowned. "Why didn't you tell her, Caitie?"

"I thought I did. Anyway, it was months ago, and it was nothing."

"Which is exactly why you need to try again. No strings, just fun, am I right?" Harper said. Kristi nodded in support.

Caitie shook her head and took a sip of wine. "I'm not cut out for casual. I'm not a natural player."

Harper burst out laughing. She was swaying her shoulders to the beat of the music, the wine in her glass moving right along with her. "Nobody expects you to be a player, you loser. Just relax and have a bit of fun. Not every date you have has to lead to something long term. I swear you read too many romance books."

But Caitie liked romance books. Or at least she would if she had time to read them. "I'm a serial monogamist." Caitie shrugged. "So sue me."

"You're not a serial monogamist, you're a fantasist. You're looking for a guy who doesn't exist. Mr. Darcy was the figment of some old spinster's fevered imagination. No real guy can measure up to that. You have to be realistic."

Caitie drained the dregs of her wine glass. "I *am* realistic."

Kristi burst out laughing. "Yeah, right."

"Come on," Harper said, grinning. "You still have a thing

for some guy you kissed when you were fifteen. And the poor kid wasn't even awake for it."

"What?" Kristi leaned forward. "I've never heard about this. Who did you kiss when you were fifteen?"

"It doesn't matter." Caitie took another mouthful of wine. She really didn't want to get into this right now.

"Oh come on. It's kind of romantic," Harper said, grinning. "Caitie told me all about it the first week we met. I tried to get her interested in a couple of the guys in our math class, and she refused to date any of them, and I quote 'because they aren't Brent.'" Harper looked at Caitie. "Or was it Brant? *Whatever*. It took me almost a whole bottle of wine to get the truth out of her. Apparently, she had a thing for this guy ever since she was a kid. And when she was fifteen, he was sleeping at her house over Christmas and she snuck into his bedroom and kissed him, and that kiss was the best she'd ever had from anybody – awake or asleep." Harper laughed. "She said he'd spoiled her for every other guy."

Thank god it was dark in the bar. Caitie could feel her cheeks heat up. Why did she ever tell Harper about that Christmas night? It was stupid and embarrassing and something she wanted to forget about.

"So why didn't you get together with this Brant guy?" Kristi asked her.

Before she could answer, Harper jumped in. "I asked exactly the same thing, and Caitie said she hadn't seen him since that night. He'd broken her heart and left her ruined for any other man."

"That's kind of sweet," Kristi said, smiling at Caitie. "And also really weird. You need to get over this guy. Or Google him."

"Oh god, you should totally Google him," Harper said. "Why didn't I think of that. What's his last name?"

"I'm not Googling him." Caitie's voice was firm. She also

wasn't planning on telling any of them she'd seen 'Brant' less than a month ago. "You're both right, it's weird and stupid and I'm over it, okay?"

"You are?" Harper sounded sceptical.

"Yep. It was just a childish thing." Caitie shook her head. "Let's not ever mention it again."

"So if you're not obsessed with Brant, that means you're open to other relationships?" Kristi asked.

"Um.. yeah?" Caitie didn't like where this was going.

"Great. Now prove it."

"What?" Caitie blinked.

"If you're not hung up on this guy you kissed once thirteen years ago, then go on a date with Damon." Kristi shrugged. "As you said, he's a nice guy."

Caitie shifted her gaze over to the bar area. Damon was still there, talking to Trent. He really was very good looking. A little hipsterish, maybe, but Caitie didn't mind that. And any time she'd spent with him had been kind of...nice. If nice was what floated your boat.

"Yes!" Harper said, high-fiving Kristi. "You definitely need to go out with Damon."

"You want me to go out with him *now?*" Caitie's eyes widened.

Harper shook her head. "No, you should arrange a proper date. One with dinner, conversation, and maybe even some laughter." Harper's expression softened. "You deserve to be happy, in your love life as well as in your work."

"That's so sweet," Kristi said, raising her glass to Harper and Caitie. "You really should give him a chance. Look what happened when I agreed to date Trent against my better judgment. I thought it wouldn't last an hour, and we've been together for two years."

"Maybe." Caitie sighed. "It's easier to bury myself in business. It's fulfilling when you're good at something, and I'm useless at dating."

"You should give it more time. It takes practice and perseverance. For every ten frogs you might find one prince. But when you finally find *your* prince, it'll be worth it." Kristi smiled and looked over at Trent.

Caitie looked around the bar. "I don't think there are many princes in Manhattan."

"True story. But there's Damon, and right now he'll have to do." Harper grinned.

They were right and Caitie knew they were. Building her business had taught her that if you wanted something you had to work hard at it, throw yourself all in, and not wait for success to come knocking at your door. Strange how she couldn't transfer that belief to her personal life. For so long she'd held herself back, afraid to get hurt, and more afraid she might bare her soul to someone who didn't treat it the way they should. If she was really honest with herself, she'd also been dreaming about Breck for too long.

If nothing else, her trip to Angel Sands had shown her what a pipe dream it was. As friendly as he'd been, and as gorgeous as he still was, Breck had shown no interest in her as anything more than his friend's kid sister. And he was right not to. They had nothing in common. They lived on different sides of the country. He loved everything to do with the sea, and couldn't get his head around her aversion to it. He would end up with someone like Rachel, an outdoorsy, All-Californian type of girl, who would match him wave for wave. Then one day they'd have beautiful babies who loved to swim in the sea, and spent their time getting covered in sand.

And he deserved it, he really did. Caitie could never give him that, not even if he did happen to show the slightest interest in her. Which he didn't.

"Okay," she said, handing her empty wine glass to Harper. "Wish me luck, I'm going over to talk to him."

"You are?" Harper's eyebrows were almost meeting her hairline. "Seriously?"

"Yep."

"I don't believe you."

"Seeing is believing. And you can watch me as I go and ask Damon out for dinner." Caitie looked at Harper through narrowed eyes. "But if he turns me down, you're a dead woman."

Harper grinned. "He won't turn you down. That man's got the hots for you."

As usual, Harper was absolutely right.

## ❦ 9 ❦

"It's going to be magnificent." David Miller shaded his eyes as he looked up at the crumbling façade of the Silver Sands Resort. The sprawling beachfront buildings stretched across half an acre. In its prime it had been more than magnificent. With white-stuccoed walls and red tiled roofs, the Silver Sands Resort used to attract the rich and famous, luring them south from L.A. for a week of relaxation. Now, almost a century after it was built, it was taking millions of dollars and a whole lot of manpower to restore it to its former glory. When Breck had first arrived it had been tired, abandoned, and waiting for somebody to show it some love. That's where Miller Construction came in.

"It will," Breck agreed. "In fact it already is." The redevelopment had been difficult. Each stage of the rebuild was being closely monitored by the Angel Sands Historical Society, as Miller Construction and the zoning committee had agreed. Though Breck was good with people – and was an expert at managing stakeholders – it still felt uncomfortable to be doing this job with half the town breathing down his back.

"It's not only about the result though, is it? It's about the process. About enjoying every moment and seeing the changes come through our hard work. I bet you'll miss this place when it's done."

His father wasn't wrong. "Yeah, well they're all our babies, aren't they? It's hard to hand them back to their owners, yet there's something fantastic about it, too. We're not rebuilding memorials here, we're creating futures. Somewhere for people to work, and enjoy themselves. Somewhere we can all look at and say this is a job well done."

David smiled. Breck knew his father got it, too. From the age of seventeen, he'd spent a lot of time with his dad at sites, watching him work his magic. At first, he'd gone under sufferance, bristling at being treated like a kid. Protesting he'd rather be at home than working on a site every weekend or school break. But as time passed, he'd realized exactly why his dad had made him go. They'd spent a lot of time together, got to know each other, and developed a shared passion. It was no different than going with a parent to a game, or enjoying golf together. They weren't just rebuilding hotels, they were rebuilding their relationship.

Pulling on their hard hats, they walked onto the site. Before construction had begun, Breck had arranged for safety notices to go up throughout the area. Protective equipment was to be worn at all times, and they weren't exempt from that, even if there was no construction going on right now.

"How are you managing being back here in Angel Sands?" David asked. "It must be strange after all these years." He looked over at the ocean. "It's strange enough for me, and I barely lived here. God only knows the memories it's bringing back for you." His voice dropped as he looked at Breck with concern.

Breck pulled a piece of loose stucco away from the wall,

holding the orange-painted rubble in his hand. It was one of the last bungalows left to renovate. Next week they'd be taking all the drywall off, piece by piece, to check the framework beneath. "It's not too bad. At first I felt like another tourist, here to visit. But as the weeks have passed I've fallen into the rhythm of things. Met up with old friends, spent time surfing. It's been good."

David smiled sadly. "The kind of teenage years you should've had."

They sat down on an old bench, overlooking the private beach. The sand was covered with weeds and driftwood, unused for years. The beach would be the last part of the resort to be restored. For now it held a wild beauty. Over the years everything had returned to its natural state.

His father was only here for a quick visit, checking out the site and having meetings with the owners. Tomorrow he'd be back in Boston, but he'd already promised to be back in California for Thanksgiving.

"I don't resent not living here after Mom died," Breck said, leaning forward to rest his elbows on his thighs. "Not any more. I know I was a jackass back then, but really, I would've been an asshole here, too. I was angry at the world, not just Boston."

"And understandably so. You'd recently lost your mom, and you were taking care of your brother. Then in comes this guy saying he wants to be your dad and move you two thousand miles east. I completely understood why you acted out so much. To be honest, I felt like I deserved it."

Breck frowned. "You did?"

"Of course I did. After your mom and I divorced, and I moved to Boston, I hardly saw you. I know I was busy building the business, and you refused to fly out there, but I could've come here to visit you. But I didn't, because I was afraid. At least in Boston I could say there were reasons for not seeing you. If I'd come to Angel Sands and you'd rejected me, all those excuses would disappear. I'd become just another dad whose kids didn't want him."

"That's all ancient history now."

"It is," David agreed. "But I also want you to know why I worked so hard to repair our relationship. As awful as your mom's death was, it was my chance to step up, to really be a father to you and Daniel. For the first time in my life I realized it wasn't too late to try again."

"I'm glad you did."

"So am I." His dad smiled warmly at him.

Breck could feel his throat getting scratchy, as though he had a cough that wouldn't come out. He rubbed his neck, feeling the stubble beneath his hand. "Did I tell you I've been hanging out with Lucas Russell? You remember the Russells? They're the ones who took us in after Mom..." he trailed off, staring at the beach.

"I remember them. They're good people. Tell them I said hi."

Breck nodded, a smile ghosting at his lips.

"And how about the California girls? Are they as good as the Beach Boys keep telling me?"

He wanted to laugh at his father's change of subject, but he was relieved at it, too. There was only so much emotion the two men could take. "They're good."

"So you met anybody special?"

"No, not really." He reached up, stroking his chin. "There isn't much time between work and hanging out with the guys." No need to tell his father he wasn't looking for that kind of relationship. His old man didn't need any more burdens.

"There's always time for girls," his dad pointed out.

"Says the perpetual bachelor."

David's cheeks reddened. "Yeah, well…" he trailed off.

Breck stared at him. "What does that mean?"

"It means, 'yeah, well'." David shrugged.

"You don't think you're a perpetual bachelor?" Breck pressed. "I remember you going out on an occasional date, but you never introduced any of them to us."

"Maria's different."

"*Maria?* You've got a girlfriend?" Breck's eyes widened at his father's admission. "When did that happen?"

David laughed. "I think I'm too old to have a girlfriend. I have a friend who just happens to be a woman."

"You're not *that* old." And he really didn't look it. For a fifty-eight year old guy, David Miller was still pretty good looking and in amazing shape. Wearing a white button down shirt, and grey pants, he looked distinguished, and far younger than his years. "But tell me more. Who's Maria, and where did you meet her?"

---

"Did you know Dad has a girlfriend?" Breck asked his brother later as they video-conferenced. The Wi-Fi speed had slowed down, and Daniel's face was blurry, each movement leaving a cloud of pixels behind him.

"Maria? Yeah, sure, she's nice," his brother said.

"You've met her?"

"Yep. We went out to dinner last Thursday. I like her. She doesn't take his shit, and he laughs a lot more when she's around."

"I've only been gone for a few months, and everything's changed," Breck protested. "I thought you both were going to fall apart without me. But look at you, living and stuff."

Daniel grinned. "Yeah, we really miss you, bro."

"Sounds like it."

"So anyway, how's it going in Angel Sands? Dad said the project's going well."

"It's great. You'll be able to see for yourself when you come for Thanksgiving." Breck tapped his fingers on the table. "Hey, should I invite Maria?"

"She's spending Thanksgiving with her kids in Florida," Daniel told him. "So we're still good to come. Anyway, no woman gets between the Miller Men and their need for Thanksgiving football. She'd probably hate every moment."

"I'm glad he's finally got somebody."

"Me, too. But I'm also glad we're spending Thanksgiving with you. I can't wait to see the old place. Has much changed?"

"Not as much as you'd think."

"And the people? Are they the same?" Daniel asked him.

Breck shrugged. "I've seen a lot of Lucas Russell. Do you remember him? And Griff and Jack, too."

"I remember the Russells," Daniel said, grinning on the laptop screen. "How are they doing? How's Caitie? Do you remember that Christmas when she gave me her iPod? I still have it somewhere. You told me it was her own gift after we'd left for Boston. I felt bad for taking it from her."

Breck closed his eyes. He'd forgotten about the iPod. That was back in the days before smart phones and music streaming. When Breck and Daniel had needed a place to stay that Christmas, they'd had no gifts at all. Their mom had been too ill to buy any before she died, and Breck had forgotten to get some since she couldn't. Breck had been almost seventeen – old enough not to care about gifts – but Daniel had been an eleven-year-old kid. Bereft at his mom's death, but also sad because he had nothing to open. Breck had felt like an asshole for not thinking about his little brother.

Then Caitie ran upstairs. It had taken her a while to come back, but when she did, she handed a gift to Daniel. Breck remembered his face as he'd torn the paper off, along with the way it lit up when he saw the box inside.

How had he forgotten that memory?

"She was a sweet girl," Breck said, a lump forming in his throat.

"And what's she like now?" Daniel asked. "God, she must be in her twenties. I can't even imagine."

"She's good," Breck said. "She lives in New York now, and runs her own business, but she came to town for a short visit a couple of weeks ago." He didn't mention how he'd taken her to the hotel, or that he'd thought about her every day since she'd gone back to New York. Any hint of that and his brother would be on his back like a monkey. He needed that like he needed a hole in the head.

"I'd love to see her again, to say thanks for all she did," Daniel said. "Do you think she'll be there at Thanksgiving?"

Breck frowned. The last time he'd seen her – when he dropped her at home after their trip to Chateau Des Tournesols – she hadn't mentioned when she'd be back.

"I don't know," he admitted. "Lucas hasn't mentioned it."

"I think about the Russells a lot," Daniel told him. "As messed up as it is, I keep thinking about that Christmas and how kind they were to us."

"Yeah, I think about it, too." He looked away from the webcam, not wanting his brother to see the telltale glint in his eyes.

"So could you call her?" Daniel asked. "Find out if she's coming for Thanksgiving. It would be really good to see her again." He grinned. "Kind of like closure."

Breck thought about the number in his phone that had been burning a hole in his pocket for weeks. Ever since Caitie had left Angel Sands and headed back to New York. He'd wanted to find an excuse to call her, but there had been nothing. Until now...

"Sure," he said softly, smiling at his brother. "I've got her number. I'll give her a call tonight."

## ❧ 10 ❧

"So, Trent tells me your work is going well." Damon poured them both another glass of wine, sliding Caitie's glass toward her. "Do you enjoy it?"

She nodded. "Yeah, it's good." This was the third topic of conversation they'd gotten to. None of them were sparking. It all felt so stilted and forced, as though she was being interviewed for a job, and not trying to get to know the man. If Harper was right, and dating was like learning to ride a bike, Caitie needed to up her game.

"How about you?" she asked, turning the conversation on Damon. "How's your work going?"

"It's boring," Damon said. "I thought graphic design was going to be all glamor and glitz, but it turns out I only get to design logos for gardening companies."

She couldn't even think of a reply to that. Instead, she stabbed a piece of steak and stuffed it in her mouth, chewing on it while she wracked her brain for another question.

*Was it really supposed to be like this?*

Ten minutes later, after the waiter had cleared their plates, she grabbed her bag and shot Damon a smile. "I, uh, need to use the bathroom. I'll be right back."

"Sure. I'll grab us some dessert menus. And I can order us some coffee, too?"

"Great." She shot him a smile and ran into the bathroom, pulling the door closed behind her, and sliding the lock. Grabbing her phone, she tapped rapidly on the keyboard, watching as the words formed on the screen, sending the message to Harper.

Caitie - *Get me out of here!*

Harper - *It's going well then?*

She could practically see Harper's grin as she replied.

Caitie - *It's awful. It's as though he made a list of questions and is determined to ask me all of them. Each time I do... crickets.*

Harper - *I told you, you have to kiss a lot of frogs. Just think, this is one Kermit closer to Mr. Right.*

Caitie tapped furiously.

Caitie - *Do you know where I want to shove your frogs right now? I'll give you a clue – the sun doesn't shine there.*

Harper - *Not California then.*

Caitie - *Funny.*

Harper - *Look, C, you got to finish the date and then you can come home. Chalk it up to experience. Be glad you got a meal out of it. Then put yourself out there and try again next week. Mr. Right's out there somewhere.*

Caitie - *What if I don't want to find him?*

Harper - *Of course you want to find him. You're a romantic. Now go finish your meal and come home. I'll put some wine in the freezer. We can drink ourselves silly and cry over lost loves.*

Caitie - *Sounds better than this date.*

Harper - *That's because I'll be there.*

Caitie bit down a grin.

Caitie - *I'll see you in half an hour. Better put two bottles in. I've got a lot of sorrows to drown.*

Harper - *That's my girl.*

Caitie pressed on the home screen, closing the conversation. As she was about to slide her phone back in her purse, it started to buzz, a familiar name lighting up the screen.

*Brecken Miller.*

It had been two weeks since she'd seen him, yet her heart started to flutter wildly. Her finger shook as she accepted the call.

"Hi Breck," she said, keeping her voice low.

"Hey Caitie, how are you?"

She leaned against the metal wall, closing her eyes as she heard his deep voice. "I'm good. It's Friday, after all. And how are you doing? Long time no talk."

"Where are you? Your voice sounds all echoey."

She glanced around at the tiled floor and walls. "Um, in a bathroom."

His laughter was low and deep. "What are you doing in there? Not taking a bath, are you?"

"No, I'm in a restaurant bathroom. Nowhere near a bathtub."

"Did I interrupt you?" He sounded amused. She could picture his face turned up into a heartstopping grin. "Do you want me to call back later?"

She shook her head even though he couldn't see her. "Now is good. I'm just...taking a break."

His laughter reverberated through the line. "If that's all your taking, we're good. What are you taking a break from? Did you eat too much?"

"I'm on a date," she admitted.

"Oh." Was it her imagination or did he sound surprised? "I really did interrupt."

He went silent. All she could hear above the creaking of the bathroom pipes were his slow breaths.

"You didn't interrupt, honestly. It's nice to hear from you." She swallowed, waiting for him to reply.

"I didn't realize you had a boyfriend." He still sounded strange.

"I don't. Damon is a..." She screwed her face up, trying to figure out how to classify him. "He's a friend of a friend. I kind of know him from the bar we all go to. He's a graphic designer. It's our first date."

"A first date? I feel even worse now. All those hormones and batting eyelashes. I should let you get back to him."

"No eyelashes were batted in the making of this date," she told him. "And I'd like to think I left my hormones behind years ago." She lowered her voice. "If you want to know, it's kind of awkward, and I've no idea how I'm going to let him down gently. And I've even less idea why I'm telling you this."

Breck laughed. "Me either. But it sounds more exciting than my Friday night. I was planning to crack open a beer and sit on the deck. I'd be happy to live life vicariously through you."

"Glad I can be of service."

"Seriously, though, Caitie. Be careful. I'm sure he's a nice guy, and you've said your friends know him, but men can be assholes when they're turned down. Make sure you do it in a safe place. And don't let him walk you home."

"I wasn't going to."

"Good. Maybe I should stay on the line. If you need any help we can have a code word. Just say it and I'll get the guys together and fly over to save you. The way we always did."

She grinned. "My four knights in shining armor. One big brother is bad enough, but when all of you were around..." She paused for a moment, remembering those days. "Unless it was you guys causing the pain, of course."

"Hey, we just liked to protect you from getting hurt."

She tried to imagine Damon being involved in any physical violence. He was way too metrosexual for that. The make-love-not-war type. "I'll be fine. I've lived in New York for a long time, and I've learned to take care of myself. I did the self-defense courses as soon as I arrived. I can get a man in a chokehold in ten seconds."

He gave another chuckle. "I don't doubt it for a minute. But I'll still feel better if you call me when you get home. Otherwise I'll be all edgy and that doesn't sit well with my cool Californian vibe."

"You really don't need to worry."

"But I will anyway," he pointed out gruffly.

"I'll call you later. Promise." She glanced at her watch. It was almost ten-thirty in New York. Only seven-thirty in Angel Sands.

"Good. You can give me the full-debrief when you do. In the meantime, have a good time." He paused, then added, "But not too good."

"I wasn't planning on it," she said. Strange how breathy her voice sounded. As though she was flirting.

She wasn't though, was she?

"I'll talk to you later." For some reason he sounded relieved. "And be safe, okay?"

"Sure," she said softly. "I'll speak to you soon."

———

"You managed to escape." Harper looked up from the sofa as soon as Caitie walked through the door. She had a large bowl of popcorn wedged between her legs, and a half-empty glass of wine on the table beside her. Picking up the remote control, she paused the black-and-white movie she was watching, the screen freezing on a close up of Bette Davis.

Caitie dropped down onto the sofa, lifting Harper's legs

and putting them over her own. "What are you watching? Is there more wine?"

"There's another bottle in the refrigerator," Harper said, grabbing her glass before Caitie could. "Didn't you drink on your date? Or is that the problem, you didn't drink enough?"

"I drank just the right amount." Caitie grimaced. "I had one and a half glasses, enough to get me through the most boring date ever, but not so much I couldn't get myself home."

"He didn't bring you home?" Harper sat up. "I thought he was better than that."

"I didn't let him. The last thing I needed was an awkward conversation on the doorstep. The one where he leans forward and tries to kiss me and I step away. Or even worse, the one where he tells me I'm a lovely girl but there's no chemistry between us. Which was true, by the way."

"That you're lovely?" Harper didn't look convinced.

Caitie slapped her arm good naturedly. "No! That there was no chemistry. It's weird, because last year I swear we got along great. Although we'd both drunk a hell of a lot more that night." She pushed herself off the sofa and walked over to the kitchen, grabbing a wine glass and the fresh bottle from the fridge. Bringing them back to the couch, she poured herself a glass, before she filled Harper's now-empty glass.

"You know, it's too late to put the wine goggles on now."

"I'm drowning my sorrows." Caitie leaned back on the sofa. "I'm not cut out for this dating thing; I'm clearly not interesting. Even Damon looked relieved when I told him I needed to go home because I have to get up early tomorrow. Seriously, Harper, I should concentrate on work. At least I'm good at that."

"Stop it. Remember what I said about the ten percent rule? You can't make any judgment based on one date. You wouldn't give up everything if you didn't win a contract at work, would you? You'd dust yourself off and try again. Put it down to the wrong place, wrong time. Learn from it. But don't tell me you're no good at dating when you've been on precisely *one* date."

"I've had other dates," Caitie protested. "It's not as if this was my first one ever."

"I know that. We've double-dated a few times, after all. But I'm talking about you doing it seriously. Not just because you're trying to appease me."

Caitie took a sip of her wine, closing her eyes as the cool liquid ran down her throat. "It doesn't matter anyway. I'm all out of dates right now."

"Then try online dating."

Her eyes flew open. "Seriously? I'm not that brave. It's hard enough going out with a friend, I can't put myself out there and meet strangers."

"So you'd rather be alone?"

"No I'd rather—" She was cut off by the sound of her cell phone ringing. She pulled it from the pocket of her jacket and checked the screen.

It was Breck.

Immediately, she covered the screen. She wasn't ready to tell Harper about him. It would only take her a moment to put two and two together, and realize the guy she'd kissed back when she was a kid wasn't named Brent or Brant. She should let it go to voicemail, pretend it was a work call, do anything to pull Harper's attention from the way Caitie's face was starting to redden, her heart sounding like a train hammering down the tracks.

"I should take this."

"Who is it?"

"Um... a friend." God, she was lame. Harper raised her eyebrows as Caitie swiped the phone and lifted it to her ear. "Hey."

She turned to Harper and mouthed, "I'll be back in a minute," intending to finish the call in her bedroom.

"Who is it?" Harper mouthed back, catching her wrist before she could leave. "Don't leave me hanging."

Caitie rolled her eyes at her friend, but stayed where she was. "Nobody you know."

"So you're not dead?" Breck asked, his voice soft in her ear.

"Yep. I'm dead." Caitie grinned. "This is me answering from beyond the grave. By the way, turns out in Heaven there are no oceans, no lakes, and no baths. My kind of place."

"Is it Damon?" Harper mouthed furiously at her.

"No," Caitie mouthed back. Trying to keep up two different conversations was harder than it looked. She really should have gone to her room.

"Very funny," Breck replied. "I've been worried about you. Kept imagining having to tell your brother that I could've saved you from a serial killer, but instead I let you sweet talk me 'round. I think I'd have joined you on the other side."

"I didn't sweet talk you."

Harper's eyes widened.

"Of course you did," Breck said, his voice full of humor. "You always have. Remember that summer when you persuaded me to help you make mud pies in the garden? Your mom went crazy when we pulled up all her begonias to decorate them."

"It's a guy, isn't it?" Harper mouthed. "What's his name?"

"Breck, I'm sorry, Can you hold on? I need to go to my room. It's really noisy in here."

"Breck?" Harper said out loud. "As in Brant?"

*Oh shit.* Caitie swallowed hard and covered the mouthpiece. "Um...no..."

The next moment, Harper grabbed the phone from her hands, and ran out of the living room and into the kitchen.

Caitie rushed after her, trapping her next to the stove, but Harper was holding the phone out of her reach.

"Hey, Breck," she shouted. "This is Harper, Caitie's best friend. Remind me, where did you two meet again?"

"Give it back." Caitie jumped once, then twice, trying to grab the phone from her. But each time she tried, Harper moved back. Then she was running again, this time down the hallway, the phone against her ear.

"Is that right? You're in Angel Sands now?" Harper was breathless from running. "Ah, yes Lucas, he's a great guy, isn't he?" She stuck her tongue out at Caitie who had caught up with her.

Harper was in the corner of her bedroom, her knuckles white from holding the phone. She was laughing, still listening to Breck.

Murderous thoughts galloped their way through Caitie's head.

"Oh, Caitie wants her phone back," Harper said, her voice as sweet as honey. "It was great talking with you, Breck. Oh, by the way, are you going to be in California for Thanksgiving? Caitie's coming back and I'm sure she'd love to meet up with you again. I'll be there, too. I can't wait to meet you." She paused while Breck replied, then said, "Oh yeah, I'm sure we can sort something out."

Smiling sweetly, she handed Caitie back the phone. Giving her a death stare, Caitie snatched it away, turned on her heel, and walked into her own bedroom. Slamming the door, she locked the knob, and *finally* lifted the phone to her ear.

"You still there?"

"Yeah." He sounded as if he was smiling. "Who was that?"

"My roommate. Or should I say my soon-to-be-ex-roommate," she said loudly, in case Harper was listening at the door. "I'm so sorry, they've only just let her go on day release. She's pathologically crazy."

"Harper the costume designer?" he asked. "The one you met in college?"

He remembered that? The day they'd visited the Chateau, Caitie had given him a brief rundown of her life in New York, but she didn't figure he would've retained all she shared. Especially not about her roommate. "Yeah, that's the one. Though it's going to be hard for her to sew when all her fingers are broken."

He laughed again. His chuckle warmed her from the inside out. "She sounds like quite a character."

"Definitely. A real character."

Breck cleared his throat. "So how did the date end up? Did he let you go without a protest?"

"Well he didn't stalk me home. So I'd call that a win."

"That's a relief. I had images of you fighting him off. I didn't fancy his chances with your chokehold."

She sat down on her bed, swinging her legs around so she was laid down. "Why are you so interested anyway?"

"You're Lucas's little sister. I kind of owe it to him to make sure you're okay. I know he'd do the same for me."

"You don't have a sister."

"Yeah, but he'd look after Daniel if I asked him to. He did when we were kids, after all."

"Yeah, I guess he would." Her shoulders slumped. She didn't know why she felt so disappointed by his reply. Of course he would look out for her the same way he always had. There was no ulterior motive, he was being protective, the same way Lucas's friends always were.

"But you're okay, right?" Breck asked her. "Not too upset about the date?"

"I'm fine." She fought hard to keep the disappointment from her voice.

"That's good."

"Yeah, it is."

"So, ah, I guess it's getting late over there. I should let you go to bed or something."

"Yeah, I'm pretty tired. But thanks for calling to check up on me. I appreciate it."

"I almost forgot why I called," Breck said, before she could disconnect. "I spoke to Daniel earlier. He was wondering if you're coming to Angel Sands for Thanksgiving. He's hoping to see you there. But asking is a bit of a moot point now, since my little chat with Harper."

"Um, yeah, we're coming. It will be good to see him. Tell him I'm looking forward to it."

"Okay, I will." He paused again. Caitie waited for him to say goodbye, to hang up, *something*, but instead all she could hear was his breathing. His breaths were low and regular. For some reason, she found their cadence reassuring, like a baby hearing its mother's heartbeat. "You sure you're okay?" he finally asked.

"I am. It's just been a long day. I had to be up early to prepare a presentation for next week; then the date from hell really topped things off. I've never been happier to see my bed in all my life."

"I'll let you go, Cait. Hopefully we'll see you at Thanksgiving."

The way he said her name made her heart skip a beat. *Cait.* He was the only one who'd ever called her that. God, she really did need some sleep. "Good night, Breck."

"Good night. Sweet dreams."

With Harper sure to be outside the door, no doubt full of questions, she was pretty sure she wouldn't be sleeping at all.

**B**reck walked out of the water and along the sand, laying his board down as he reached for his towel. He grabbed his water bottle, opening it and taking long gulps. His skin felt rough, beaten up by the early-morning wind and the salt from the sea. Pouring some water into his hand, he splashed it on his face, rinsing away the dried-on granules.

"I'm getting too old for this." Lucas threw himself onto the sand next to Breck, throwing his arms above his head until he was laying prone. "Remind me why we do this again?"

"Because it's the closest thing to God?" Breck suggested. "Plus the beach is so perfect at this time of the morning. No tourists, no litter. The only sounds are the sea, the birds, and your complaining."

Lucas grinned. "It sure is beautiful." The wide expanse of sand was barely touched by humans that morning. The only footprints were from surfers, running in and out of the ocean. Between the hours of ten at night and eight in the morning, nature ruled the beach.

"You love it. You're the guy who comes out here in the rain and wind, no matter the time of year. You told me the other day you hate summer, because when school's out, the kids take away from the early morning tranquility," Breck said.

"I said that?" Lucas grinned. "I didn't even know I knew the word tranquility."

Breck bumped his shoulder. "Shut up. You're always pretending you're not as clever as you are. We both know you're the cleverest guy on the beach."

"Nah ah. I'm sitting next to him."

Reaching behind him, Breck unzipped his wetsuit. Snapping his arms from the sleeves, he rolled it down to his waist.

"Anyway," Lucas said. "I've got something to ask you."

"Sure, fire away."

"I told Mom about your dad and brother visiting for Thanksgiving, and she's got it in her head that you should come over and spend the day with us. I know you probably want to catch up with your family, but it would really get her off my back if you'd agree to come."

Breck blinked. "Your mom wants all three of us to come? Won't that be extra work?"

Lucas shrugged. "She's already invited half the town. What's three extra people among friends?"

"A lot of people to cook for?" Breck grinned. "But yeah, that would be great. My dad always liked your folks. Plus Daniel already said he wants to catch up with you all. Are you sure your mom doesn't mind cooking for us?"

"You clearly don't remember my mom's cooking. It's you who'll mind it." Lucas grinned. "Remember the Christmas she forgot to defrost the turkey?"

Breck swallowed. "Yeah, I do." He remembered it all too well. He would never forget that Christmas.

"Oh shit," Lucas said, realization crossing his face. "I didn't mean..."

"It's okay." Breck smiled at him. "Old history. We don't need to talk about it now."

"Are you sure you're okay spending a holiday with us?" Lucas asked. "I don't want to upset any of you."

"It'll be good," Breck said, his voice firm. "Let's make some new memories and forget the old ones." He hadn't come all this way to turn his back on his fears. He was going to face them head on.

Even if they hurt.

"Okay then, that's sorted." Lucas grinned. "You'll make Mom really happy. Thanks, man."

"No worries. What are your plans for the rest of today? Do you have time to grab some coffee? I was going to head over to Déjà Brew to meet Ember. Wanna join?"

"Sure." Breck nodded. "Let's go."

---

"Hey, guys. What can I get you?" Ally smiled at Breck and Lucas across the counter. On the far side, her boyfriend Nate was talking to his teenage daughter. It made Breck grin to watch as the kid tied him up in verbal hoops.

"Two flat whites, please," Breck said, handing over his card.

"Hey Breck, hey Lucas."

He turned to see Rachel walking through the door with Ember. The two of them were carrying a pile of bridal magazines. Breck raised his eyebrow at Lucas who shrugged.

Why did he have the impression this was a set up?

"Hey," he said, raising his hand at them. "How's it going?"

"Good. Just doing some research," Rachel said, holding up the pile of magazines.

"Can you add their orders to my tab?" he asked Ally.

"Sure." Ally nodded. "What do you guys want?" she called

over to the girls.

"A cappuccino please," Rachel answered quickly.

"Make that two," Ember added.

"You didn't tell me we were going to be wedding planning," he said to Lucas with a grin. "If I'd known I would've brought my own magazines."

"It's not that kind of wedding," Lucas said, winking. "And anyway, I didn't know you could read."

"He probably just looks at the pictures." Ally grinned, clearly enjoying the banter. "You guys go and sit down, I'll bring your coffees over when they're ready."

"Table service?" Lucas asked. "Whatever next?"

"I wouldn't want you to miss a moment of the wedding planning." Ally said, a twinkle in her eye. "Now shoo."

When they sat down, Ember looked up from the magazine she was thumbing through. "Did you pay the deposit for the band?" she asked Lucas.

"Yep." He nodded. "And I sent them the list of songs we wanted them to play, like I promised." There was a teasing note to his voice. "Don't worry, sweetheart. We got this covered."

"Thanks to Caitie." She sighed. "She's been a godsend. I swear, every morning I wake up to an email saying something else is handled. She's like some kind of Wedding Angel."

"Maybe she should become a wedding planner," Rachel said. "Sounds like she's good at it."

"She wouldn't have the time, would she?" Breck asked. "Not with her business being as successful as it is."

"Oh do you know her well?" Rachel asked, tipping her head to the side, her brows knitting together. "I didn't realize."

"We all grew up together," Lucas told her. "Breck and his brother spent as much time at our house as they did at their own when we were kids."

"There you go," Ally said, sliding a tray on the table in front of them. "Two flat whites and two cappuccinos. Anybody need sugar?"

They all shook their heads.

"In that case, enjoy." She smiled at them. "Oh, Lucas, when you get a chance, Nate wanted to ask you something about his suit."

"Sure. I'll go and speak to him now." Lucas stood and grabbed his coffee cup, taking a mouthful of flat white. "I'll be back in a minute."

"Oh, guess what?" Ally said, turning to Ember. "I think I found the perfect wedding gift for you guys. Wanna look? It's on the laptop in the kitchen."

"Sure," Ember agreed. "What is it?"

"You'll see. I haven't ordered it yet, in case you don't like it." The two of them headed to the kitchen, leaving Breck alone at the table with Rachel.

"So..." she smiled at him. "What are your Thanksgiving plans?"

"My dad and brother are flying in from Boston for a few days."

"That's so nice. Thanksgiving's always a good time to be with family." She pressed her lips together. "My folks are going to be in Hawaii."

"I'm really sorry to hear that. Can't you join them there?"

She shook her head. "I don't get enough time off. Only a couple of days and then it's back to school."

"Oh right. I'd forgotten you were a teacher."

"Yeah, it's one of the pitfalls. On the plus side we get a lot of time off in the summer. It almost makes up for it." She smiled. "And Lucas's mom has invited me to Thanksgiving which is nice, so I won't be on my own."

Breck bit down his dismay. "Oh right. She's invited us, too."

"She has?" Rachel's face lit up. "That's great. I'll see you there." She took a sip of her cappuccino. "I was scared I was going to be the only single person there. It'll be much easier if you're there, too."

"I think Caitie's coming in. She's single," Breck pointed out.

"Oh yeah. So she is." Rachel pulled her bottom lip between her teeth. "I was going to ask you something, actually."

"You were?" Breck glanced over her shoulder to see if Lucas had finished talking to Nate yet, but they were still deep in conversation. He shifted in his seat to get comfortable.

"I don't know if Lucas and Ember have officially decided who's walking down the aisle with who, but I was hoping you'd escort me. With us both being single and all." She tipped her head to the side. "We could do each other a favor."

Breck felt cornered. "Griff and Jack are groomsmen, too," he said, trying to find a way of letting her down gently. "I'm not sure what any of us are doing yet."

"Griff can walk Caitie down," Rachel said, shrugging. "And Jack can escort Ember's mom, since her dad isn't around any more." She gave him another smile. "Come on, it'll be fun. I promise not to trip over my dress."

Why did his throat feel dry at the thought of his friend walking Caitie down the aisle? It didn't matter who went with who. It didn't mean anything – weddings were just rituals, after all.

"I..."

"Who's tripping over a dress?" Ember asked, joining them back at the table. "Not me I hope."

Rachel shook her head. "I was asking Breck if he'd be my escort at your wedding. I know him better than Jack and Griff, after all."

Ember beamed, oblivious to Breck's discomfort. "Oh that would be lovely. Thanks, guys. That gives me one less thing to sort out."

"See?" Rachel said to him. "It's meant to be. We'll need to get together to talk about the first dance, though." She glanced at Ember. "Have you chosen it yet?"

"*God Only Knows* by the Beach Boys." Ember raised her eyebrows. "It was Lucas's idea."

"I love that one. It's the perfect beat to dance to, don't you think, Breck?" Rachel leaned forward, catching his eye.

About three years ago when he was working on a hotel in the Catskills, Breck had been driving home one night down the dark, winding roads, when his headlamps had caught a deer standing right in the middle of the blacktop. The deer had frozen still, unable to save itself from the incoming truck. He'd had to swerve to avoid it.

Right now he knew exactly how that deer felt. Rachel and Ember were staring at him, their expressions as bright as those headlamps. And he had no idea how to get out of this.

"Yeah." He let out a lungful of air. "It's all good."

Rachel grinned. "Great! Maybe we can get together and talk about it some time. I'll call you. There's a place in the hills that serves a great lunch. We could go there."

"Okay." His chest tightened. "That would be fine."

It was only for one day, right? Two if you counted lunch. He could do it for his friend, the way he knew Lucas would do it for him.

It wasn't as though Rachel was an ogre. She was a perfectly nice woman who was friendly, kind, and full of bubbly energy. So what if she didn't make him feel the way Caitie did. Maybe that was a good thing, because god knows he didn't like feeling so out of control.

Like he said, it would be fine.

So why wouldn't the knot in his stomach go away?

## 12

"So, I've got something to tell you." Harper pulled the strap across her lap, clipping the buckle in. Harper'd chosen the window seat, leaving the middle free for Caitie. She sat down beside her, sliding her phone and book into the pocket on the back of the seat in front of her. They were almost the last to board the plane; the flight attendants were already doing their final checks, pushing up trays and blinds as they tried to make themselves heard among the din of the full-to-bursting airplane. Caitie looked around, noticing the businessmen mixed in with noisy families, their faces lit with anticipation. Everybody needed to be somewhere at Thanksgiving.

"Is this a guessing game, or are you going to tell me?" Caitie grinned. She was amused at the anxious expression on her friend's face. Harper never worried about speaking her mind.

"I'm not flying back on Saturday like we'd planned."

"You're not?" Caitie frowned. "Are you leaving earlier? Don't you dare leave me to a Russell family Thanksgiving on my own. Not when it's the first one I've been to in years."

"No, I've extended my ticket. I have a few meetings in L.A. next week, so I won't fly back until next Friday. That's when your return flight is, right?"

"Yeah. I've got that big presentation in L.A. next week." The pitch Caitie had been working on for months was finally coming to fruition. The choice was between her and another company, and the theme park owners wanted both of them to present their bids in person. "But why do you have meetings?" Caitie looked at her friend a tad confused.

"I've got a meeting at a studio. They have some vacancies in the costume department."

"In L.A.?" Caitie shifted in her seat, a grin spreading across her lips.

Harper nodded, her eyes full of excitement. "Yes," she squeaked. "The head of the department was in New York a couple of weeks ago and saw my designs off-Broadway. She emailed me, and I thought why not call her since I'll be in California for Thanksgiving." She widened her eyes. "I never thought she'd say yes to meeting up."

"That's great," Caitie said, leaning forward to hug her best friend. "I never thought you'd consider giving up theater work, though."

"Nothing's guaranteed. I just want to have some options open, since we both know you're going to win this theme park contract."

"We do? I wish you'd tell my nerves." Caitie sat back, letting her head fall against her seat. "I'm not going to be able to sleep all week. Every time I look at the presentation I see something wrong."

"You're going to be great," Harper said, taking her hand. "You've got this, honey. I can't think of anybody better to revamp their holiday offerings. Your ideas were amazing when I saw them."

Caitie wasn't so sure. She couldn't remember the last time

she'd felt this anxious about a contract. But this wasn't her usual movie or event. This was big. It meant having to dedicate all her time to the one job, while Felix, her assistant, ran the rest of her business. It was going to take some getting used to.

Their plane taxied to the runway. The flight attendants made their way down the aisle, running through the safety information. As soon as they were seated and the plane sped up for takeoff, Harper turned to her again.

"Imagine if we both end up in LA. Wouldn't it be great?"

Caitie couldn't help but smile at her. It was impossible to imagine her life without Harper. They'd been there for each other through thick and thin. She was lucky to have her.

"It would be amazing."

"We could get an apartment with a pool. Imagine how much better we'd both look with a suntan." Harper grinned. "Wouldn't that be amazing?"

Caitie laughed. "I can't imagine you with a tan. And I won't be going near that imaginary pool in our imaginary apartment."

Harper wrinkled her nose. "Ugh, yeah. I guess a beach house is out, too?"

"Yep."

"Ah well. An apartment in L.A. will be fine. We'll still have year round sun."

"There's just a little matter of us getting our contracts," Caitie pointed out. "I'm sure you'll be fine, but my competition is huge. There's no guarantee they'll go with my proposal."

"Even so, there's plenty of work out there for both of us," Harper said with a shrug. "We could move out here anyway. You'll still have Felix in New York. It'll be fine."

"Hmmm."

"And there's a little matter of Breck," Harper added, her eyes twinkling. "Another good reason to move to California."

Caitie blinked. Harper hadn't mentioned Breck since the disastrous phone call last week. Not that either of them had the chance to talk very much. Caitie had been working late every night on her proposals, and Harper had been finishing her Etsy orders.

"Breck?" she said, her voice weak. "What does he have to do with it?"

"He's in Angel Sands. Which as we both know is only a couple of hours from L.A.."

The seatbelt light went off, and Harper released hers and leaned forward. Sitting on Catie's right was a businessman who was doing his best not to listen to their conversation.

"But that doesn't mean anything," Caitie told her. "He's a friend, that's all."

"He was the love of your young life, Caitie. The one who got away. Don't you think you should work out if there's still something between you?"

"There isn't." Caitie shook her head. "He sees me as Lucas's little sister. Someone to be friends with and take care of." She wished it was different. That her heart didn't ache every time she thought of him.

"Are you sure?" Harper sounded disappointed.

"Yeah. He was like another older brother to me growing up. He'd tease me the same way Lucas did, and he'd take care of me in the same way, too. There's nothing more than that between us. I just need to get used to it." And she would. As soon as her heart realized the truth.

"God, he really did a number on you, didn't he?" Harper tipped her head to the side, her eyes soft with compassion.

"It wasn't his fault. It was a childhood crush. He didn't even know I had it. He didn't encourage it, didn't tease me over it. I just sat there and suffered in silence."

"Until you kissed him," Harper said.

"Yeah. And wasn't that a weird thing to do? Creepy even." Caitie grimaced. "I've no idea why I did it."

"It's not weird. You were in love with the guy." Harper folded her arms across her chest. "I for one think you did the right thing."

"I think it was more than that," Caitie admitted. "His mom had died and I could see he was full of pain." Caitie took a deep breath, remembering that Christmas. "I wanted to make things better. I only went in his room to check if he was okay, and there he was laying in bed. I walked over to check if he was breathing, and that's when I felt the urge to kiss him."

Harper's eyes sparkled. "That's so romantic. Tell me more."

God, this was embarrassing. Even if Harper didn't think so. "The curtain was partially open," Caitie continued, her voice soft. "There was a shaft of moonlight across his hair, making it look golden. I reached out to touch it, and it was so soft. I thought I'd woken him up, he murmured something before breathing out. But when I looked, his eyes were still closed."

"Is that when you kissed him?"

Caitie nodded. "I was only going to kiss his cheek. I leaned down, ready to press my lips against it, and he turned his head to face me." She blinked. "The next thing I knew, I was kissing him." Soft lips. Even softer breaths. And for a moment it felt as though he was kissing her back, his mouth moving beneath hers. It sent a spark of electricity down her body, shooting through her legs and making her toes curl.

It was delicious. And she could still remember every moment of it.

"Are you sure he was asleep?"

"Yeah. He still had that rhythmic breathing going on.

That's when I realized what a creep I was. So I scurried back to bed, and I must have been exhausted because I didn't wake up until late the next day." She took a sharp inhale. "By morning, him and his brother were gone."

"And you've never loved anybody since," Harper said softly.

"I know how stupid that is." Caitie tried to smile. "Believe me, I think I'm an idiot, too."

"It's not stupid. It's beautiful. And if you don't tell him how you feel I'm going to cry myself to sleep. Caitie, maybe this is destiny. Meant to be. You need to be brave and put yourself out there." She leaned back in her seat, a smile on her face. "And if you don't, maybe I will."

---

"Lucas said he'd meet us in the pick-up zone," Caitie told Harper, as they pulled their suitcases through the airport exit. "He didn't want to try parking. It'll be even crazier than normal with it being Thanksgiving and all." There hadn't seemed much point in renting a car when they were staying with family all weekend.

She wasn't exaggerating about the craziness. LAX was jam-packed with passengers, making personal space a luxury nobody could afford. Even the sidewalk outside was three-people deep. Over in the taxi lane, two guys were arguing over who was there first. So much for being thankful, they'd be lucky if they got out of here alive.

"Hey, Cait. Over here."

Caitie and Harper turned their heads in unison, looking at the silver-grey truck parked on the other side of the pick-up lane. The driver's door opened, and Brecken Miller climbed out. His long, muscled legs were encased in dark blue pants, paired with a long-sleeved white shirt. He was wearing those familiar aviator sunglasses, and his hair was brushed back from his face. His skin held the natural sort of tan you only found in California, the evidence of long days spent riding the waves.

"That's not Lucas. Not unless he's had plastic surgery." Harper was staring, open mouthed.

Caitie took a deep breath, preparing herself for Harper's reaction. "That's Breck," she said.

"*Your* Breck?" Harper's mouth dropped open even more. Any minute and she'd be able to fit Breck's truck in there.

If her heart hadn't been stuck halfway up her throat, Caitie would have reminded her friend he wasn't *her* Breck. But she was too busy watching him cross the road, striding over the blacktop as if he owned the place.

"Hey, how was your flight?" he asked when he reached them.

That smile. All warm and full of promise.

"It was good, thanks." She looked around. "Is Lucas with you?"

"He was supposed to message you. I had a meeting in L.A., so when I heard you were flying in, I offered to pick you up. Seemed crazy for him to drive all the way here when I was in town."

"Well that was convenient." Harper grinned, tipping her head to the side.

"Ah, you must be the famous Harper." Breck offered his hand. Harper took it, shaking firmly.

"That's me. And I already know you're Breck. Caitie's told me a lot about you."

"She has?" Breck's smile was still broad. Though she couldn't see his eyes, Caitie knew he was looking at her. It made her feel warm and nervous, all at the same time, especially after her discussion with Harper.

"Harper's always full of questions," Caitie said. "You'll find that out on the drive home. If you were hoping for a nice scenic drive and some music, you're going to be disappointed."

Harper elbowed her in the waist. "Caitie thinks anybody who shows an interest in her is too talkative. I call it being a friend."

Breck rubbed the back of his neck. "Well, talkative is good. I was up early this morning to get to L.A., and I'm already running on caffeine fumes. I'll welcome the distraction."

"Ooh, is there a coffee shop on the way to Angel Sands?" Harper asked. "I'm dying for a frappé. Can we stop at one?"

"Sure." Breck shrugged. He turned to Caitie, grabbing the handle of her suitcase. "You okay? You look pale."

"I always look pale. Especially in California." She shrugged good naturedly.

"You look good, though," he added. "Cute sweater."

She glanced down at the pink cashmere top she'd pulled on that morning. It was one of her favorites, hugging her in all the right places. "Thanks. It was freezing in New York when we left. We had to layer up."

"It's not exactly scorching here either," Breck said. "The temperatures have dropped like a brick."

"We'll have to cozy up to keep warm," Harper said, that smile still playing at her lips. She kept looking from Caitie to Breck, as though she was trying to take everything in.

He lifted their suitcases into the back of his truck and pulled the passenger door open. There were two rows of seats, and Harper almost pushed past Caitie to climb into the back.

"What? I'm tired," she said, when Caitie gave her *that* look. "You can sit in the front with Breck and keep him entertained."

As though to make her point, Harper snapped her seatbelt on and leaned her head back on the rest, closing her eyes and crossing her arms over her chest. "Wake me up when we get to the coffee shop."

An hour later, after waking up temporarily for her frappé, Harper was snoring again in the backseat. When Caitie turned to look at her, Harper's head was back, her mouth wide open. She really was out for the count. Biting down a smile, Caitie turned back, taking the opportunity to look at Breck's strong profile. "I'm sorry about her. She has no control switch, she's either full on or at a complete stop."

"She seems nice," Breck said. He pulled his eyes from the windshield to look at her before directing his attention back at the road ahead. "I feel bad that I bored her to sleep. I swear she started snoring mid-conversation."

Caitie laughed. In the short time she was awake, Harper had managed to grill Breck about everything; his childhood, his time in Boston, the contract he was working on. He'd been in the middle of describing the Silver Sands Resort when Harper drifted off for the second time. "She was out late last night and we were up pretty early this morning. I'm surprised she didn't sleep on the plane." Except she wasn't *that* surprised. Harper had been too busy arguing with her for that.

"She seems like a good friend," he said. "She's very proud of you."

"What gives you that impression?"

"The way she talked about your work. She was bringing you up constantly. And she kept looking at me to gauge my reaction."

Caitie wrinkled her nose. "Sorry if she's a bit over the top."

He glanced at her from the corner of his eyes. "You don't like people talking about you, do you?"

He had the unerring ability to turn any conversation

between them into something personal. She liked it and hated it. Any conversation she had with him made her feel special, but it made her feel exposed, too. "I haven't really thought about it," she said. "I guess I'm a fairly private person. In my line of work I have to keep things confidential. I've learned not to talk about everything, because it'll usually turn around and bite me."

"But it's okay for people to be proud of you," he said. "It's not false pride, is it? Look at everything you've achieved. Your own business, a life in New York. Don't you realize how you come across to other people? Lucas never stops talking about you. Even Griff talks about how clever you are, at least as often as he describes you as hot."

She started to laugh. "Griff calls me *hot*? Eww. I'm not sure if that's a compliment or not coming from him."

Breck wrinkled his nose. "He'd think it was a compliment. And let's face it, you're beautiful. I barely recognized you at the beach club when you were here last time."

"Maybe that's because I looked so out of place," she said. Had he really called her beautiful? "It's not like I spend a lot of time at the beach club, I never did. Not even as a kid."

He was looking at her again, and the warmth in his eyes made her heart skip a beat. Being in such close proximity to him was making her feel dizzy, as though there wasn't enough air in the car.

"That's not why I didn't recognize you," he said softly. "It's because in my mind you're still the fifteen-year-old kid who cried with me the day my mom died. I still see her there – I still hear her in your words – but you've grown into an amazing woman. I should've known you would. You don't have that much empathy and compassion as a child without it following you through life. I wish you could turn it on your-self sometime. See yourself the way other people see you."

The emotion in his words silenced her. She inhaled a deep

breath, the air drying her lips and her tongue. Caitie wasn't sure anybody had ever said anything so open, so honest, or so lovely to her before. She was almost jealous of the girl she'd been.

"Are we there yet?" Harper asked. She had leaned forward, her head positioned between the driver and passenger seat. "I must have fallen asleep again."

Had she heard their conversation? Caitie narrowed her eyes, looking at her friend. If Harper had been listening, she'd never hear the end of it.

Caitie couldn't bring herself to be sorry Breck had said it. Hearing his kind words had buoyed her up in a strange way. Heated her from the inside out. He was a good friend, a kind one, somebody she was lucky to have. And if Harper wanted to pretend they were any more than that, good luck to her.

## 13

"How many people should I set the table for?" Caitie asked. Standing in the kitchen was like being in the eye of a tornado, disaster looming before her. Deenie was running from pot to pot, shooing away anybody who tried to help. Harper had already been pushed out into the living room, ordered to help Caitie's dad choose the wine, which was Deenie Russell code for 'I don't want to shout at you.'

Caitie didn't get any such consideration. She was used to her mom's haphazard ways. Russell family Thanksgivings were always a mess up until the last minute, when somehow, Deenie managed to bring it all together. The outcome was edible, it was the process which needed a little work.

"Let's see, there's us, Lucas and Ember, and Breck and his family. Oh wait, there's Ember's friend Rachel, too. What does that make? Ten?"

"A small one this year, then," Caitie said, biting down a smile. Her mom was notorious for inviting everybody who had no place else to go for the holidays. There had been years while Caitie was growing up when they didn't have enough plates or chairs for people to sit in, and they'd knock on their neighbor's houses to borrow them. "It's nice that you've invited Breck and his family."

"I couldn't stand the thought of them sitting on his sofa with takeout." Deenie shrugged. "Thanksgiving is about being together and sharing whatever you have. Anyway, it'll be lovely to see Daniel again. The last time I saw him he was eleven years old and cute as a button."

"I imagine he won't appreciate being described like that now," Caitie said dryly.

"It's nice to have them back. I worried about them a lot over the years. It was such a shame we lost touch."

The timer on the stove went off, interrupting her. Deenie pulled on her mitts and opened the door, a cloud of hot smoke escaping from the oven. It curled its way up to the ceiling, lingering there. Caitie peered across to see what was burning.

"Why don't you go on and set the table?" Deenie said from where she was kneeling in front of the stove. "Go on, shoo. Out of my kitchen." Deenie turned and gestured at the door to the dining room. "There's nothing to see here."

"Did you burn the turkey?" Caitie tried not to laugh.

"No, I didn't. Now get out and stop distracting me. I've got work to do."

Caitie scooped up the silverware, laying it on the tray next to the wine and water glasses. She carried it through to the dining room, kicking the kitchen door shut behind her. Even with the door shut, Caitie could hear her mom still muttering to herself about the food.

In a little while Breck would be here. The thought made her heart beat a little faster. Breck, Daniel, and their father. People who had been out of her life for so long, yet that Christmas way back in time had been a defining moment.

Breck's desperate loss.

Daniel's quiet grief.

Her own inability to figure out what to do. How to make things right. Because there was no way to make things right for them. Oh, she'd tried that Christmas morning with the stupid present, and again much later when she'd tiptoed into the guest room and wrapped herself around Breck. But the fact was, she'd felt useless in the face of such a mountain of pain. As if there was no way to scale it.

She grabbed the forks, the handles clanging together as she walked around the table, laying one at each place setting. She wished she could lay her own feelings out as easily. They were a mess inside her, a mixture of memories and emotions, things she'd thought she'd left behind when she'd grown into a woman.

"Happy Thanksgiving, little sis." Lucas grabbed Caitie from behind, making her shriek. He squeezed his arms around her waist, lifting her with ease until her feet were inches from the floor.

"Put me down." She wiggled in his grasp. He was strong, more so than she remembered.

"No way. Try and escape." His voice was teasing. She loved hearing him so happy.

"I can't." She twisted, but his hold on her waist remained firm. Even kicking her legs did nothing to aid in her release. All it did was make him laugh.

"Come on, Lucas, you can put me down now."

"Remember when we used to do this as kids? I swear you were stronger back then. New York's taken the edge off you. Made you a weakling."

"Tell that to my self-defense teacher," she said, still trying to wriggle out of his grasp. Okay, what was it they taught her? She tried to concentrate. She'd been trained for this. All she needed to do was hook her leg behind his knee and jab her elbow into his stomach. She did it in quick succession, and he released her with a groan.

"Christ..." He doubled over, gasping for breath.

Her eyes widened. "Did I hurt you?" She reached out for him and he went to grab her again, all pretense disappearing beneath his grin.

But this time she was on high alert, and slipped out of his grasp, darting behind him to get him into a chokehold.

"What the heck?" he managed, his voice strangled. "Where did you learn that?"

"Caitie, put your brother down," Deenie said. She showed no surprise at the sight of her twenty-eight-year-old daughter choking her thirty-year-old son. "Our guests are here. Lucas, I need you to offer them all a drink. And, Caitie, can you take some appetizers out onto the deck? It's warm enough to sit out there for now."

Caitie released him from her grasp, trying not to smirk at his look of surprise. "I took a self-defense course when I moved to New York," she told him.

"Smart thinking." He nodded. "And it's reassuring to know you can take care of yourself." He rubbed his neck where she'd been holding him. "Remind me not to underestimate you again."

She grinned. "I will."

Five minutes later, Caitie walked out to the deck, carrying two plates full of raw vegetables and dips. She came to a stop, staring at the people in front of her, her heart full as she took each of them in.

Lucas was helping her dad with the champagne, twisting the cork out with a pop. He poured it into the glasses her dad was holding out, and Harper took them and passed them around. Breck and his family were seated around the patio table, looking out at the yard so she could only see the back of their heads. Opposite them were Ember and her friend, Rachel, who was looking pretty in a pair of tight jeans and a strappy silver top. Caitie looked down at her own outfit –

tight black pants, paired with a cream sweater and a thin, gold chain. She felt like winter to Rachel's summer. The New York to her L.A.. She'd been pleased with the clothes when she'd put them on that morning, liking the way the fabrics outlined her curves. Now she wasn't so sure.

"Do you want some champagne, Caitie?" Harper walked over, holding a glass in each hand. The bubbles were hissing and popping inside, begging for escape, just like Caitie. In unison, Breck, Daniel, and their father turned to look at her. She was taken by the strong family resemblance.

Breck was the first to stand. Scraping the chair across the deck, he walked over and took the tray of snacks from her hands. His fingers brushed against hers, sending a bolt of electricity up her arms. He smiled and it took her breath away.

"Happy Thanksgiving. Let me take these for you." He leaned forward and brushed his lips against her cheek. Her nerve endings were on fire, her face tingling from the sensation of his breath against her skin. She wanted to close her eyes and savor the moment.

"Caitlin?"

The second man joined them. Younger than Breck, yet with the same sandy hair and sparkling eyes. His voice was quieter and his stance less dominant than his brother, but there was no mistaking who it was.

"Daniel Miller? Jeez, you don't look like I remember you." She grinned at him. "You're a sight for sore eyes."

"Since I was pre-pubescent the last time you saw me, I guess I'll be grateful for that." He smiled shyly, and it brought back the familiar emotions in Caitie's heart. Though she was only four years older than him, in those days it had been a huge gap. Enough to make her feel maternal and try to make him smile.

"I can't believe you're here." She threw her arms around

him. "Breck told me you were coming back for Thanksgiving. I'm so pleased to see you."

"Me, too. It's worth putting up with him just to say hi to you again."

"I'm David Miller. I don't expect you to remember me." Breck's dad offered her his hand. "But I remember you. Breck was right, you've grown up to be a beauty. It's a pleasure to meet you again."

Ignoring his hand, Caitie hugged him. "I'm so glad you could come. Breck's told me a lot about you."

"All bad, I expect." Though his tone of voice was the same, David's accent was different than Breck's. Full of Boston character. He winked. "Don't believe any of it."

"You should believe every word," Breck said. "It's all true." He smiled at Caitie, and she grinned right back. God, it was so good to see them again.

"Shall we sit down?" Caitie's dad pointed to the table. Only Ember and Rachel were still sitting. "If we don't eat all these dips, Deenie's gonna be angry. And none of you will like her when she's mad." The way his expression turned to one of horror made everybody laugh. They followed him back to the wooden table where Daniel pulled out two chairs, offering them to Harper and Caitie, before sitting down beside them.

"Breck, come and sit over here," Rachel called out, patting a chair next to her. "I was telling Ember about the restaurant we went to last week. The one in the hills."

Caitie froze, sitting completely still in her chair. The hair on her arms stood up, goosebumps forming along her flesh. It took all the control she had to not let the dismay show on her face.

Breck and Rachel went on a date? She watched as he walked over to her side of the table, his gait easy and his expression neutral. She tried to swallow, but her mouth was too dry. The temptation to down the entire glass of champagne was almost too strong to ignore.

She took a deep breath and silently chastised herself. Why wouldn't he date? It was a free world, after all.

"The Five Olives?" Breck asked, leaning on the table, next to Ember. He'd ignored the seat next to Rachel. For some reason that gave Caitie a grim sense of satisfaction. "It's a nice spot. Not too pretentious, good food. It feels more like a café than a restaurant."

"Did you think so?" Rachel said. "I thought it was beautiful. Really romantic, overlooking the ocean. And the food was to die for. We shared a platter, it was amazing. Breck, we should take Lucas and Ember there some time."

Harper elbowed Caitie in the waist. "You okay?" she asked quietly. Biting her lip, Caitie nodded, trying to blink away the salt water stinging behind her eyelids. She was being stupid, she knew it. What did it matter if Breck was going out with Rachel, or any other girl for that matter? He could spend time with whoever he wanted to.

"Breck tells me you're a Holiday Consultant," Daniel said quietly.

She smiled at him, grateful for the distraction. "That's right."

"What exactly is that?"

Her laugh was almost genuine. "I get asked that a lot. It's a bit of a niche job, I guess. Not one many people have heard of, but there are a few of us around. I advise companies on holiday trends and traditions. If a movie company wants to dress a set to look like Christmas in the 1940s, I help them, source the stuff, and give them historical background. But I also look at future trends, talking to retailers and letting them know what I think they should stock for the holidays next year. Whether red and green are in or out, if they should concentrate on silver and white. Which, by the way, is going to be huge this year, so start stocking up now."

Daniel laughed. "We don't really celebrate Christmas, so I don't think I'll be needing many decorations."

Harper leaned forward. "You don't celebrate? Are you Jewish?"

"Nah, we're nothings. Christian if you really wanted to give me a religion. But Breck usually travels at Christmas, and I tend to spend a lot of time in the lab. Dad just holes up and watches sports."

"That's awful," Harper said. "Why wouldn't you want to all be together?"

"I don't know. We've always concentrated on Thanksgiving. We spend it together every year. It's our holiday, you know? Christmas has always seemed a bit overrated." He cleared his throat. "And it's the anniversary of Mom's..." He blew out a mouthful of air. "It kind of puts a dampener on things."

Caitie gave him a sad smile. "That's understandable."

"Hey, don't look so sad," Daniel told her. "You sound as though you're great at your job. Breck's told me how well you've done. It's just that Christmas has so many memories for us, bad as well as good. Thanksgiving feels so much less loaded."

Of course it did. After everything they'd been through as a family, it made total sense. It didn't stop her from feeling sad. Christmas had always been a time of joy for Caitie. As a child, it had been full of magic and wonder, with dreams of sugarplum fairies and visits from St. Nicholas. As a teenager, it had been imbued with a deeper meaning, taking care of Daniel, and stealing that kiss from a sleeping Breck. Now it was her job – her life if she was being honest – and she loved everything about it.

"You don't even watch movies?" Harper asked. "*White Christmas? Miracle on 34th Street?*"

Daniel shook his head. "It kind of passes us by."

"Well jeez. These guys must be your worst nightmare, Caitie. They could put you out of a job."

She laughed at Harper's shock, even though she felt a bit of it, too. "I'll try not to panic too much."

There was a break in conversation as Caitie thought about them never celebrating Christmas. How they still must feel so much pain while everyone else is celebrating.

"Can I show you something?" Daniel asked, breaking the silence. "It's stupid, but I've looked after it for all these years."

"Of course. What is it?"

He pulled a phone from his pocket. Except on second glance it wasn't a phone at all. It was phone-shaped, with rounded edges, but instead of the whole face being a touch-screen, there was a small screen at the top with the rest of the front being dominated by a circular control wheel.

"Is that an iPod?" Harper asked, reaching out to touch the wheel. "God, I haven't seen one in years."

"Do you recognize it?" he asked Caitie. "It's the one you gave me that Christmas." He pressed the button in the middle of the wheel, and the screen came to life, the menu forming in dark letters.

"It still works?" she asked, the corner of her mouth lifting up.

"I took good care of it," he said. "It meant a lot to me. I still have the playlist you made, too. Look, here." He pressed another button, and a list of tracks came up on the screen. Just seeing the song titles formed a lump in Caitie's throat. She'd chosen one song from each CD in her collection, loading them onto her dad's computer. It had taken more than an hour to burn them into a playlist and download it onto the iPod.

"Those are beautiful songs."

"I played them constantly when we first went to Boston," Daniel told her. "They got me through some dark days." He pulled some earbuds from his pocket. "Do you want to listen to one? I'll share my headphones with you."

"I'd love to."

They took an earbud each, and Daniel pressed play. Almost at once, *Hallelujah* came on – the Jeff Buckley version – and the soulful pitch of his voice took her breath away.

A tear rolled down her cheek. When she looked at Daniel, she could see his eyes were watery, too. As they listened to the haunting tune together, she gave him a half-smile, and he took her hand in his, squeezing it tightly.

She wasn't sure what made her turn her head. A need to include the second brother? To feel if seeing him still hurt? Taking the last mouthful of her champagne, she swallowed it down, shifting her eyes to where Breck was still leaning against the table.

He was looking at her with the strangest expression on his face, his brows dipped with an intense, deep stare. She gazed back, unable to pull her eyes from his. Every part of her body was leaning toward him, needing to touch, to connect, to feel.

As the music continued in her ear, she felt a deep ache forming in her chest. It was painful and beautiful, but more than anything, it felt real.

## ❧ 14 ❦

"Do you have plans for tomorrow?" Rachel asked Breck after dinner, when everybody was clearing up. "I don't have work until next week. I thought maybe we should work on our first dance." She grinned at him. "I'm desperate to see your moves."

Breck blinked. He'd been too busy watching Caitie as she carried the dirty plates into the kitchen to notice Rachel walking up to him. There was something hypnotic about the way Caitie's hips swung in those tight-cut pants. "Sorry, what?"

Rachel bit her lip. "It doesn't matter."

He felt like a dick. "I'm sorry. It's been a long day. I'm all ears now, what was it you said?"

"I was wondering if you'd like to come to my place tomorrow." Her face was pink. "Maybe grab something to eat and... ah... practice our dance."

Thank god he had a built in excuse, he felt bad enough already. "Sorry, I can't. I promised to take Daniel surfing in the morning, and Dad and I have to visit with some customers." He tried to ignore the hurt expression on her face.

"Oh. No problem." She attempted a smile. "It was only a suggestion."

"You could come, too," Daniel suggested. How long had he been standing there? He had a smirk on his face as though he'd been listening for a while. "Do you surf?"

"No. I like watching though." Rachel's smile returned. "Breck's a great surfer."

Daniel raised his eyebrows. "Do you watch him a lot?" he asked, shooting Breck an amused glance.

"A few times. Sometimes I go with Ember when Lucas and Breck go out. It's fun to watch when they catch a wave."

"Then you should definitely come," Daniel said. "Shouldn't she, Breck?"

Breck shot his brother a dark look.

"What time are you going?" she asked him, not noticing his expression. "Early?"

It wasn't Daniel's fault he couldn't find a kind way to get Rachel to back off. Still, from the corner of his eye Breck could see his brother smirking. Noticing his scrutiny, Daniel made a silly face. Breck squeezed his eyes shut, wishing Rachel wasn't such a close friend of Lucas and Ember's. Maybe then it would be easier to say no.

That was one of the problems of living in a small town like Angel Sands. Sometimes it felt as though everybody was up in your business. He didn't want to upset somebody he was going to come into contact with again and again.

He'd just be kind and hope she got bored of the chase.

Caitie walked past them again, carrying another empty dish. She gave him and Rachel a small smile and went to hurry past.

"You need any help clearing up?" Breck asked her.

"No. We're good," Caitie said. She turned her head so he couldn't see her face. "You guys can carry on talking, you're guests here."

His eyes followed her as she walked away again. It was almost impossible to ignore the way her sweater hugged her body. It made him swallow hard, and try not to imagine what it would be like to peel it off her.

This was such a bad idea. He had one woman who couldn't take no for an answer, and another he couldn't get out of his mind, no matter how forbidden she was. You couldn't make this stuff up.

"Son, I think I'm going to head out," his dad said, joining them in the dining room. "It's almost nine in Boston, and I'm beat. Plus I'd kind of like to Skype with Maria before she goes to bed."

"Okay. I'll go say thanks to the Russells and then I can run you home."

"No need for you to leave early," Daniel said. "I'll take dad home. I'm sure Lucas can drop you off later. That's if you trust me with your truck."

Breck frowned. "Are you sure? You're only here for a couple of days. I'll take you."

"Dude, Dad'll be holed up in his room on his laptop and I'm heading to bed with a book. Just stay here and have fun with your friends. We'll see each other in the morning."

"He's right, son," his dad agreed. "You should stay. I heard Lucas talking about playing some cards."

Breck was torn between spending time with his family, and spending time with the Russells. As if to add to the confusion, Caitie emerged from the kitchen again, and their eyes immediately met.

"Are you leaving?" she asked, disappointment in her voice.

"*We* are," Daniel said, putting his arm around his dad. "Breck's going to grab a ride with Lucas later."

The furrows in Caitie's brow seemed to smooth out. "Oh, okay. It's a shame to see you go so soon."

"We've got a bit of jet lag," Daniel told her. "Plus, Dad's got a hot video date with his girlfriend. Thanks for having us over. It was so good to see you again." He pulled her in, hugging her tightly. "Let's stay in touch, okay? Now I've got your number, I'll give you a call."

"That would be wonderful." She squeezed him back. "And thanks for coming, it was great catching up with you."

Breck pulled his keys from his pocket and threw them to his brother, who caught them mid-air. "I'll see you later, bro."

After Breck's family left, Deenie and Wallace went up to bed, claiming exhaustion. Only six of them remained. Lucas grabbed some beers, handing one to Harper, before passing Caitie and Breck both a bottle. Rachel shook her head, and Ember poured them both a glass of wine instead.

"Okay, so who's up for a few rounds of poker?" Lucas asked.

"I'm game," Caitie said, taking a mouthful of beer. "If you can handle me."

"I'm certain you can't handle me. But I'm up for it if you are." Harper grinned.

Rachel shook her head. "I'm terrible at cards. Maybe we can put on some music and dance instead."

Caitie's expression was classic. Her wide eyes and open mouth made Breck want to laugh. He was half inclined to agree with Rachel just to watch Caitie's reaction.

"I'm no good at cards either," Ember agreed. "Do we have to play? Lucas gets all angry and starts shouting whenever he loses."

When Breck looked at Caitie again, she was biting down a smile. Her teeth digging into her bottom lip. As he watched it slowly unfurl, he had to tighten his hands into fists to stop himself from touching her.

"We could watch a movie," Lucas suggested. "Dad's got some old Clint Eastwood DVDs in his office."

"Can't we watch something nice?" Rachel said. "A romantic comedy, or something? Oh, maybe there's a Christmas movie on Netflix."

Breck swallowed hard. Watching a Christmas movie sounded like his idea of hell.

"We don't need to watch something Christmassy," Caitie said quickly, glancing at him from the corner of her eyes. "It's only Thanksgiving." She shrugged. "Breck, what do you think we should watch?"

With the threat of watching a holiday movie removed, he could feel himself breathe more easily. "Why don't we see what's in the study?" he suggested. "Though I'd definitely prefer an action movie to romance."

"Me too," Caitie agreed.

"I'm easy," Harper said. "I'll probably fall asleep no matter what you put on. It's been a long day and we started drinking at lunch time. I never realized your folks were so hardcore, Caitie."

"Just don't make it too scary." Ember grimaced. "I need to get some sleep tonight. I want to hit the Black Friday sales tomorrow."

"Oh I don't know," Rachel said. "I kind of like scary movies. As long as I've got somebody to cuddle up to."

As the guys walked out of the room, Breck's mind was made up. Definitely not a horror movie, and definitely not a Christmas movie. He was pretty sure that was going to rule out most of Wallace Russell's antique DVD collection.

---

As the door closed behind Breck and Lucas, Rachel sighed from her spot next to Ember.

"Breck is so lovely. Where has he been all my life?"

"In Boston," Harper said, deadpan. Caitie tried not to laugh.

Rachel ignored them, grabbing Ember's wrist. "Did I tell you what he said at the end of our lunch the other day? We were talking about the best places to surf in winter, and he told me he loves going to Hawaii in December. Well, of course he can't go before your wedding, but he's thinking of flying out there after. Do you think he might invite me?"

Caitie set her half-drunk bottle of beer on the end table. "I'm going to look for some snacks in the kitchen. Anybody want anything?"

"I'll help you," Harper said, jumping up.

"Don't worry about getting anything for me," Ember said, rubbing her stomach. "I'm still full from dinner. And I have a wedding dress to squeeze into." She frowned. "Ugh, I probably shouldn't eat for a week."

"I'm fine, too," Rachel said. "I want to look my best when we walk down the aisle."

"I bet you do," Harper muttered, her voice too low for anybody but Caitie to hear.

Caitie sped up her exit, pushing the door to the kitchen open with more force than necessary.

"Are you okay?" Harper asked, pulling the door closed behind her. "You were so quiet at dinner I thought you might have fallen asleep."

"I'm fine," Caitie reassured her, pulling a pack of chips from the cupboard. She grabbed two bowls and opened the packet, even though she had no appetite at all.

"Do you know that Rachel girl well?" Harper asked as Caitie started to shake the chips into the bowls. "She's been hanging around Breck all day. Are they an item?"

Caitie stopped mid shake and turned to face her friend. "I've only met her a couple of times before. She's Ember's friend. They work together at the elementary school." She pulled her bottom lip between her teeth. "And I've no idea if they're an item, though they seem pretty close."

The two of them had seemed attached at the hip since lunchtime. Every time Caitie had glanced across the room Rachel had been talking with Breck. He didn't seem to mind, either. He was his usual, amiable self, making jokes and talking with everybody.

But every time he'd smiled at Rachel, it had felt like Caitie's chest was about to implode.

"Maybe they're just friends," Harper suggested, though she didn't sound convinced. "That would be normal, wouldn't it? If she hangs around with Lucas and Ember a lot she'd be bound to get to know their friends. The way you did when you grew up with Lucas."

"I never whispered in Griff's ear the way Rachel whispered in Breck's," Caitie pointed out. "And Breck is her partner in the bridal procession. He's going to walk her down the aisle."

"He is?" Harper wrinkled her nose. "Ugh. Maybe they are a couple." She reached for Caitie's hand, sliding it between her own. "I'm sorry, honey. That must hurt like hell."

"I'm fine," Caitie said again, hoping she sounded convincing. "He's a grown man. He's allowed to have a relationship with anybody he wants. It's not as though I expected him to save himself for me." She gave a short laugh. "It wouldn't have worked anyway. He lives here and I live in New York. And I don't know if you were listening to Daniel earlier, but he said none of them like Christmas very much." She shrugged. "Maybe it's better this way. We're clearly not compatible."

"Right..." From the way Harper was staring at her, it was clear she didn't agree at all. "You tell yourself that."

"What else is there to tell myself? That I should have told

him how I felt earlier? Maybe that way he wouldn't be in love with someone else."

"Now wait a minute," Harper said, crossing her arms in front of her chest. "Who said he was in love with her?"

"Isn't that how relationships work?"

"Not at first, no. They start off with flirting. And Rachel was doing a lot of that today. Breck not so much. He responded to her, smiled at her at the right times, nodded his head when she spoke, but he didn't initiate anything. If they're a couple it's her doing the driving. And it's very early days."

Caitie frowned. "You got all this from watching them interact?"

"I'm a people watcher. It's what I do to have fun. And I can tell you Breck isn't in love with her, even if they've got something going on."

"It doesn't matter." Caitie crumpled up the empty chip packet and tossed it in the trash. "He probably likes how uncomplicated it all is. She lives in Angel Sands and so does he. He likes surfing and she likes to watch. She isn't a Holiday Consultant and he doesn't like Christmas. Maybe they're made for each other."

"So you're giving up on him?" Harper asked.

Caitie's eyes caught hers. "I'm not the kind of girl who chases somebody else's man. If he wants to be with Rachel I'm good with that."

"His eyes followed you around all day. Wherever you went, that's where he was looking," Harper said nonchalantly.

"What?" Caitie whipped around to look at her.

"And I noticed you doing the same. Neither of you could keep your eyes off each other."

"That's not true," Caitie protested.

"It was kind of hot, if it didn't make me want to bang your

heads together." Harper grinned. "You're both so oblivious to what's going on. I'd laugh if it wasn't so sad."

"I did not look at him constantly."

"Oh come on," Harper said. "You couldn't take your eyes off him. Even when we went around the table and all said what we were thankful for. You said you're so happy to be surrounded by friends, both old and new."

"Well I *am* happy." Well, she was until she saw Rachel spending all that time with Breck.

"Yeah, but the way he smiled at you when you said it, I swear it could have turned the turkey to ashes. That man's got a thing for you, even if he doesn't realize it yet."

"Oh, shut up." Caitie shook her head.

"I say it like I see it, and it all fits. The phone calls, the protectiveness on your date, the way he couldn't stop smiling when you were kind to his little brother. He's got it bad."

"Then explain why he's dating Rachel."

"I didn't say he had any sense. He's a typical man. I don't know many guys who would turn down somebody so determined. And if you ignore the huge gap where her brain should be, she's very attractive."

"Don't be mean," Caitie told her. But she couldn't help but smile. "I wasn't kidding about them being better suited. I bet she doesn't turn into a gibbering wreck whenever she's near the ocean."

"Oh yeah, she's perfect on the surface, that's for sure. But that's all she is. Surface. But you're the iceberg, Caitie. The still water that runs deep."

"That's why you're my best friend," Caitie said. "Because you only see the good in me. But this whole conversation is pointless. Whatever you think's going on in your head about Breck and me isn't true. I'm his friend's little sister, the girl who looked after his brother one Christmas. That wasn't attraction you were seeing, it was kindness."

Harper shrugged. "You think whatever you like. Now are we going to watch this movie or not?" She took a bowl from Caitie and pushed the door to the living room open. "Hey everybody, who wants snacks?"

## ❧ 15 ❧

"Are you joining us for lunch?" Deenie asked, peering around the door. "Jeez, honey, the air smells stale in here. You should open a window or something."

Caitie looked up. It took a while for her eyes to adjust. For a minute, her mom looked blurry. The result of too many hours staring at her laptop screen, tweaking her presentations and proposals.

"Is it lunchtime already?"

"Lunchtime has come and gone. We've been waiting for a while. I'd called out for you."

Now her door was open, the aroma of turkey soup was wafting into the room. Combined with the smell of freshly-baked bread, it was mouthwatering.

"I'm sorry, I didn't realize. I must have been too far into the zone. I hope it's not ruined because of me."

"Don't be silly, you can't ruin soup. And the bread's cooled nicely. But if we keep your father waiting any longer, he might explode."

Caitie laughed. "He's the most patient man I know. Remember that experiment he did at work that took years?"

"The one they had to abandon when all the dishes were contaminated? Oh yeah, I remember that. He sulked for months."

"Yeah, well, I can empathize with the sulking." She glanced at her laptop again. "I feel like all I've done for the past few weeks is work on this proposal. If I lose the contract..." She trailed off. She didn't want to think about that. And if she was honest, she didn't want to think about winning it either. She needed to get through to Thursday night, then she'd let her mind wander.

"You need to get out of the house. You've been here since Wednesday and you haven't left once. Honestly, you're going to drive yourself crazy. Go out, get some fresh air, and take a walk. Something. Anything to take a break. Even Harper went shopping on Black Friday, for goodness sake." Harper had left earlier that morning, planning to visit some actor friends in L.A., before her meeting at the studio on Monday.

"My first presentation is in two days, Mom. There's no time to take a break."

"Are you prepared for them?" Deenie asked, the same way she used to before Caitie's school tests.

"I'm trying. I've gone over every minute detail at least three times. I've timed my speech, checked the spelling, and I've even made sure to memorize everybody's names."

"Then you're ready. Looking at them constantly isn't going to do you any good. Whereas, getting out of the house and thinking about something else will help to recharge your batteries."

Caitie sighed. She wasn't going to win this battle. She knew her mom was right. Reading everything over and over was only driving her crazy, and making her more nervous. "Okay, I'll go for a walk on the trail after lunch. You want to come with me?"

Deenie shook her head. "Nope. Your father and I will

walk later. Why don't you call one of your old friends, or maybe your brother?"

Caitie shrugged. "I'll go alone. I'd prefer to have some silence. Be at one with nature or something." She didn't feel much like company. Hadn't since Thanksgiving. Maybe she was still sulking about Breck.

Deenie laughed. "When have you ever been one with nature? You're more comfortable tapping away at a laptop than spending time in the great outdoors."

"Careful, or I'll go back to looking at the laptop."

"In that case, I'll shut my mouth. And feel free to take my car." As Deenie turned to walk out of the doorway, she stopped and looked back at her daughter. "Oh, and can you do me a favor while you're out?"

"Sure. What is it?"

"Brecken left his sweater here on Thanksgiving. Can you drop it off on your way to the trail? I'll give you his address. He's over near Silver Sands."

"Yeah sure, I'll take it over." Caitie tried to keep her voice nonchalant, even though she felt anything but. She wasn't sure what perturbed her more, the thought of seeing Breck or his close proximity to the beach.

"Thanks, honey."

An hour later, Caitie was driving down Main Street, heading to the other side of town before the beach gave way to the Silver Sands Resort. One of the newer parts of town, made up of apartments and bungalows, she could remember when the homes were first being built. Before then, that side of Angel Sands was practically abandoned. The only people who went over there were surfers – headed for the waves at Silver Sands – and school kids who liked to scare themselves stupid exploring the eerie buildings of the old resort, a location even Scooby Doo would be proud of.

The GPS on her phone led her down the curving roads of

the development, past the taller apartment buildings, and toward the water. Her chest tightened as the ocean loomed in front of her. Slowing the car down to a crawl, she tried to take in a deep breath.

Of course Breck would choose to live near the ocean. Where else would he go? As a kid he'd spent most of his time on the beach, and by all accounts, he still did the same thing in his spare moments as an adult.

She turned the final corner onto his road, where a row of bungalows were lined up against the sidewalk. Each had a wooden deck curving from the front to the back, steps leading straight down to the beach. They were bigger than her grandparents' old cottage, now Lucas and Ember's home, but somehow they reminded her of it.

When she reached Breck's bungalow, she stopped the car and switched off the ignition. But rather than get out, Caitie closed her eyes, trying to center herself. The sound of the waves penetrated through the Honda's windows, and her pulse sped up in response. Though the car had stopped, her hands were gripping the steering wheel so tightly her knuckles were bleached white.

Glancing to her right, she could see his navy sweater folded neatly on the passenger seat. "Just give him the goddamn sweater and leave," she muttered to herself. "You can be out of here in under two minutes."

Leaning forward, she banged her head against the center of the wheel, her eyes squeezed tightly shut. God, what was she doing? She was a grown woman. She owned her own business. She was about to pitch for the biggest job of her career. And yet the sound of the waves crashing against the sand was enough to make her want to run away like a child.

Her arm shook as she released the wheel and reached for the door. She missed it on her first try, finally managing to keep herself still enough to grab it. One small tug and the door creaked open. The smell of salt and sand immediately entered the Honda, along with the amplified sound of the ocean. The assault on her senses made her stomach roll.

Closing her mouth, she held her breath as she climbed out of the car, taking Breck's sweater from the passenger seat. After a long minute, she finally made it to his front door, and rang the bell, leaning against the door frame to steady herself. After a minute of waiting, she realized Breck wasn't there. Was it wrong she felt disappointed?

Maybe it was a blessing in disguise. She could put his sweater down on the bench in front of his door and leave. But instead, she lifted her head and caught a glimpse of the golden sand running along the back of his bungalow. A fresh breeze hit her, carrying notes of ozone and saline in its wake. Unable to hold her breath any longer, she gasped, the smell invading her mouth, her nostrils, and her skin.

Without even thinking, she walked forward, drawn to the oceanfront in spite of herself. The sound of the waves was muted by the pulse drumming in her ears, yet still it made itself known. Her breath got shorter, her chest more labored as it tried to get the oxygen it needed. She felt her heart rate rise as it pushed the blood around faster in an attempt to mitigate the loss of oxygen.

She'd almost made it to the back steps before she'd collapsed. As her knees folded beneath her, Breck's sweater fell onto the sandy wooden planks. Reaching out for the handrail, she managed to stop herself before she completely fell. The effort knocked the wind out of her, and made her eyes water up. Through her blurred vision she could make out the yellow of the sand, the blue of the ocean, and the hazy forms of the people at the waterfront.

Even as the panic began to overwhelm her, she knew how stupid she must look. And she hated it. Hated the way she reacted to something as innocuous as the beach.

It felt like she was back *there* again. That she was the girl who wanted to be like her brother. The one who sneaked out with his surfboard, ignoring the flags on the beach. Who found the ocean had no mercy for those who didn't respect it.

She was drowning again, but this time on land. The pressure on her chest was unbearable. The only way she'd stopped herself from tumbling down the steps was from grasping onto the rail, but the dizziness taking over her body was twisting her away from the edge.

"Cait? Is that you?" The voice seemed to come from far away. "Caitie, Jesus, what's wrong? What's happening?"

The next moment was a rush of sensations. Breck's arms wrapping around her, wet and hard, as though he'd run up from the water. The slamming of a door as he carried her away from the deck. The softness of upholstery as he pulled her down against him. All the while he was murmuring, touching her, his hands soft against her skin. Urging her to breathe, to calm down, to breathe again. Slowly, she felt reality coming back into focus. She tried to open her eyelids, but a fresh flood of tears escaped, pouring down her face and dropping onto her sweater.

"Caitie, try and breathe, okay?"

When she opened her mouth, her chest started to hitch, but the rapid, shallow breaths were useless. Her lungs were screaming out for the oxygen they lacked.

"Breathe slower," he told her, his voice calm and low. "In and out. That's it, slowly. Caitie, try and look at me."

She blinked twice, her eyelids slowly raising up. Breck's face was inches away from hers. His eyebrows were drawn together, the skin between them pinched into a line.

The tears started to multiply, and her breaths turned into sobs. They wracked her frame as Breck pulled her against him. He was all hard muscle and wet skin – bare from the chest up.

"I'm sorry," she sobbed against him, full of humiliation. "I'm such an idiot."

"You don't need to be sorry. Just try to breathe, okay? Your heart is hammering. It can't be good for you. Try to slow everything down." He started stroking her hair, his touch gentle. The rhythmic motion calmed her. For a few minutes, she let him hold her, her face pressed against his chest, his hands smoothing the strands of her hair as she breathed.

"What happened?" he asked once her breathing was steady. "What made you react like that?"

She squeezed her eyes shut, feeling her cheeks flood with warmth. Nobody had ever seen her like that before. She hated that he was the first to see her weakness. Yet the look of concern on his face made her answer him honestly.

"I had a panic attack," she told him. "I've had them before. They were regular when I was a kid."

"It looked like you were dying. Scared the shit out of me," he said. "How the heck do you cope with them?"

"I don't get them very often anymore," she said, taking a deep lungful of air. Though still too high, her heart rate was slowly dipping. "I almost had one when I came to Lucas's engagement party, but I managed to calm down before it set in."

"Do you get them at work? In New York?" he asked.

"No, they're pretty specific to here. The ocean's the real trigger, the biggie. That's why I try to avoid it if I can." She licked her dry lips. Her whole body felt like a wrung-out dishrag.

"I knew you hated the beach, but I didn't think it was that bad." She could hear the frown in his voice. "Sweetheart, you can't live like this. You can't. It's fucking awful to watch you go through this."

She looked up, her face still wet with tears. Breck winced as he took in her disheveled appearance, cupping her face between his hands, as if he wanted to wipe the tears from her cheeks.

"It's okay," she told him. "I'll be fine once I get away from the beach. I always feel better once I leave."

"You're not going *anywhere* like this." His voice was firm. "It's not safe for you to drive right now."

There was something so reassuring about the way his hands held her face. She wanted to melt into them. His fingertips brushed the tears from her cheeks, his thumb running a line along her bottom lip, his eyes dark as he watched them part. Her breath caught in her throat.

This time, her speeding pulse had nothing to do with panic, and everything to do with the way he was touching and looking at her.

His stare was as intense as her emotions. Her chest hitched as his pupils dilated and eyes narrowed. Every second that passed was punctuated by the beating of her heart and the soft touch of his breath against her skin. The reality of him pushed out every other thought in her head, until Breck was the only word on her lips.

"Cait..." He traced her mouth with his thumb again, this time pressing the tip against her soft flesh. She opened her lips, submitting, inviting him in. His thumb slid inside, her lips closing over it. As the pad grazed her tongue, his breath hitched.

"You're so damn beautiful." He pulled his thumb from her lips and leaned forward until his mouth was a breath away from hers.

The brush of his lips against hers was so gentle she could barely feel it at first. But then he pressed harder, until the soft skin of her mouth surrendered, her lips moving in time with his.

His hand clenched and unclenched at the nape of her neck, grabbing at her hair. The other traced the line of her throat, feathering softly where her neck met her shoulders. His fingers were oh-so-soft against her sensitive skin, leaving a trail of ice along her spine. She felt the hum of his breath against her lips as he deepened their kiss, his tongue sliding against the tender flesh of her mouth.

Caitie's pulse was drumming rapidly in her neck, echoing the rapid beating of her heart. She felt overwhelmed by him. Was it possible for somebody to make you feel so safe and on edge at the same time?

They kissed until her lips were stinging, and their lungs were burning with the need to inhale. They parted and gasped until the need had been sated. Breck pushed her back against the couch and started kissing her again. She was laying on her back, Breck half-laying across her, her arms looped around his torso. His own were sliding down her sides, lingering at her hips, where he pressed against the thin fabric of her pants.

The sweetness of their desire, in contrast to the ache of her anxiety, was like a balm to her soul. She gave herself to him again and again, letting him kiss her before kissing him back, until their lips were moving as one. She didn't want it to stop, not ever.

It felt unbelievably perfect.

## ❧ 16 ❧

Breck kissed her like there was no tomorrow, desperate to feel every part of her against him. Her lips were soft and yielding, her breath warm against his mouth. With every slide of his hand, he could feel himself falling deeper. She was the kind of woman men like him dreamed about. Soft, yet tough. Beautiful, but she didn't know it. Kissing her was like coming home, and it made his heart ache.

Caitlin Russell. How many times had he thought about her as his best friend's little sister? But she wasn't so little any more. She was a woman; the way she was responding to his touch was enough to tell him that.

He kissed her like she was the oxygen he needed, loving the way she kissed him back. Her touch was hesitant at first, growing bolder as she ran her fingers down his spine. When she reached the base and found the sensitive nerves clustered there, his back arched.

His whole body was aching for her. Blood rushed to his groin, pulsing through him, as she pressed her hands against his back. He lowered himself down and kissed her again, careful not to rest all of his weight against her. Caitie's hands slid around to the back of his shorts, urging him against her, until his desire was hard against her core. Wrapping her legs around him, she hooked her ankles at his thighs, rocking until the friction was almost unbearable.

Minutes passed as they kissed wordlessly, neither of them willing to break this sensuous spell. Everything about her excited him, yet calmed him at the same time. She was a whirlwind that somehow set everything right with the world, and he wanted more.

When he caught her eye, she nodded, letting him know she wanted it, too.

Grabbing the hem of her sweater, he tugged it off, over her head. Beneath it, her skin was pale, almost translucent, her breasts swollen beneath a pale-blue lace bra. He cupped them, feeling her nipples harden beneath the fabric. Pinching her swollen flesh between his thumb and forefinger, he made her writhe and moan. The friction they created, the teasing, the delicious movement of their rocking – it was enough to blow his mind.

Lowering his head, he brushed his lips across her bra, loving the way her nipples pressed against his flesh. He sunk his mouth onto her, sucking her through the lace, until she moaned loudly, her body bucking beneath his.

She was beautiful, perfect, everything he wanted.

*She's also your best friend's sister.*

Hell no, he wasn't going to think about *that*. Not then.

He moved his head up until he was kissing her again, his hands reaching around her back to unclasp her bra. The only sound in the room was his harsh breaths and her deep moans, drowning out the distant hum of the waves.

Until the sound of his phone broke their spell.

It was still in a waterproof pouch inside his board shorts. He could feel it vibrating against his skin. Caitie froze beneath him at the sound, her desperate cries fading to nothing. For a moment, he frantically tried to figure out how to recapture the moment.

"Do you think you should get that?" she asked, pulling back from him.

"It's not important." He immediately missed the warmth of her body.

"It could be," she said. "You really should answer."

Sighing, he pulled the plastic pouch from his shorts, unzipping it. A name was written across the screen for them both to see. Breck felt his stomach fall.

*Rachel Foss.*

---

Those two words felt like a bucket of ice water being poured over her. Her muscles – so relaxed only moments before – tensed up until they felt almost painful. A feeling of shame washed over her. She was half-naked beneath Breck, and the girl he was dating was calling him.

What the hell had she done? She wasn't that kind of girl.

Caitie sat up quickly, wrapping her arms around her chest. Frowning, Breck pressed the end call button and threw it on the table beside the couch. It started to ring again. Breck sighed, sitting up to grab it.

"You should answer her." Caitie sat up and grabbed her sweater from the floor. "I need to go, anyway. I've got so much work to do." God, how the heck had she ended up like this? She felt sick at the thought of Rachel. Even if what Harper had said was true, you still didn't do this to another woman.

It was the girl code. And she never broke it.

"I can call her back later. You don't have to go yet, do you? I can make us coffee and we can sit out on the deck—" He stopped short. "Shit, bad idea. I can still make the coffee. Or we can drive out to some place. Whatever you prefer." His voice was thick, as though he had something to hide. She could detect more than a note of panic in it.

She pulled back, mortified. "I've got these big meetings starting on Tuesday. I really need to work on my presentation. Thanks for the offer, though." The air was buzzing with awkwardness, she could almost taste it. What the hell had they been thinking?

Or maybe they hadn't thought. That was the problem. They'd listened to their bodies instead of their good sense.

Breck sat up, rubbing his face. "When do you leave?"

"I drive to L.A. tomorrow afternoon." She couldn't quite meet his gaze, too ashamed for him to see her heated face.

"And after that? When are you going back to New York?"

"Friday. I'm catching a morning flight with Harper. I'm hoping by then I'll know if I've got this contract or not."

"But you'll be back here soon? You've got the wedding to organize. It's less than a month away."

"Yes, I'll be back. I have to meet with the suppliers at the hotel in mid-December, then I'll fly back for the wedding at Christmas."

"That's a lot of travel."

"I'm used to it. I've been working on this proposal on and off for six months, plus I have other clients in L.A.. I can do a lot by Skype and email, but sometimes face-to-face is the only way."

"I hear you." Breck tugged a t-shirt over his head. He took a deep breath in. "Look, Caitie, what happened ..."

She couldn't talk about this now. "It's okay," she answered quickly. "It was a mistake, I know it was. Just a reaction to my panic attack. I was hyperventilating and you were trying to help me, it was nothing more than that."

"You think I kissed you to stop you from panicking?" He frowned.

"No, I think you kissed me because we were in a heightened situation. I'm grateful you were here. I really am, but we both know it shouldn't have happened." She rubbed her neck, glancing over at the hallway door. She was desperate to get out of there before she made an even bigger fool of herself than she already had.

Breck frowned, his lips parted as though he was trying to find the right thing to say.

"I won't say anything to Rachel," she told him quickly. "I know you're not that kind of guy."

"What kind of guy?" Breck frowned, wiping a bead of water from his brow. His wet hair was hanging over his forehead, eclipsing some of the lines there.

God, she wished her heart would slow down. It was hammering against her chest as though it was desperate to get out. "It doesn't matter." She attempted a smile. "Thank you for taking care of me when I couldn't take care of myself."

"Cait..." He was still frowning.

"You won't say anything either, will you?" she quickly added. "I don't want things to get awkward between any of us. Not when Lucas and Ember's wedding is getting so close. They deserve to have their big day without any drama."

"Drama?" he repeated. "What kind of drama? And of course I won't say anything. Not if you don't want me to."

She let out a mouthful of air. "Thank you." She could see herself in his living room mirror. Her hair was a mess, tangled and knotty. Her face though – that was glowing, in spite of the tears and shock from earlier. Her lips were swollen from their kisses, her skin flushed from the exertion.

"Are you sure you don't want some coffee?" he asked. "Or a soda? I've got a full fridge if nothing else." He looked anxious, as though he didn't want her to leave.

"I'm fine, honestly. I've been working all morning, and I

really need to get back to it. I only left the house because Mom made me... oh, I brought your sweater back. You left it at our place on Thanksgiving."

"I saw it on the deck outside. I'll grab it later. Thanks for dropping it off."

"It was a good holiday, wasn't it?" She changed the subject, hoping it would help.

"Yeah, it was." A ghost of a smile passed his lips.

She'd stood to make her way to the door. "And it was so nice to see Daniel again. Has he gone back to Boston?" If she kept talking, she wouldn't have to think about what she'd done. And wouldn't that be a good thing? She walked into the hallway, Breck following close.

"Yeah," he said from behind her. "He and Dad left yesterday. Dad was desperate to get back to his girlfriend, and Daniel wanted to get back to his research."

They'd reached the front door. "Hey. Are you sure you can't stay?" Breck asked as she reached for the handle.

"I really can't." She opened her mouth then closed it again, unable to find the right words. Clearing her throat, she forced herself to look him in the eyes. "Thank you. I'm so sorry I interrupted your day. I'm sure this was the last thing you wanted to deal with."

His jaw twitched. "You didn't interrupt anything."

"Well, enjoy what's left of the day. I'll see you at the wedding."

He opened the door, stopping halfway. "Look, Cait..."

"Knock knock!" The door was pushed from the other side, revealing Rachel standing there in cut-offs and a cropped sweater. "Oh, you're home. I tried calling you. I was in the area and thought I'd stop by."

"Oh, yeah, I missed your call. I was talking to Cait." He looked back at Caitie, the strangest expression on his face.

"And I was just leaving." Painting a smile on her lips,

Caitie tried to walk past him, but his muscled frame was blocking her way. "I came by to drop his sweater off. Mom asked me to. He'd left it at our house on Thanksgiving." She was aware how stupid she sounded, babbling and making excuses. Maybe if she kept talking for long enough a hole would open up and kindly swallow her.

Rachel stared at her. "Hi, Caitlin." She looked confused. "I didn't realize you were here."

"Only for a second," Caitie told her, wishing she was anywhere but here. "I need to go. I'll leave you guys to it. Have a great afternoon."

This time Breck let her pass, moving back against the wall as her body slid against his. For a second their gazes met. His eyes were cloudy, unreadable, and they made her feel worse than ever.

She turned away and took a deep breath, determined not to look back as she walked onto the porch. Not because the ocean lay beyond his bungalow, with the waves and sand and everything else that made her want to cry. No, it was Breck himself it hurt to look at.

Breck and Rachel.

So why was it that as soon as she got into the car and turned the ignition, she glanced at him through the Honda's window? He was staring right at her, ignoring Rachel and the way she was trying to grab his attention. His jaw was tight, his eyes dark, and his gaze unwavering. Something about it made her whole body start to tremble.

She'd always thought Angel Sands was bad for her. Now she *knew* it was. The sooner she got out of there the better, before she ended up making a bigger fool of herself than she already had. Tearing her gaze away from his, she moved the car into reverse and began to pull away. As far as she was concerned, she couldn't get out of there fast enough.

"You need to call him," Harper said as they let themselves into their suite. Caitie had arrived in L.A. earlier that afternoon, and picked her assistant Felix up from the airport, where he'd flown in from New York. They'd travelled onward to meet Harper at the studio where she'd been in meetings all day in the costume department, and finally they'd checked in and been shown to their rooms.

"I can't," Caitie said, glancing along the corridor to make sure Felix hadn't heard. Luckily he was already in his room, hopefully oblivious to her problems. "What would I say? Sorry I kissed you before your girlfriend showed up." She shook her head. "I think I've humiliated myself enough already."

"She's not his girlfriend," Harper said, pulling her case through the door.

Caitie blinked. "You said there was something between them on Thanksgiving. Look at how much time they spent together. And why would she turn up unannounced at his door if they weren't dating?"

The door closed behind them as they walked into the huge living area. At the far end large glass windows overlooked the sprawling city, full of high rise buildings and intersecting roads. In the center of the room were two cream leather sofas, facing each other with a polished glass coffee table between them.

"Well this is nice," Harper said, grinning. "I could get used to this." She walked over and sat on the nearest sofa. "And there's no way they're dating if he kissed you. He's not the kind of guy who'd ever cheat on a woman, I know enough to tell you that."

"I wish I could feel certain." Caitie slumped in the sofa opposite, leaning her head back on the cool leather. She hadn't been able to get their kiss out of her mind. The way he'd touched her, kissed her, set her on fire. Her chest ached every time she thought about him. In spite of herself, she'd fallen for him all over again.

And it hurt.

"I'm certain enough for the both of us," Harper told her. "I know people. And a kiss that hot needs to lead to something more. So call him and put us all out of our misery."

"What about Rachel?" Caitie asked, her mouth dry.

"What about her?" Harper shrugged. "Look, it's obvious she has a crush on him, but that's all it is. If he isn't interested then he's free to kiss whoever he wants." She grinned. "And he wants you."

"This is so messed up. I liked it better when he was a fantasy."

"Did you really?" Harper tilted her head to the side, a smile playing at her lips.

"No." Caitie couldn't help but smile back. Because her fantasies were nothing compared to that kiss. She could still feel his lips against hers, still taste him on them. And when she closed her eyes, she could feel his strength as he held her, touched her, made her needy in a way she'd never been before.

"Are you sure they're not dating?" Caitie asked, hope blooming in her chest.

"I'd stake your life on it," Harper said, her eyes twinkling. "But there's only one way to find out. Call him. *Ask him*. Don't let this chance slip away." She leaned forward and pulled Caitie's phone from her purse, holding it out to her.

Caitie looked at it for a moment. Harper was right, dammit. She was a grown, strong, intelligent woman, not a teenage girl with a crush. Tomorrow she'd be pitching for a multi-million dollar deal. Surely she could call Breck and ask him how he felt.

"Okay," she said, letting out a mouthful of air. "I'll call him."

"Yes!" Harper pumped her fist. "God this is romantic. He's the first boy you kissed. I'm melting here, thinking about the two of you."

"Don't count your chickens," Caitie warned her. "It's just a call. And if it turns out he really is dating Rachel Foss, it'll be all your fault." She took the phone from Harper's grasp and turned on her heel, heading for the bedroom. "Wish me luck."

"You won't need it," Harper shouted. "You've got this, my friend."

---

"I'll never get bored of this view." Lucas leaned back in the wooden chair on Breck's deck, staring out at the ocean. Breck passed him a bottle of beer, and Lucas leaned forward to take it, before leaning back on his Adirondack chair.

He'd spotted Breck from the beach as he'd run along it, and had stopped to shoot the breeze with him. Breck welcomed the distraction. For the past day and a half his head had been a mess of thoughts.

Of Caitie. Of that kiss. Of how holding her in his arms had made him feel. If he closed his eyes he could still smell the sweet scent of her. His fingers tingled with the memory of how soft her skin had been. For ten minutes he'd been in heaven, his need to taste her overwhelming every sense he had.

And now? He was beyond confused.

It was Caitie he couldn't stop thinking about. His best friend's little sister. She was under his skin in a way he'd never expected, and his body itched with a need he couldn't shake off.

If it was anybody else maybe he'd scratch it. But not her. You didn't have a fling with your buddy's little sister, everybody knew that. Especially when you weren't a relationship kind of guy.

But the thought of not touching her again. Not feeling her soft lips against his... it was driving him crazy. God, he needed to get her out of his mind.

"You okay, man?" Lucas asked, bringing him out of his reverie.

"Yeah." Breck nodded. He needed to be careful. Lucas wasn't stupid. He already knew something was up. What had he been saying? Oh yeah, he'd been admiring the beach.

"The view's what sold me on this place," Breck said, keeping his voice even. He could get through this. "The inside isn't much to look at, but who cares when you have this on your doorstep? You don't get this back east."

The sun had hit the line between the ocean and the sky, casting orange shadows across the waves. Only a few more minutes and the moon would be visible. It was the end of another day.

"I can't imagine living anywhere but California," Lucas

said, his voice soft. "Or Angel Sands now that I'm with Ember. But I'm not sure we're going to be able to live on the beach forever."

"Why not?" Breck asked, crossing his legs in front of him. "I thought you loved your cottage."

"I do, but it's small. Too small for a family."

"You got something you want to tell me?" Breck asked, grinning. "Do I need to bring a shotgun to your wedding?"

Lucas laughed. "Nah, nothing like that. But we want to start a family soon. Ember loves kids and I love making her happy. Plus I kind of like the idea of being a daddy, too."

"I never thought I'd see the day," Breck said, lifting his bottle to his lips. "Remember when we all planned to live at the beach together? You, me, Griff, and Jack? Imagine how bad that place would have smelled."

Lucas wrinkled his nose. "Yeah, it would have been disgusting."

"Have you thought about extending the cottage? Or demolishing it and building something new?" Breck asked. "I could take a look if you want me to, make some suggestions."

"Yeah, that could work." Lucas nodded. "Though I'm still thinking about the risks of bringing kids up so close to water. I need to work it through."

"Just say the word and I'll come over." Breck shrugged. "We can go over now if you'd like?" It wasn't as though he had anything else to do, and he'd probably welcome the distraction. His mind had been way too full of a certain woman for his own comfort.

"I wouldn't do that to you, my friend. Rachel's visiting with Ember and they're talking about you. When she started waxing lyrical about your abs, I decided to make myself scarce."

"She's never seen my abs." Breck shook his head. "And they're not that great."

He shifted in his chair, uncomfortable at the thought of Rachel talking about him. Things were getting out of hand. He needed to find a way of letting her down gently. Maybe after the wedding. It was only three weeks away, he could avoid her until then.

"That's not what she said," Lucas carried on, oblivious to Breck's discomfort. "Washboard tight, is how she described them. I had to get out of there before she said something I couldn't unhear. I don't want to have a detailed description of any other part of your anatomy."

"She's never going to see other parts of my anatomy." Breck drained his bottle, and threw it at the can in the corner of the deck. It hit the rim, before sliding inside with a clatter. "So you don't have to worry there."

"You know she wants to, right? She's got her heart set on getting into your bed. Before you know it, you'll be walking with her down the aisle for a second time."

"Shut up." Breck sighed loudly. "Seriously, I'm not interested. She seems like a nice girl and all, but she's not my type."

"Who is your type?" Lucas asked, smiling at him.

*Your sister*, Breck wanted to say. He winced at the thought. Lucas would never accept him going there. "I'm not sure I have one."

"Come on, you must've had girls back in Boston you dated. And I remember you hanging around some when you lived here. You're not exactly a monk."

Breck laughed. "No, not exactly." He regretted throwing his bottle in the trash. He wished he had something to hold, to mess with. His hands felt jittery and empty. "I guess if I needed to choose a type, I'd say I like a girl with class. Intelligence. Someone with a sense of humor who isn't afraid to push me, and doesn't take my shit. A girl with her own interests, who's ambitious, strong, and doesn't want to hang around me all the time. At the end of the day, I guess I want what everybody wants. A girl to sit and talk to as the sun goes down."

"And then you take her to bed and have hot sex." Lucas raised his eyebrows.

"Classy." Breck groaned. Why was it when Lucas said that, Breck's mind automatically flew to Caitie?

"I'm just telling it like it is. There's no point in having a relationship without the sex. The talking is nice, so's the being together, but when you get down to things, it's all about sexual compatibility."

Breck blew out a breath. This conversation was moving into uncomfortable territory. A stark reminder of why he shouldn't shit on his own doorstep. What kind of guy thinks about sex with his best friend's sister?

"Anyway, back to your list. For a guy who said he doesn't have a type, that's pretty extensive criteria. Are there any girls out there who can even match up to them?" Lucas asked.

"Apart from Ember?" Breck raised his brows.

"Ah, as gorgeous as she is, even my girl doesn't meet your criteria. You're never going to get all that with one girl."

*Only with the wrong girl.* "Now you know why I'm single."

"You're going to end up being a lonely, old man. Maybe you should call Rachel. At least you'd have someone warm to cozy up to."

"I'll pass on that, thanks."

Breck's phone buzzed in his jeans pocket. He pulled it out, planning to forward it to voicemail. Probably Rachel calling again. After his conversation with Lucas, he definitely didn't want to chat with her anytime soon.

But it wasn't Rachel calling. Caitie's name lit up the screen. Angling it so Lucas couldn't see his sister's name, Breck quickly accepted the call.

"Hey, you okay?" he asked her, aching to hear her voice.

"I'm good." She sounded upbeat. Different to the woman who'd walked out of his bungalow without a backward glance. "Just getting ready for the big presentation tomorrow. I thought I'd call really quick and say hi."

"Well hi." Out of the corner of his eye, he glanced at Lucas who was looking at his own phone, scrolling through messages. It didn't make Breck feel any less awkward that he was talking to his sister where he could overhear. "Did you get there okay?"

"To L.A.? Yeah, the roads weren't too bad after the holiday weekend. And the suite I've got is pretty swanky. So at least I can panic in luxury."

"You're panicking?" He felt anxious himself. "Is it near the water?"

That comment garnished Lucas's attention. He glanced at Breck with interest.

"No, I mean panicking about the presentation. We're in the middle of a built up area. There's a pool, but we're not overlooking it, and if I close my eyes, I can pretend it's not there."

Lucas had given his full attention to Breck. He could feel the back of his neck prickle up under his friend's scrutiny. Breck was intensely aware of everything he said, trying to veil his words so Lucas wouldn't realize it was Caitie he was talking with. If he'd felt awkward before this was a whole new level. And exactly why getting involved with Caitie was the worst idea ever.

So why did talking to her feel so good?

"Well, I'm glad you're okay. It's great to hear from you."

Caitie breathed, soft and deep. "So, I wanted to thank you again for looking after me yesterday. And to apologize for running off so quickly."

Breck shifted in his seat. He was holding the cellphone so tight against his head it was digging into his temple. The thought of Lucas overhearing the other side of the call was making him sweat. He needed to cut this off. *Quick.* "Um, I've got someone with me right now. Can I call you back later?" he asked.

"Oh. Right. Yeah, of course," she said quickly, sounding as though all the air had gone out of her. "I should go anyway. I have a ton of work to do. I'm sorry I interrupted you."

He hated the way her tone had turned on a dime. From being friendly to guarded again. How the hell had he managed that?

Lucas cleared his throat. His eyes were full of amusement.

"I'll talk to you later, okay?" He needed to end this call now, before any more secrets spilled out. His lips were so dry they felt cracked. "You take care now."

"Yep. Bye." She ended the call before he could reply. Breck slid the phone back into his pocket. His face felt warm, but his soul felt cold. He felt like an asshole for dismissing her so fast, but what other choice did he have? Lucas was still staring right at him, a grin on his face.

"Tell me that wasn't a girl you're interested in, and I'll call you a liar."

---

Caitie switched off her phone and plugged it into the charger, before she slumped back onto her bed. Embarrassment covered her like an unwelcome blanket, weighing her down, and making her muscles tremble. She should never have listened to Harper. Breck must have thought she was such a fool. Some little school girl, following her brother's friend around with puppy dog eyes.

*"I've got someone with me right now."*

Of course he had. And it didn't take a genius to guess who it was. Thank god she hadn't made a complete fool out of herself before he'd told her exactly what she needed to know.

She needed to push him out of her mind. Him, Rachel, and all of Angel Sands. They weren't important. She'd take a shower, go to sleep, then get up and hit it out of the park with her presentation. When it was over she'd go home to New York. To her safe place.

Things weren't so painful there.

She wasn't picking up her calls. Breck pressed her number for the fifth time since Lucas left and winced as it connected to her voicemail. *Again.*

"Cait? It's Breck. Call me back." His chest tightened. Was she pissed with him? Annoyed because he had to end their call abruptly? What choice did he have – another minute and Lucas could have guessed who it was. Neither of them wanted that.

He leaned on the rail circling the deck, and looked out at the dark ocean. The night air did nothing to cool his heated skin. He wasn't sure anything would. Drumming his fingers on the wood, he took a deep breath, willing his mind to calm down. But he knew tonight, like last night, when he closed his eyes to sleep it would be *her* he saw behind them.

Sighing, he grabbed his phone again to check if he had reception. All four bars were lit up. She was probably busy getting her pitch ready for tomorrow.

He breathed in, letting the air fill his lungs. He couldn't do this anymore. Couldn't keep telling himself she was off-limits, and that he should forget her. God knew he'd tried. But she was there, in his mind, in his body, in everything he looked at. He knew he shouldn't want her, but he did.

There was only one thing for it. When her presentations

were over, he'd drive up to LA and hash this thing out. Maybe he could talk to her, get her out of his system, and somehow find the common sense that had been desperately eluding him ever since his lips touched hers.

Yeah. They could talk. That would work. Because god knew nothing else would.

## ❧ 18 ❧

"So that's it," Felix said, blinking as they walked out of the building and into the parking lot. "Now we wait and see."

"I guess so." Caitie pulled her sunglasses down, filtering out the bright November sun. It was blinding here in L.A.. "It's going to kill me to wait. They must know who they're going to hire. What's the point in making us hang on for a week to find out? And did you see how smug the people from Holiday Hope looked? Do you think they know something we don't?"

Felix unlocked the rental car with his key, and opened the trunk, loading their boards and folders inside. "They don't know any more than we do," he said, taking her laptop bag and stashing it in the back. "I had a quiet word with Claire, their exec assistant. They've been told the same thing as us."

That was the great thing about Felix, he wasn't afraid to talk to the enemy. "I guess we're all in the same position."

"Except we aced it and they didn't. According to Claire, their proposal was pulled apart over the last three days. They were up all last night rewriting it."

"Really?" Caitie relaxed for the first time all day. "That's the best news I've heard all week. I was positive they were doing so much better than us. Every time I saw their CEO in the corridor he gave me such a cocky look. At one passing he said something about offering me a job when they'd won the contract." They climbed into the car. "What I wouldn't give to see his expression if they don't win."

Felix turned the engine on. "It'll be almost as good as your expression when *we do* win."

It took them an hour to get back to the hotel. The L.A. traffic was living up to its reputation. All the freeways running through the city were almost at a standstill. When they arrived, Felix stopped the car in the semicircular driveway, and the doorman walked forward to open Caitie's door.

They climbed out of the car and Felix popped the trunk, passing her the laptop bag.

"So I'll see you back in New York," Felix said. He was taking the red-eye back home.

"Are you sure you're okay to take the boards back?" Caitie gestured at the trunk.

"Yeah, I'm going to check them. It's all good."

Caitie leaned forward to give him an uncharacteristic hug. "Thanks for all your hard work. And for being my rock this week. I couldn't have done it without you."

Felix blushed. "We're a team, and I enjoyed it. If we get this gig, hopefully I'll be able to help with that, too."

"If we get this gig, Felix, you'll be doing a lot more than helping with it. I'll need you to take the lead on some of the other contracts," she told him. "I wouldn't trust anybody else." Funny what a difference a week could make. Though she'd had some faith in Felix before, now she was seeing him in a completely different light. There was no doubting his ability, not when he'd shone in all of his presentations. "If we win, you'll be getting a big promotion."

"Fingers crossed."

"Amen to that." She released him from their embrace. "Have a good flight. I'll talk with you tomorrow."

Felix got back into the car, and Caitie gave him a wave, watching as he pulled away. Her whole body ached, the result of constant talking, walking, and being on her best behavior for the last four days. Like an actress performing the longest show of her life, she'd taken her final bow and now her muscles were making her pay the price.

She was grateful for the coolness of the air conditioning as she stepped into the lobby. She stopped for a second, closing her eyes to appreciate the sensation on her skin.

"Cait?"

Her eyes flew open. She blinked to see if they were working. Because the man standing right in front of her looked and sounded like a doppelganger of Brecken Miller.

He smiled at her, and she realized it *was* Breck. Nobody else could make the muscles in her legs feel this weak.

He was dressed for business, wearing dark grey pants and a crisp white shirt. The collar was unbuttoned at his throat, no tie, and the sleeves were rolled up. The skin surrounding his eyes crinkled as he smiled at her. A thousand questions lingered on her tongue. Why was he here? What did he want? Why the hell was her heart beating so fast? She ignored them all, and smiled at him.

"How did your presentations go?" he asked, coming to a stop in front of her. She never failed to be surprised by his height and his strength. She wasn't the smallest woman in the world, but he always made her feel tiny in comparison.

"They went well. We just finished the final one," she told him. "Now we have to wait for their decision."

"Always the worst part. It's like being a kid again and waiting for exam results. I swear it doesn't get any easier. When do you find out?"

"They said I'd get an email by next week, but I'm guessing that's when the loser will find out. If I haven't heard anything by Tuesday I'll assume the worst." She couldn't shake off how strange this was, standing in the lobby of her hotel talking to the man she'd dreamed about for the past few nights. Him being here couldn't be a coincidence, L.A. was way too big a city for that.

"You'll get the job." His voice was certain. She wondered what it would be like to come home to him every day. To unload her worries and hear his reassurances. There was something so strong about Breck, so certain. He was a rock in the middle of a tempest. "And if for any reason you don't, you know you did your best. It wasn't meant to be."

"You sound like my mom."

"Deenie's a wise woman."

"She thinks Elvis is still alive. And the moon landings were all a conspiracy. Wise isn't always the first word that springs to mind when talking about my mother."

Breck laughed. Why did he have to be so handsome? It was really distracting. "Elvis is definitely alive. I saw him driving a truck in New England last year. White suit and all."

Another wave of exhaustion washed over her. She reached out to steady herself against a chair. Breck stared at her white-knuckled hand, frowning. "Sorry, you must be tired. I was in L.A. for meetings and wanted to make sure you were okay. I've left you a few voicemails."

Caitie bit her lip. "Oh yeah, I'm sorry, I've been so busy this week..."

Busy avoiding thinking about him and Rachel.

"It's okay. I know how it can be. But I didn't want you going back to New York without us having a chance to talk." Breck shifted his feet. "Can I take you out to dinner or something?"

She swallowed hard. There was nothing more she wanted

to do than spend time with him, but that would be crazy. It was already impossible to get him out of her mind. She didn't want to make things even worse. "I'm supposed to be going out with Harper. It's our last night here." She looked around nervously. "Maybe you could join us?"

He put his hands in his pants pockets and shook his head. "It's okay. I don't want to butt in."

"You should come, Harper will be pleased to see you. I just need to take a shower. Do you want to come up to our room? We've got a living room and a minibar. You can sit down and wait while I get ready."

"If you're sure I'm not putting you out."

"Not at all. Follow me."

As they walked across the lobby, Breck took her laptop bag, slinging it over his shoulder. He pressed the elevator button, putting his arm around her as they waited for it to arrive. She stiffened at his touch.

"Breck?"

"Yes?"

"Does Rachel know you're here?"

"What?" He dropped his arm from her waist. "Why would she need to know I'm here?"

"Because you should have told her you were coming."

He rubbed the back of his neck, frowning. "Why would I tell Rachel where I am?"

"Because if you're dating somebody you should be honest with them. And I know this is really innocent between us, just two friends meeting each other, but Rachel might not see it that way." She tried to smile to show him it didn't hurt, but her muscles wouldn't play ball.

The elevator arrived with a ping. The doors slid open, and they were both silent as the overfull car emptied. It was only when they were inside, with the doors closed, that Breck spoke again. "You think I'm dating Rachel?"

"Aren't you?"

"What makes you say that?"

The elevator started to ascend. Caitie leaned back against the handrail, her eyes on the digital display. "It's obvious, isn't it? I'm so embarrassed about what happened between us last weekend. Did she figure it out? Does she know? I can't believe we did that when you're with her."

"Jesus, Caitie, do you think I'd cheat on her? Or on anybody? Is that what you think of me?" The expression on his face said it all.

Harper was right. He wasn't *that* guy. Her stomach turned at the disgust on his face.

"That's not what I think of you," she said quickly. "You're a good guy, Breck, and I know you'd never hurt anybody. Not willingly. But I..." she trailed off, trying to find the words. "Rachel's constantly around you. I assumed there was something to it." She couldn't look at him. Her face was flaming with embarrassment. Why was it that whenever he was around all common sense deserted her?

"So is Lucas and Ember and everybody else we hang out with." Breck's voice was low. "But there's nothing going on between me and them, either."

She covered her face with her hands, not wanting him to see her complete discomfort. Could she make things any worse? She'd practically accused him of being a cheat when he'd done nothing wrong at all.

The elevator stopped at her floor, the doors sliding open to reveal the corridor. They stepped out and stopped, the elevator closing behind them.

"Cait," Breck said softly. "Will you look at me?"

She leaned against the papered wall. "I can't."

"Please," he said. "Please look at me." He prised her fingers away from her face, curling his hands around hers. She scrunched her eyes shut as tight as she could. She felt too exposed, embarrassed. Her heart was about to burst out of her ribcage.

"There's nothing going on with me and Rachel," he told her. "I'm not dating her, seeing her, or whatever else you think might be going on. She's a friend of a friend. That's it. Nothing more than that."

Her body was such a mix of emotions she had no idea what to do next. Embarrassment melted into shock, and maybe something else, too. A need for him that had only gotten stronger this week they'd been apart.

She'd kissed him as a teenager, and it had felt like her world had tipped sideways. But it had nothing on kissing him as an adult. A woman. Somebody who was his equal.

His fingers were warm as they wrapped around hers. "I'm not dating Rachel," he repeated. "I'm a single guy. I've no idea where you've got the idea Rachel and I are an item."

She opened her eyes. His face was so close to hers she had to blink to bring him into focus. "I'm sorry," she whispered. "You must think I'm crazy."

He smiled softly. "A little. I never would've kissed you last week if I was with someone. I wish you'd known that."

She opened her mouth and closed it again, unable to find the right words. She felt as though she was being absorbed by his eyes, drowning in them. Her whole body was vibrating at his closeness.

"Maybe I did, somewhere deep inside. I don't know," she whispered. "It was all so unexpected. One minute I was dropping your sweater off, the next minute we were... doing whatever we were doing."

"Kissing," he said. "We were kissing and touching. Making each other feel good."

An image flashed into her brain. Breck above her on his couch, her legs wrapped around his. For those few minutes when they had been together, everything had felt so right.

"This is my suite," she said, pointing at the door on the opposite side of the hall. Grabbing her card, she jammed it into the slot. The lock mechanism whirred to let them enter.

"Are you sure you want to come in?" She gave him a small smile. "You know what Harper's like." Her gossip radar would be going through the roof.

"Do you want me to come in?"

"As long as you're prepared for the scrutiny."

He shrugged. "I think I can handle it."

She pushed the heavy oak door open. "Then let's do this." Walking inside, she kicked her shoes off and sunk her feet into the carpet. Her ankles sung with joy at the relief. She could feel Breck right behind her, hear his gentle breathing as he followed her. The door slammed behind him as he set her laptop bag on the floor.

"Hey, you're back. How'd it go?" Harper walked out of the bathroom wearing a white towel, her hair wrapped in a makeshift turban. Her eyes widened as she looked at the pair. "Hi, Breck." She tugged at her towel as if she could make it bigger. "I didn't realize we had company."

"Hey." He sounded amused. Caitie bit down a grin.

"Are you joining us for dinner? I can call and add you to the table." Harper's voice dropped. "Scrub that. You guys stay here and order room service. The place we're going to sucks." She was backing away from them slowly, as though they hadn't noticed she was standing there almost naked.

"But you said it was impossible to get into. You couldn't wait to go." Caitie frowned.

"Nope. Seriously, you'll hate it. They have karaoke and everything. You're so much better off staying here and having a quiet meal." She widened her eyes at Caitie. "Okay?"

"Um... okay."

"Cool. I'll go put something a little more appropriate on." She walked backward, lifting her hand in a wave. "It's good to see you again, Breck." Her back hit the door, and she spun around and opened it, sliding her towel-clad body inside. "Oh, Caitie, can you help me with something in here? It won't take but a minute."

Caitie bit her lip at the absurdity of the situation. "Sure." She glanced at Breck. "Would you like a drink?"

"I'll help myself," he said, raising his eyebrows as though he knew Caitie was in for the third degree. "You go ahead."

He walked to the kitchen area, while Caitie trailed Harper into her room. From the corner of her eye she watched him pull the fridge open and grab a bottle of water. Her face was burning. Stepping into Harper's room, she pulled the door closed behind her.

"Before you ask, I've no idea what he's doing here. I got back from my meeting and he was waiting in the lobby."

"I wasn't going to ask. I just need help zipping my dress up."

"I don't even know how he figured out which hotel we're staying in." Caitie frowned. "Unless someone told him."

"I *may* have checked in on Facebook," Harper admitted. "And Foursquare."

"But your profile's private."

"Not to friends."

"I'd forgotten you friended him." Caitie sighed. "Why did you do that again?"

Harper pulled her dress on. "Because we're friends?"

"But even *I'm* not friends with him on Facebook." Caitie frowned. "And I know him better than you do."

"And by the way," Harper continued, ignoring her reply. "His relationship status is single. From what I can tell he's been that way for a while."

"I know. He told me there's nothing going on with Rachel. That they're only friends."

"Did he now? That's interesting." Harper turned around, pointing at her dress.

"What's interesting about it?" Caitie yanked the zipper up, being a little rough on her friend and the fabric.

"Oh, that he bothered to come all the way here to set you straight. He wants you to know he's available." She was loving every minute of this.

"Stop that right now. I can tell what you're doing." Caitie was smiling, though. Because she liked the idea that he cared what she thought. That he wanted her to know he was available.

"What am I doing?" Harper asked.

"You're making assumptions. We haven't even had a chance to talk. Not properly. For all I know he really *was* in town for meetings and decided at the last moment to drop in." Caitie licked her dry lips. "I don't want to get my hopes up."

"Well, I guess we'll never know unless you get out there." Harper inclined her head at the door.

"First I need to take a shower. Otherwise nobody's going to want to come near me."

"I'll entertain Breck as soon as I've dried my hair." Harper pulled the turban from her head. "You go ahead and freshen up."

"Promise me you won't say anything."

"Like what?"

"Like anything about what happened on Sunday. Just make small talk or something."

"Sure." Harper smiled. For some reason that made Caitie feel uneasy. "Oh, and how did the presentation go?"

"It went well. We find out next week." Caitie looked at the door again. "Seriously, promise me you won't mention what happened between us."

"Funny how you're more worried about Brecken than this

multi-million dollar deal. Says a lot, don'tcha you think?" Harper grinned.

Ignoring her, Caitie walked through the adjoining door to her own bedroom. Of course her business was more important than anything else. It was just that every time Breck was near, he messed up her mind. And damn if she didn't like the way he made her feel.

## ❧ 19 ❧

Half an hour later, Harper ran out of their suite like she was being chased by a bull, her scarf trailing behind her. Caitie turned to look at Breck right as the door opened up again.

"Forgot my phone," Harper said, running across the living room. "Don't mind me." She grabbed it and turned on her heel, leaving all over again, her breath coming out in pants.

When the door closed behind her for a second time, Caitie bit down a smile and slowly turned to look at Breck. He was leaning on the wall, arms folded across his chest, the skin at the corner of his eyes crinkling up as he smiled at her.

"Hello," he said, his smile widening.

"Hi."

She felt breathless as the air around them snapped and crackled. The hairs on her neck stood up. Breck slowly pushed off the wall and walked over to the sofa where she was standing, his strides long and confident.

Caitie didn't move. She wasn't even sure if she could. Her muscles were tense with anticipation, her skin tingling with need. There was a half-smile on his lips as he reached out for her chin, using the pads of his fingers to tip her face up.

"Cait..." His voice caressed her ears. She loved the way her name sounded on his lips.

"Did you know you're the only one who calls me that?" she asked breathlessly.

"Do you mind?"

She shook her head slowly, his fingers still holding her. "No. I like it." Too much.

He took another step forward, his eyes firmly on hers. "I like it, too," he said. "The same way I like you."

Her chest tightened. Standing so close to him felt overwhelming. She could smell the woody scent of his cologne, feel his firm touch as his fingers caressed her jaw. Everywhere she looked, all she saw was him.

"Where were we last week?" he asked her.

The corner of her lip quirked up. "Remind me?"

He chuckled and lowered his head until his lips were a breath away from hers. She could see the thickness of his eyelashes, the strong line of his nose, the warmth of his skin where it was kissed by the California sun.

"I think it was a little like this," he murmured, brushing his lips against hers.

"It's coming back to me..."

"Or maybe like this." He slid his hand along her jaw, his fingers curling around her neck. Slowly, tantalizingly, he deepened their kiss, his mouth moving against hers. She could feel it down to her toes, her body aching and needy at his touch. He slid his hand down, fingers feathering her spine, pulling her closer until her body pressed against his.

God, he felt good. Firm, strong, and everything she needed. He kissed her again, his mouth greedy. She looped her arms around his neck, rolling on her toes to kiss him back.

She could feel his fingers on the small of her back where her blouse had pulled away from her waistband, warm and soft against her skin. He pushed up, splaying his strong palms against her, pulling her closer, closer, until she wasn't sure where he ended and she began.

She needed more. So much more. She pulled her own hands down and tugged at his shirt, sliding them beneath to feel the hard ridges of his stomach.

"Cait," he whispered against her lips.

Her need was thrumming, aching, driving her for more. She moved her hands up, around, wanting to feel every inch of him. When it still wasn't enough, she tugged at the buttons of his shirt, unfastening them one by one until it fell open, revealing his strong, hard chest, his warm skin dappled with sunbleached hair.

She devoured him with her eyes, feeling the need for him aching at her core. As if he could sense her desire, he pushed his leg between hers, the hard ridge of his thigh muscles giving her blessed relief.

"We should go to my room," she whispered. "If you want to, that is."

His eyes caught hers. His dark desire made her breath catch in her throat. "I want," he said gruffly.

She took his hand and pulled him to her room. He stopped her once, wanting to kiss her again, as though he was an addict and she was the only fix. Then they were through the door, and her back was against her bedroom wall, he pressed his body against hers as he kissed her again.

If she thought for too long, she'd question how they got here. Caitie Russell and the boy she'd trailed around after for years. The boy who had saved her from her brother, the only one who'd ever held her as she cried. The one who knew all the secrets she'd never told anybody else. For so long he'd been a fading memory, one she'd tried – and failed – to grasp onto. Her first kiss. Her first crush. All those emotions were magnified by that terrible Christmas. And now he was looking at her as if she was the most precious thing he'd ever set his eyes on.

He shrugged his shirt off, letting it fall to the floor. Her lips turned dry as she looked at him, taking in his broad shoulders and torso, and how it tapered to his waist. Breck reached for her, his biceps flexing as he did. She circled her hands around his arms, feeling them hard as steel beneath his warm skin. He was full of strength and warmth, a man who dominated everything he touched. He only had to walk into a room to control it.

But now he was in her room, and whether he knew it or not, he was controlling everything about her. He only had to look at her to set her on fire. A simple touch to make her melt inside. The boy she'd crushed so hard on had become a man, and he was breathtaking.

Silently, he unbuttoned her blouse and pushed it from her shoulders, revealing her ivory laced bra. Breck ran a finger down her spine, making her shiver. When he reached the base, her nerve endings practically exploded.

"You're sensitive," he murmured. "I want to kiss you there." His fingers continued their journey, unbuttoning her pants and pushing the waistband past her hips, her thighs, until the fabric was pooled around her feet. She stepped out of them, all too aware she was only wearing a bra and panties.

From the darkness of his stare, he liked them.

"It's your turn," she whispered.

With his eyes still on hers, he unbuckled his belt and pulled it out of the loops, stepping out of his pants until all he was wearing were a dark jersey pair of boxers.

His chest was bare, his stomach rippled and taut. A thin line of hair led from his navel to his waistband. The fabric beneath was straining from his excitement, and she ached to touch him. But when she reached out, he caught her hand, holding her with a firm grip. "Not yet. I want to touch you first."

His eyes were focused on hers, refusing to move. Her cheeks were flaming, and her body buzzed. Caitie's back arched as she felt herself being pulled toward him, desperate for his touch.

"I've been dreaming about this for days," he said softly, reaching out to feather his fingers across her chest. "Thinking about how you felt that day when we were together." His thumbs slid across her bra, teasing her nipples until they peaked. "Remembering how you looked when I kissed you." He pushed the fabric down, exposing her breasts. "The way you gasped with your mouth open, and your eyes closed."

He bent down, cupping her breast so her nipple stood out further. He captured it between his lips, grazing it with his teeth. The sensation made her moan.

"Yeah, you sounded like that." He sucked her smooth skin, his tongue swirling against her pebbled flesh. He repeated the same with her other breast, spending long moments worshipping her. By the time he moved down her body, she was a bundle of desire, her skin fizzing and popping with every touch. He trailed kisses down her stomach, his hands grabbing hold of her hips, until he reached her flimsy panties.

She held her breath as he pressed his nose against her, breathing in. The gesture was so intimate, it almost scared her. Yet the strength of longing in his eyes was enough to reassure her.

"Let me see all of you."

He was kneeling before her, yet still the one in control. She unhooked her bra, pulling the straps down her arms. She hooked her fingers at the sides of her panties, dragging them down her thighs.

As soon as she kicked them off, Breck grabbed her knees, hitching her legs apart. His face moved between them, kissing the sensitive skin inside her thighs. She felt the roughness of his stubble, the softness of his lips, the probing of his tongue as he circled her skin.

Then he was *there*. Blowing softly against her scant hair. His tongue dipped against her, licking the spot that made her legs feel weak. She had to reach down to steady herself against him. Breck moved his tongue along her, the tip firm every time he pressed into her. Her breath came fast and fevered. She started to rock with his movements, as pleasure pooled its way down her body.

"Oh God," she moaned, both hands tangled into his hair. He pushed two fingers inside of her, the movement intensifying her pleasure, until it felt as though she was about to explode. "Breck, don't stop."

"Wasn't going to." The vibration of his words heightened the sensation. Another thrust of his fingers and she was done, her world closing in to a single, perfect spot. She closed her eyes, her head falling back, as she moaned his name over and over again.

He held her hips tight to stop her from collapsing. As she was still riding the wave, her body convulsing, he lifted her up, carrying her to the bed. He stripped his briefs off and lay his body on hers, before they began all over again.

His kisses were fervent and desperate, as his hardness pulsed against her. His thighs teased her legs apart, as his hand reached down to hook her ankle behind him. Every time he touched her it was as if her skin was on fire. It threatened to engulf them both.

"Do you have something?" she asked him.

"Yes." He broke from her complete embrace and reached for his pants, his other arm still holding her. A moment later she heard the rip of foil and a snap as he pulled it out.

Another moment and he'd rolled the rubber on. But instead of pushing in and taking her, he paused, waiting until she opened her eyes and met his gaze. He held it, his eyes dark and needy. The emotions inside of her swelled, threatening to spill over. She had to bite her lip to stop the tears from forming.

This was Breck, *her* Breck, touching her as if she was some precious stone. Staring at her as though she had all the answers to questions he hadn't even begun to think up. As he slid inside her, his thick girth filling her, she wrapped her arms around his neck, holding on tight.

This wasn't *just* sex. Her world was shifting as she lay in a hotel room. Everything was spinning, left becoming right, and her mind was reeling from the motion.

He started to move his hips, his mouth capturing hers. At that moment she knew deep in her heart this wasn't purely physical. He was the boy she'd dreamed of, the man she hoped for. The only one who knew her from the inside out. Though he'd protected her all those years ago, he had the ability to break her right now.

His breath quickened, his fingers digging into her hips as he moved hard and fast. She felt the pleasure forming again, expanding deep inside her. This time he was moaning, too. His lips formed her name as he kissed her, their skin slippery from perspiration and need.

His desire was her desire. His peak was her peak. And as she came again, he joined her, clinging to each other through their explosion. His arms cradled her as though he couldn't let go, and she felt herself falling into him, hoping he never would.

It felt wonderful. It felt perfect. It felt like she was falling for him. And maybe that was the scariest thing of all.

## ❦ 20 ❧

As far as he was concerned, Breck planned to hold her all night. If she tried to move, or roll away, he was determined to move with her. The thick bands of muscle in his arms flexed as he pulled her even closer. Her body relaxed against his, her breathing low and rhythmic. Breck felt his own slow until they were in sync with hers. But the thoughts in his mind were too fevered to allow him to cross the final bridge to sleep.

He could still taste her on his lips. Still feel her on his mouth. The sound of her moans – soft and deep – as he brought her to release still reverberated in his ears. She was filling him up, the thought of her replacing every worry and fear he'd ever had. Caitie had always had that effect, even back when she was a girl. She'd been the moment of stillness before the lashing of rain began. He brushed his lips across her temple, breathing her in. She smelled sinfully good.

He pulled her a little closer, a little tighter, all too aware morning would be creeping in soon. Only a few more hours until she was getting on a flight back to New York, and he'd be driving along the Pacific Highway to Angel Sands.

What then? They hadn't made any promises, hadn't exchanged any words of love. But from the moment he'd kissed her, he knew it wasn't a fling. The ache in his heart told him that much.

He closed his eyes, pulling her closer, trying to think it through. On paper, nothing about them worked. She hated the ocean. He hated Christmas. And if her brother found out about this, he was going to hate them both. And yet somehow, laying in her bed, being together, they felt perfectly compatible.

The bedroom door cracked open, a shaft of light hitting the carpet. Harper was silhouetted in the gap.

"Caitie, are you awake?" she whispered.

Next to him, Cait snuggled closer, her mouth brushing against his bare chest. He wasn't sure whether to be amused or alarmed, knowing they were seconds away from Harper finding them in bed together. Breck opened his mouth, intending to alert her, but she'd crossed the room to the bed before he could say anything.

"Cait, wake up." Harper grabbed his arm, shaking it, before jumping back with a yelp. "Oh shit. Breck, is that you?"

"Yeah, it's me. She's asleep." He kept his voice low

"So I see." He could almost hear the raised eyebrows in her voice. "I guess you two made up."

Caitie mumbled and turned in his arms. He didn't like the way she was facing away from him. "I didn't realize we needed to."

"Well, after you hung up on her the other day I thought you did. Plus there's the small problem of Rachel. You'd better *not* be doing the horizontal tango with both of them. If you are I'll rip your balls off. That's if Lucas doesn't do it first."

Breck chuckled. There was something about Harper he couldn't help but like. She was forthright, but more than that, she was fiercely loyal. Everybody could do with a friend like her. "Yeah, well I wasn't planning on telling Lucas anything. Not if I want to make it out of that conversation alive."

"I thought he was your friend."

"He is."

"So why would you lie to him?" she asked, a frown in her voice.

"I'm not planning on lying to him," Breck told her. "But I'm also not the kind of guy who broadcasts my business all over town. I figure that what's going on between us is kind of private." His voice lowered. "I promise you my intentions are honorable."

Harper nodded. "I'm glad to hear it. You might not know it, but underneath all that armor Caitie has a heart of gold. And she really likes you, Breck. Please don't hurt her."

Breck blinked. What a weird conversation to be having while the woman he was holding was asleep. "I like her, too," he whispered, dropping his head to press his lips against Caitie's hair.

There was silence for a moment. Harper shifted from one foot to the other. "Well, this is awkward." She grimaced. "*Again.* Sorry for disturbing you. I'm going to head to bed and pretend I never saw any of this, okay?"

Breck grinned. "Works for me."

"Harper?" Caitie sat up. The sheet fell down and exposed her breasts. "Oh shit, what are you doing here?" Hastily, she pulled the sheet back up, jamming the fabric under her arms. Wide eyed, she turned her head to look at Breck. She looked like a deer caught in the headlights. "Is this a private party or can anyone join in?" she asked.

Harper put her hands up. "Sorry, it's my fault. I didn't

realize Breck was here. I wanted to check on you before I went to bed. We've got an early start in the morning."

Caitie blinked, as though getting used to the dim light in the bedroom. "Yeah, I'm okay. I set an alarm." She glanced over to the table beside the bed, where her phone lay face down. "And anyway, Breck's leaving early. He has to get back to Angel Sands."

"Long distance love. Oh my heart." Harper lifted a hand to her chest, mock-swooning.

"Shut up." Caitie rolled her eyes. "And get out of here. I don't interrupt you at night."

"I didn't interrupt anything," Harper protested, a twinkle in her eyes. "As far as I can see, it was coitus finnitus. Breck was practically smoking a cigarette."

"Harper, get out!" Caitie said, though there was a smile in her voice.

Breck started to laugh. He couldn't help it. The absurdity of the situation had got to him. Here he was, holding the girl he'd slept with for the first time, the girl he'd not been able to get out of his mind for days, while she bickered with her roommate about whether or not she'd interrupted sex. It was like he was back in college, except his muscles ached more. It was a good thing he liked Harper.

"I'm going. But before I do, I'd like to say I told you so, *Cait*."

A tissue box flew through the air, narrowly missing Harper's arm. "Get out!"

"Okay, okay."

As soon as Harper left, Caitie rolled onto her back and covered her eyes. "Oh God, I'm mortified."

Breck frowned. "Why?" He tried to pull her hands away from her face. He didn't like not being able to see her.

"Because I'm twenty-eight years old, and my roommate

just walked in on me and a guy. I swear, she's not normally like this. Back in college we used to give each other space. Guess not anymore. You must think I'm so immature."

He laughed. "I was just thinking this whole exchange reminded me of college."

"Kill me now."

Breck finally succeeded in pulling her hands away. Caitie stared at him through melted-chocolate eyes.

"Hey, I didn't mean anything by that," he told her. "Your friend is clearly crazy, but she loves you. That much is also clear."

Caitie's expression softened. "She's a good friend."

"She is. And she'll be an even better friend when you make sure to lock your door."

That made her laugh. "Touché. And thank you for not being an asshole about it. Some guys would be angry at her for barging in."

"I try to not be an asshole whenever possible. Though if she'd caught us mid action, I might've had to change my mind." He ran a finger down her chest, lingering at her nipple. "Speaking of which..."

He kissed her until their words melted away. Until her breathing caught and his heartbeat quickened. By the time he'd slid his way into her, all thoughts of interruptions were gone. They were so caught up in each other that nothing else mattered.

---

The next morning Breck drove them to the airport, parking up and carrying their luggage as they walked into the terminal. He'd stood with them as they checked in, then Harper leaned forward to hug him in farewell. "I'm going to run through security and grab a coffee," she said. "I'll see you when you get through, Caitie."

Caitie nodded. "Sure. I won't be long." She turned to look at Breck, her eyes catching his as Harper walked over to the security line. "I can't believe I have to leave."

He reached out, tracing her bottom lip with his finger. "I'm glad we had last night." They'd woken twice to make love, their limbs entangled, their fingers entwined. No wonder they both looked exhausted.

"Call me when you make it home," he said, moving his hand to cup her jaw. Her eyes were shining brightly. "Let me know you're safe."

"Okay." She nodded. He hated the way she looked so sad. He wanted to smooth away all the lines, and make her smile again.

"It's not long until you're back again," he said, kissing the tip of her nose. "I'll see you at the wedding, and maybe before if we can make it work."

Caitie nodded. She was still trying to clear her schedule so she could fly back to the Chateau for the final wedding arrangements the following weekend. It was touch-and-go if she could make it. Between that and his construction work, neither of them had a free day until the end of December. It was frustrating as hell.

"And after that," he said, smiling, "We'll make a plan. Because I plan on seeing a lot of you, Caitlin Russell."

She lifted her gaze to his. "You want to see me again?"

"Of course I do. Last night was..." He searched for the right word. "Amazing. But it's only the beginning. I can't get enough of you. I don't want to. And in the meantime, I'll be calling you every night."

The corners of her lips curled up. "I've heard about calls like that."

He laughed. "Yeah. Me too." He ran the tip of his tongue

along his bottom lip, thinking about last night. "I like you, Cait. Really like you."

"I like you, too."

"But there's something you need to know about me."

She blinked. "There is?"

He felt his chest tighten at her gaze. So open, so warm. She looked as innocent as a flower. "I'm terrible at relationships," he told her. "I guess that's why I'm single. I haven't had one yet where I haven't let a girl down. I don't want to do that to you."

"You won't." She smiled at him. "I won't let you."

She didn't get it. "I'll give you everything I can to make this work. But if it isn't enough, you need to tell me. Because there are some things I can't do."

"Like what?"

He swallowed hard, thinking about all the girls he'd met who thought they could change him. Make things better. He'd tell them he didn't want to celebrate Christmas, that he wanted to be alone, but each one of them thought he'd be different with them.

And he wasn't. *Ever.* And that's why he sucked at relationships.

"I know how important Christmas is to you," he said, his brows dipping down. "To your job, your home, your life. But I can't be there with you for it. I can't support you." He shook his head. "I can't even stand to think of the day."

"It's okay." Her voice was soft. "I understand."

But she didn't. Not at all. He could tell from the way she was staring at him that she had no concept of the hatred he had for the day. No understanding that it was going to take every bit of strength he had to attend Lucas and Ember's wedding.

And after it was over, he'd hide out at the beach until the whole damn holiday was over.

Her phone beeped, and she pulled it out of her pocket. "It's Harper," she told him. "Apparently the line for security is huge. I should go..."

"Yeah." He nodded. No point in trying to explain the rest now. It could wait.

"I'll miss you," she told him.

"Not as much as I'll miss you." He lowered his head, brushing a kiss against her soft lips. "Call me, okay?"

"Of course."

"And when the wedding is over, we'll make some plans."

Her phone beeped again, making her sigh. "That sounds good." She pulled her lip between her teeth. "And let's not tell Lucas about this. Not until after the wedding. Just in case he gets upset."

"Okay." He kissed her again, longer this time, pulling her close to try and memorize every fall and rise of her body. She kissed him back, her lips curling in a smile against his, before they broke apart and she grabbed her laptop bag.

"I'll see you soon," she said.

"And we'll talk tonight." He grinned. "And every night until I see you again."

"That works for me." She rolled onto the balls of her feet, pressing her lips to his one more time. "See you later, Breck."

"Not if I see you first."

Caitie was still smiling as she walked through the security scanner and headed to the end of the conveyer belt to pick up her things. Her whole body felt alive, in a way it hadn't for a long time, all lit up like a firefly in summer. She slid her laptop into her bag and looped her belt back through her jeans, grabbing her phone, ready to stuff it in her pocket when she saw another message had come through.

This one was from Felix. Four simple words that made her heart leap in exultation.

*We got the contract!*

She read it again, her grin widening as she slid her bag over her shoulder.

Everything was slipping into place and she couldn't be happier. And a lot of that was thanks to Brecken Miller.

---

"Hey, where are you, bro?" Daniel's voice blasted through the car speakers. "I tried calling the office but they said you weren't there."

"I'm on my way back from L.A.." Breck rested his elbow along the open window of the car. The weather was pretty temperate for early December, the sun's rays unfettered by clouds. A cool breeze wafted from the coast, through the car's open window. It ruffled Breck's hair as he drove along the Pacific Highway.

"More meetings? Man, you must be sick of those. Remember back when you first started working for Dad and you said you never wanted to be in management, that you'd rather get your hands dirty and build stuff all day?"

Those days were over for Breck's career. He could hardly remember the last time he held a brick in his hands. "Yeah, well somebody has to bring the customers in. Anyway, I wasn't only there for meetings. I met up with a friend."

"And you stayed over? Interesting. Tell me more. Who is she?"

"Nobody you know."

"Really? So how come I saw Harper checking you in on Facebook? In the L.A. Suites with Caitie Russell and Brecken Miller. I think I know them both, bro."

"Daniel..."

"So, who was it? Harper or Caitie?"

"I mean it, Daniel. I'm not talking about this."

"That means it's Caitie." Daniel tried to hide a laugh, and failed miserably.

"What makes you say that?" Breck's voice was sharp.

"I thought you didn't want to talk about it."

"I don't."

"But since you asked, if it had been Harper you wouldn't have been so cagey about it. But Caitie is awkward. You're her brother's friend. You've known her for years. You can't mess with her and disappear. There are consequences to being with Caitie. And right now you don't even want to think about them, which is why you don't want to talk about it."

"Thank you for your insight, *Dr. Phil.*" The traffic had gotten heavy and brake lights shone from the cars ahead of him. Breck slowed down. "Was there any other reason you called, apart from dissecting my love life?"

"So you're admitting you have a love life? Very interesting. At Thanksgiving I thought you were messing around with that girl with the blonde hair."

"Rachel." Breck groaned.

"But if you slept with Caitie that means you're serious about her. So Rachel must have been a red herring."

"Even if I slept with her – which, by the way, I'm not saying I have – what makes you think it's serious?"

"Because if you were just messing with Caitie, Lucas would kill you. Harper would kill you. Hey, even *I'd* want to kill you and you're my brother. I don't think you'd do anything with her unless there was a connection."

"You're ruining my drive home," Breck said, shaking his head. "I've got some of the best views in all of America, and your constant blabbering is driving me crazy. Can we talk about something else? Or even better, could you hang up?"

Daniel laughed. "Okay, I'll let you concentrate on the road. I'll talk to you later." He cleared his throat. "Oh and Breck?"

"Yeah?"

"Don't you dare break that girl's heart."

## ❧ 21 ❧

"Try to not freak out," Lucas's said, his voice strained. "But there's no way we can make it to the Chateau this weekend. It's all Mom's fault. She insisted we try her fish... or whatever it was. And whatever it was, it's coming up right now."

Caitie walked out onto the balcony to improve the reception "Eww, too much information." She wrinkled her nose.

"Hang on..." He started to retch. The sound was enough to curdle her own stomach.

"Are you throwing up? I think I'd rather listen to you having sex than vomiting in the bathroom." She shuddered. "Wait, I take that back. I really wouldn't."

"Can I call you back?" There was a loud thump, as though he'd dropped the phone.

Caitie frowned. "Lucas?" she called. When there was no response she tried a little louder. "Lucas? What about the tastings? We're due to agree on the final menu tomorrow—"

All she got back was silence. Sighing, she slid her phone in her pocket and walked back into the office, her pulse dancing around like an acrobat. This was the last thing they needed.

The wedding was in exactly ten days, and the kitchen needed to order in all the food in the next two days to make sure everything was ready. Without Lucas and Ember here to taste the chef's suggestions, and agree on what food to serve, there was no way they could meet the deadline.

Martine, the hotel's wedding coordinator, looked up as she walked in. "Is everything okay?" she asked as Caitie slumped back into her chair.

"My brother and his fiancée are sick. They can't make it tomorrow."

Martine winced. "Ouch. Is there any way they can get better before then?"

"Not without some kind of miracle. He could hardly talk on the phone without being sick in my ear." Caitie cringed. "There's no way they can drive here and face eating the food." Caitie swallowed, trying not to panic.

"So we'll have to do the tastings without them." Martine smiled at her. "You have good taste, you can make the decisions."

"On my own?" Caitie's eyes widened.

Martine shrugged, her face soft with sympathy. "It's that or the guests go hungry. Which would you prefer?"

This was the last thing she needed. Caitie had spent the last week running herself ragged, decorating houses and hotels for their Christmas events. When she'd had a moment to herself, she'd had to spend it making plans for her move to California, ready to start her new role at the Hollywood Hills Theme Park in January.

Then there was Breck; the light at the end of her over-worked tunnel. They'd talked every night, each laying in their own bed, their bodies aching from a combination of hard work and need. The sound of his soft voice in her ear was like a balm to her soul, warming her from the inside out.

God, she missed him. And this weekend wasn't making it

any better. Knowing he was so close, and yet they couldn't see each other. Not without having to explain to Lucas why Breck was spending time with Caitie here in the mountains. So instead she had to suffer with the knowledge the man she wanted to spend time with was only a short drive away.

She'd arrived at Chateau des Tournesols earlier that day. The plan was to stay two nights. Enough time to finish up the arrangements, coordinate the décor, and finalize the menu for the wedding dinner. With the big event almost here, she was feeling the pressure.

And thanks to that phone call, it had risen to the boiling point.

"We also have to agree on timings," Martine reminded her. "Unless we walk through the event, I won't be able to estimate the number of staff we'll need. With the wedding right before Christmas, I'm already having trouble pinning wait staff down. Either they're travelling to be with family, or they've already agreed to work at other events."

Blowing out a long breath, Caitie stared at the plan they'd written out. The rehearsal dinner the night before, the ceremony, and post-wedding drinks. All of which was followed by an elaborate sit-down meal and dancing. Each step required intense organization and a whole barrel of staff. "Okay," she finally agreed. "We'll have to go ahead and do it without them."

"I can get a couple of my team to stand in for the bride and groom," Martine said, giving her a reassuring smile. "And if you know what your brother and his bride want, hopefully we won't go wrong."

"Luckily, they're fairly easy going. I've spent enough time with Ember to know her tastes." And if Caitie messed everything up, which was highly likely, then somehow they'd have to forgive her.

"Okay. I'll tell the chef to go ahead for the tastings tomorrow. We'll do the run through of the ceremony in the after-noon. That way we can check the lighting, the warmth, and make sure everything's right for the actual wedding."

"That sounds good."

The door behind her creaked open. Martine sat up straight, a careful smile plastered on her face.

"Everything okay in here?"

Caitie turned to see Juan Dias walking through the door-way. She had met him before. As the owner of Chateau de Tournesols – and a friend of Breck's – he'd taken her on a personal tour of the hotel the last time she'd been here.

"Caitie, it's great to see you again. Is Martine taking good care of you? Is there anything you need?" He shook her hand. It was only when she smiled that she realized he wasn't alone. Behind him were two more men. And one of them was giving her the dirtiest grin she'd ever seen.

God, he was a sight for sore eyes. The most beautiful man she knew. And though she had no idea what he was doing here, she'd never been so happy to see Brecken Miller.

"Martine's been a great help," Caitie said, trying to catch her breath. "We've had a few snafus, but we're ironing them out."

"Snafus?" Juan looked alarmed.

"My brother's too sick to join us this weekend. His fiancée, as well. So Martine and I are going to have to plan this without them."

His eyes flickered to Martine's. "Do you need any help? I can give you extra staff."

While Martine and Juan continued their conversation, Caitie found her eyes drawn to Breck's. She wanted to ask him why he was here, and find out who the guy with him was. Who was she kidding? What she really wanted to do was drag him to her hotel room and show him how much she'd missed him.

Breck and the man with him walked toward her. "Cait, do you remember Aiden Black? He's in charge of the Silver Sands Resort."

She smiled at the man next to Breck. He didn't look much older than them. Way too young to own such a huge resort. "Hi, I think we met at Lucas and Ember's engagement party. It's good to see you again." She stood to shake his hand.

"You, too," he replied, a smile catching his lips. He was slightly shorter than Breck, but shared the same build. Muscled and lean. But where Breck's hair was sandy blond, Aiden's was dark. With his warm skin and full lips, he had the sort of face that was more at home on a movie poster than in a hotel.

"So what are you guys doing here?" Caitie asked.

"I wanted to show Aiden some of the finishes we used on this place," Breck said, his voice deep. "When I heard you were here I wanted to come say hi."

Juan turned his attention to Aiden and started talking rapidly, showing him the tiling in the outer office. The two of them bent their heads together, Aiden nodding as the hotel owner continued to point things out. Neither of them were paying Breck – or Caitie – the slightest attention.

She tried to suppress a smile. Breck knew she was going to be here. She loved that he'd come up here just to see her in the flesh.

"I guess you heard about Lucas," she said, biting her lip. "Terrible food poisoning. He and Ember can't make it up here as planned."

"They can't?" He raised an eyebrow. For some reason he didn't look at all surprised. "That's a shame."

"It really is," she agreed.

"So I guess you'll need some help now that they're not here. I'm free all weekend, and more than happy to be of service."

She narrowed her eyes, wondering if he had anything to do with her brother's sickness. She shook her head at the thought. She knew far too much about her mom's experimental cooking. Food poisoning wasn't an isolated incident at the Russell house.

"It's a shame you didn't know before you left. That way you could have packed a bag," she said lightly.

"Strangely enough, I do have one packed. I was planning on going away for the weekend."

"I'd hate to interrupt your plans," she said, smiling. The frisson of excitement in her belly started to grow. "If you have some place to be."

Though his expression was serious, she could see the amusement in his eyes. "It'll be a worthwhile sacrifice to make sure one of my closest buddies gets the wedding he deserves."

"You're my knight in shining armor," she whispered. "Thank you."

"The pleasure's all mine." He lifted his hand. "We'll let you get on with the arrangements while I show Aiden around the place. Catch you later?"

She grinned. "Not if I see you first."

---

Later that afternoon, Caitie was searching through her suitcase for her toiletry bag when there was a knock on her hotel room door. Juan had suggested she try out the Bridal Suite, but the thought of being in that room before her brother was way too disconcerting. Instead, he put her in a junior suite at the front of the hotel.

"Hey," Breck said, as soon as she opened the door. "You okay?"

"Yeah, I'm good. You finished working?"

"Yep. Aiden just left, and Juan's headed to his office to finish up for the day. I wasn't sure I'd ever get to shake them off."

Caitie stepped back and he walked inside, whistling as he took in the view from the windows. "Christ, that looks inviting." He grinned. "You wanna swap rooms with me?"

"I kind of thought we'd be sharing a room," Caitie said, biting her lip. "Unless you don't want to."

His expression softened. "Of course I want to. Why do you think I'm here? Did you really think I'd come all this way to show Aiden some flooring tiles? It took everything I had not to pick you up at the airport and whisk you away to the nearest motel." His eyes dropped, taking in her professional skirt suit and pale silk blouse. It was opened at the neck, revealing her delicate throat and chest. "I like it when you're dressed for business. You look damn hot."

"It's just a suit."

"It makes me want to bend you over a desk and show you who's boss."

She tilted her head. "I think we both know who's boss."

He doffed an imaginary cap. "Yes, ma'am."

"This room you've got. Where is it?" she asked.

"Across the hall."

"So you'll be sneaking over here in the middle of the night like a teenage kid in his parents' house?" she asked.

"Nope. I'll be bringing my suitcase in here and unpacking it, before spending the weekend with the girl I've been thinking about ever since I saw her last." He ran his finger down her neck, letting it linger in the hollow of her throat. "And then I'm going to act out every single thing we talked about on Skype, and show you where teasing gets you."

She looked at him through her eyelashes. "You didn't complain at the time. You kept asking for more."

"But now that I'm touching the real thing, I realize the

screen has been a poor substitute." He unbuttoned her shirt, pushing it from her body, before slipping his hands inside. They were warm as they caressed her stomach, her hips, and her waist, before moving up to her bra.

"This is designed to drive me insane," he said, tracing his fingers around the fabric. "As if you're naked, but you're actually covered. It's messing with my mind."

"It's a nude bra. It doesn't show through white silk."

"It's a tease." He grinned, pushing the straps from her shoulders, before he pressed a kiss to her skin. "But you know how much I like to be teased."

He moved his lips down, brushing against her chest before reaching the swell of her breasts. Nudging her bra away, he captured her nipple between his teeth, wetting it as he pulled her into his mouth. Her eyes rolled back with pleasure.

He carried her to the bed, throwing her on it so she bounced softly on the mattress. In that moment it felt like everything in her world was finally coming together.

The contract, the wedding, the man. Was it possible to have it all?

---

"Have you ever thought about exposure therapy?" Breck asked, as he poured them both a cup of coffee. "I was reading about it the other day. You could start with something easy, like dangling your legs in the pool or something. Work your way up to the open water."

Caitie looked up from her laptop. She'd been catching up on yesterday's emails. "Not really." She frowned, wondering why he was bringing this up.

"You know, the hotel's got an indoor pool."

"What?" This time, he had her full attention.

"An indoor pool. It's got to be the easiest place to start. Dipping your toes in, physically and metaphorically."

"That sounds very deep."

"Nah, we'd start at the shallow end."

"Very funny." She shook her head. "And I'm perfectly happy avoiding pools, for now."

"But are you happy?" He handed her a steaming mug. "Or are you afraid?" He sat in the chair opposite her, crossing his legs.

She pushed the screen of her laptop down. "Of course I'm afraid. That's the whole point, isn't it? I can't go near water without having a panic attack. You've seen that for yourself. It seems stupid to expose myself to things which make me afraid."

"But what if you weren't afraid anymore? What if you could get over it?"

"Breck, I've had a phobia of deep water for more than half my life. If I could get over it, don't you think I would've by now?"

"Tell me about that day." His voice was low, his eyes kind. "It must have been terrible. Lucas had told me about your time in the hospital, and the aftermath once you were home. I can't imagine what it must have been like for you."

She didn't want to talk about it. She really didn't. Yet there was an invitation in Breck's expression that she couldn't bring herself to turn down. A need to understand, to help, to be the white knight on a steed. He couldn't shake that look off if he tried. Her mouth was dry, her lips cracked. Everything in her body was telling her not to speak.

But this was Breck. *Her Breck.* The same boy who'd always come to her rescue; the man she couldn't stop thinking about. And he was staring at her as if he needed to know. If she couldn't give him honesty, what could she give him? He was possibly the only person in the world she could be this open with.

"I grew up wanting to be like Lucas," she said softly, her hands wrapped around her coffee mug. "Even as a toddler, Mom said I used to follow him everywhere. Of course he thought I was annoying. As we got older, he was always the outgoing one, never without a group of friends around him. When you guys started surfing, I wanted to do it, too. Lucas would tell me to leave him alone, that I couldn't do it because I was a girl."

Breck said nothing. He stared intently at her, absorbing every syllable she uttered.

"I wanted to prove him wrong. To show him I could surf as good as him. There was this one day when you all had to go to school on a Saturday morning. I can't even remember what it was for."

"Detention," Breck said flatly. "We were caught smoking beneath the bleachers."

"So, I took his board down to the beach. I'd watched him enough times. Thought it would be simple. You guys made it look so easy, you know, with your strong legs and perfectly balanced bodies. When I got down to the beach, it was almost empty. I was so focused, so ready to go, I didn't notice the flags. Plus the sea was calm, hardly any waves. It seemed like the perfect time to go and make a fool out of myself." She took a mouthful of coffee to counter the dryness in her throat. Her voice was getting thicker by the minute. "Of course now I know a riptide often makes the water calmer, before it drags you out."

She took a deep breath and blew it out. Breck reached for her, grabbing her hand.

"I took the board out until I was waist deep and tried to scramble on it. Naturally, I fell in right away. That's when it happened. It felt like something was grabbing my whole body.

I was yanked under until I was totally submerged. It was like being in one of those tube slides, not able to grab onto anything, and not able to stop. Your whole body's being propelled through the water as it crashes against you. I kept moving my arms, trying to get to the surface. I wanted to call out, but I was surrounded by water. My chest was burning, screaming at me to open my mouth, but I knew if I did, that would be it.

"I don't know how long I was under. A minute or two, maybe. Enough for me to get completely disoriented, for my head to be so light I could hardly think. And all I wanted to do was scream."

Breck tugged her hand, until she was moving toward him. Wrapping his arms around her, he pulled her onto his lap.

"It was a tourist who saved me. He'd watched me go under. Even though it was dangerous, he swam out to save me. Mom said they never found out his name. Somehow, he managed to grab hold of me and pull me back to the beach. By that point I was unconscious, and had inhaled some water. They had to perform CPR. I didn't fully wake up until I was in the hospital." She closed her eyes, breathing him in. "And I guess you know the rest."

"Did they not offer you therapy? You'd almost died. What about your mom, didn't she understand how scared you were?"

"It's amazing how good an actor a kid can be. I didn't want therapy, and I think my mom was relieved I wasn't going down to the beach on my own any more. I felt like it was all my own fault. I shouldn't have stolen Lucas's board. I shouldn't have gone to the ocean by myself; it was a self-inflicted injury. To tell them about my fears would've made it seem like I was seeking attention."

"You were ten years old," Breck whispered, burying his face in her hair. "You weren't looking for anything. You were a scared kid, somebody who needed help. God, if I'd known how frightened you'd still be, all these years later..."

"Breck, it's nobody's fault. And I'm okay now. I'm still alive, still breathing. I'm okay."

"But you're not okay. If you were, you wouldn't panic every time you saw a body of water; you wouldn't avoid lakes and pools. You'd just take them in stride."

"It's a coping mechanism."

"But you're missing out."

The fervency in his voice made her lift her head up. He looked upset, enough for her to reach out and cup his face with her palm. "I'm okay, Breck."

"I want you to come to the pool with me," he said. "You don't have to go in. You just have to look at it. You can't ignore your fears like this."

"Breck..."

"Do it for me?" he asked, leaning in close. "I won't make you do anything else. I'll hold you. I'll do whatever else you want. Just let me do this with you."

There was a hint of desperation to his tone, and it reflected in his eyes. He tightened his arms around her, pulling her closer, until it felt as if every part of her body was touching his. She breathed him in, this man, the one she couldn't help but fall in love with.

"Okay, I'll come down to the pool with you," she said, her voice shaky. "But you have to promise not to let go of me."

"Baby, I swear on my life I'll never let you go."

## ❦ 22 ❦

"Are you sure about this?" Breck asked, taking her hand as they walked across the ceramic tiles. His voice echoed, bouncing around the room. They were wearing matching white bathrobes, covering up the bathing suits Breck had bought from the hotel boutique. The air around them smelled of chlorine.

The pool was closed for the evening to the guests. But Breck had asked Juan for a favor, and he'd allowed them to have private use of it. It was the only way Caitie would contemplate trying this – there was no way she wanted the hotel guests to witness her reaction.

"I'm not sure," Caitie admitted, biting her lip. Her stomach was churning like crazy. "How about you?"

"Only if you are," he said quietly. "I can already feel you shaking. I don't want to push you into a panic attack."

"If I don't do it now, I might never do it." She took a deep breath, trying to ignore the way the chemicals lingered in her throat. She *needed* to do this. To prove to herself the water couldn't hurt her. She was twenty-eight-years-old, a strong, professional woman. She hated having a weakness like this.

It was time to face it.

"Let's do it." Breck gave her a smile.

He pushed the double glass doors open and they stepped inside the pool area. The water was gently lapping against the edge of the tile, the glass ceiling dappled with reflections from the surface. Even the walls were covered with intricate mosaics of waves. The sudden assault on her senses made Caitie stop in her tracks.

"You okay?" Breck's mouth was touching her ear. She could feel his words against her skin.

"Give me a minute." She closed her eyes, taking in the sounds of the water gently moving in the pool. Breathing in, she inhaled the watery chemical smell. Finally, she opened her eyes. As she looked around, from tile, to water, to Breck, she waited for the familiar palpitations to arrive. For the congestion in her throat to make it difficult to breathe. But the panic stayed away, kept at bay by a combination of determination, and Breck's steady hold on her.

Was it possible she could *actually* do this?

"Let's get a little closer," she whispered. Breck hesitated. He held her in place, his hand tightly grasping hers.

"Shouldn't we leave it here for now? I don't want to push our luck."

"I want to get closer to the water." Emboldened by her lack of panic, she stepped forward, pulling a reluctant Breck with her. Strange how their roles had changed within seconds of walking inside.

She took another breath in. This time the chemicals weren't so disturbing. As though her body was getting used to them. "I want to touch the water." Even though she whispered her request, the determination was thick in her voice.

"Are you ready for that?"

She looked up at him. Concern radiated from Breck. He wanted to protect her from everything.

"I don't know," she whispered. "But you're the one who said I can't live like this anymore."

"I did."

"So let's see if I can stand it."

First one step, then another, and a moment later they were at the edge of the pool. Their reflections danced in the water, the gentle movement distorting them.

Gently, she pulled her hand from his, getting down on her knees to stare at the water. She kept a sensible distance between herself and the edge – not willing to risk an unexpected fall. But still, she was closer to a body of water than she had been since the day of her accident.

"I'm not panicking." She looked up at him with bright eyes. "I'm okay."

For the first time since entering the swim area, he allowed himself to smile. Breck squatted down next to her, putting an arm around her shoulders. "You made me promise not to let you go."

"I think I'm going to dip my toes in." Excitement bubbled through her. Why had she avoided doing this for so long? Without waiting for a response from Breck, she scrambled until she was sitting, and extended her feet until they were almost touching the surface. She'd barely skimmed the water, the very tip of her toe leaving a trail in its wake. Feeling emboldened, she dipped both of her feet in the pool.

An unexpected image flashed through her mind. The memory so vivid she thought she was there. The riptide coming out of nowhere, pulling her under. Her ten-year-old self no match for the power of the ocean.

"Breck, I need to go." She could feel the familiar tightening in her chest. The pounding, the speeding, everything inside of her going too fast. Her body froze, unable to move away even though she wanted to. Her hands and thighs started to tremble.

"Cait, try to breathe." His arms wrapped around her waist, pulling her away from the edge. "Cait, stop crying. Try to inhale. Okay?"

Tears began to flow down her cheeks. Just like all those years ago, she couldn't breathe. She couldn't open her mouth.

Drowning. She was drowning.

"Cait." His voice was louder, a hint of panic causing it to be sharp. "Cait, look at me. You need to breathe." He grabbed her chin, yanking her face until her wide eyes met his. "Breathe, babe, come on."

The first inhalation she took was like a shot of adrenaline to her veins. Everything sped up – her sobs, her shallow breaths – all of them trying to catch up with the racing of her heart. She was shaking, her whole body convulsing. Breck lifted her into his arms.

"Christ, you're freezing." Carrying her, he rushed from the pool area, heading down the corridor to their room. She clung to him, still trying to catch her breath, as he fumbled with his keycard, before pushing it into the lock. "Keep breathing, Cait," he told her.

"I... am..." It was almost impossible to talk between the gasps and shivers. He kicked the door open, ran in, and set her on the bed. He wrapped himself around her as she lay in his arms.

"It's so cold." Her teeth started to chatter. Breck rubbed her skin, trying to create some warmth. But even when he pulled their robes off and lay on top of her, trying to give her his body heat, she still shivered.

"You need to get into a hot shower. Do you think you can do that?" he asked. "You need to warm up. You're so damn cold."

"I don't know... I..." She started to shake again. "I think so. Stay with me. Don't leave me."

"I'm not going anywhere, baby. I'm here. I've got you."

His voice was like a balm, soothing her, while he held onto her tightly. She clung to him, as he took her to the bathroom, turned on the shower, and pulled their suits off.

A moment later, she was standing naked beneath the hot, steamy spray. Breck was in front of her, his arms wrapped around her, rubbing her back and murmuring soft words in her ear. Caitie's arms were around his waist, her face buried in his chest. It took a few minutes before she was warmed up, and her breathing was under control.

Of course, that's when the crying started again. A whole myriad of emotions hit her at once. Shame, embarrassment, anger. Like a poisonous cocktail they swirled together, rising up, until the only way to express them was to let the tears spill out.

"God, I'm so sorry," she whispered against his chest. "I'm so, so sorry."

"Shush, there's nothing to be sorry about." He ran his fingers through her wet hair, massaging her scalp.

"I shouldn't have done that. I thought I was so clever. You told me not to push it and I didn't listen. I had to keep going. To try. I'll never learn, will I? I'm a coward."

"Cait," Breck said, his hands cradling her head. "You're the bravest and strongest woman I know. I'm humbled by you. You went in there and faced a fear that's had a hold on you for seventeen years. Don't let me ever hear you calling yourself a coward. You're amazing." He moved his fingers in circles against her scalp. Dropping his head, he brushed his lips against hers. "Every minute I'm with you I become more entranced by you. You're everything."

The emotion in his voice made her want to cry harder. He was touching her so gently, his lips soft and his hands softer. As though she were a fragile bird, waiting to be rescued. She was hyper aware of how close they were standing, of how naked they were. Of how much she felt for this man who was cradling her against him.

As they stood there, their bodies slick with water, the air thick with steam, she didn't have time to think any more before the words came spilling out of her. "I love you."

He stilled against her. His hands froze in her hair, his breath caught in his throat. She felt her heart beating hard in her chest, but this time not from panic, but from fear.

*Had she really said that out loud?*

Her body that had been so cold, began to heat up. Water poured down from her hair and onto her face. When she looked at Breck, he was smiling.

God, was he smiling. His eyes were warm and intense, like dark pools threatening to engulf her.

"Caitlin Russell, the feeling is mutual."

---

"We should definitely go with the ham and turkey en croute, don't you think?" Caitie asked, taking another mouthful of the pastry-wrapped bites. "God, this is delicious, plus it fits perfectly with the Christmas theme. What side dishes do you recommend?"

Breck frowned, trying to swallow the food down. *Christmas.* The thought of it was like a pitcher of ice water being poured down his spine.

He opened his mouth to tell her how he felt about Christmas. That he avoided it every year, traveling somewhere exotic for the holidays while everybody else gathered with their friends and families.

He couldn't look at a tree without thinking about his mom. Couldn't listen to a Christmas song without feeling like a seventeen-year-old boy again, all alone, responsible for his little brother. Afraid and shocked.

But she was smiling at him as though it was the best thing ever. And to her it was. Unlike him she loved Christmas. So much so she'd made a career out of it. Her face was lit up as she looked at him.

No, he wouldn't spoil this for her. Not when she'd only just recovered from her panic attack from the night prior. If she could face her fears, he could, too. He'd eat the food and enjoy it, even if it tasted like ashes in his mouth.

Because she was worth every damn swallow.

"I'd recommend carrots and peas cooked in coriander and wine, paired with croquette potatoes. It's simple and looks elegant once plated. Even the colors will be festive," the chef suggested.

Martine sat next to them, scribbling things down. They'd already chosen the first course – a simple goat cheese salad that had made all their mouths water. After the main course, they moved onto the cake.

"It's a three-tiered cake," the chef told them. "The first layer is fruit, the second is chocolate, and the third is raspberry and vanilla. My plan is to ice it with white frosting, and decorate it with silver snowflakes and glitter, keeping with the theme." He slid the plate over to them, gesturing to the forks. "Try them."

After they'd tried all three layers, Caitie asked Breck, "What do you think?"

He looked up at her, keeping his expression neutral. "I don't know. I'm not a fan of sweet things." In particular, not a fan of Christmas sweet stuff, but he kept that little morsel to himself. "I'm pretty sure it would work."

"I think they're perfect," Caitie said. "And I love the way the decoration fits with the festive theme. Thank you for working so hard on this. I know it hasn't been easy with me being across the country."

"Are you working right up to the wedding?" the chef asked.

"Pretty much. I landed a new contract. I'm redesigning the Christmas theme for the Hollywood Hills Theme Park." She blushed as she said it. Breck couldn't help but smile as he looked at the pink in her cheeks.

Her enjoyment of the festive season was obvious as she talked with the chef and Martine. She glowed as she took them through her plans for the table décor and the winter wonderland theme that would be the highlight for the dancing following dinner.

Breck leaned back as Caitie chatted animatedly with the others. He watched as she smiled, leaning forward to point at Martine's list. Caitie had this aura about her when she worked. A way of drawing people in, of getting them excited. It was a side to her he hadn't seen before. An enticing one. She was as dedicated to her work as he was to his. He liked that a lot.

"Will you be back here before the big day?" Martine asked.

Caitie shook her head. "No, I'm flying in late on the twenty-first. I can't get away any sooner. But Lucas and Ember are only an hour away if there are any last minute issues. And I'm only a phone call away. Hopefully by the time I fly back to New York tomorrow, we'll have already agreed on almost everything."

And so the afternoon continued. Once they'd finished the tastings, they moved onto the wedding venue. They'd chosen to have the ceremony inside, in the ballroom. Though the weather in California was pretty reliable, they didn't want to take the chance that the one inclement day in December might fall on the twenty-third.

"We'll have the tree here," Caitie said, pointing to the

corner. "The one I've ordered is thirty feet. The Christmas Interiors Company will decorate it when it arrives."

"They're the ones doing all the decorations, right?" Martine asked.

"Yes, they're doing this room, the entrance hall, plus the dining room. I've known the owner for years. He's the best."

"Grant?" Martine said. "Oh yes, he's a darling. Plus his wife, Catriona, is gorgeous. They'll do a good job."

"How do you know all these people?" Breck asked, frowning. "Don't you work mostly in New York?"

"How did you find the best contractors when you started working in California?" Caitie asked in return.

"Word of mouth, friends of friends. The hotel construction industry is pretty incestuous."

"So's the Holiday industry," Caitie said. "As is the hotel catering industry. We're stepping over each other all the time."

"You're not wrong there," Martine said, smiling. "Everybody knows everybody in this business. If you make a wrong move, word hits the streets within minutes. It was disconcerting when I first started working in hotel events. But it can be handy, too. Especially when you need to call in a favor."

"I've been calling them in left, right, and center for this wedding." Caitie sighed. "Some I wasn't even owed. I'll be repaying people until 2030 at this rate."

"You can repay me for as long as you'd like," Breck whispered, his voice thick and low, when they were alone. Martine was in the corner, measuring the chairs.

"You think I owe you something?" Caitie replied, smiling. He loved that she was back to her old, happy self. He'd done the right thing not burdening her with his own problems. She didn't need to know that every time he looked at a Christmas cake he wanted to smash it with his hands.

"I don't know," he said, pressing a kiss to the tip of her nose. "Do you?"

"What I've got for you is freely given," she replied, grinning. "Isn't it better that way?"

She had this way of talking that made every cell in his body tingle. Caitie was naturally sexy, and the fact she had no idea of her allure only made her sexier. Every time he was with her he wanted to touch her. And every time he touched her, he wanted more. "Shall we go to bed?" he whispered.

"It's only five o'clock."

He grinned. "All this talk about weddings has tired me out."

"You're crazy," she said, though the smile on her face told him otherwise.

Not caring what anyone else thought, he kissed her softly. "Crazy about you." And he was. Over the top in love with this girl. And damn if that didn't make him scared and excited all at the same time.

---

The next morning, the two of them were laying in the long grass atop a blanket. Breck's body was curled around Caitie's, his arms wrapped around her torso. In a few hours she'd be leaving for New York again. She was dreading it.

"So what do you think?" Breck murmured against her hair. "Are you ready for the wedding?"

"Just about," she said. "Martine's a real gem. She's got everything under control. There's a few things we need to iron out over the next couple of days, but apart from that, we're there."

"Lucas owes you a lot," Breck said. "Ember, too."

She smiled. "I owe them, too."

"What makes you say that?" He stroked her arm with soft

hands. Her skin tingled as his fingers trailed from her shoulder to her wrist. That's what he did to her with the slightest touch. Set her on fire until there was no way to douse the flames.

"Because organizing this wedding led me to you. If I hadn't come to Lucas's engagement party, we might not have met again. And we definitely wouldn't have gotten together."

"Oh, we would have." Breck sounded so sure. "We were meant to be. I knew you were who I wanted as soon as I saw you at the Beach Club. Actually, I didn't even know it was you. All I saw was a beautiful girl who took my breath away the moment she smiled at me. The rest was history."

He took her breath away, too. She closed her eyes, letting the winter sunrays warm her skin. The air around them was completely still, not even a blade of grass moved. "I knew it was you the moment you turned around," she told him. "I'd been staring at your back, trying to figure out who you were, but as soon as I saw your face, I knew."

He moved her hair, pressing his lips to the side of her neck. They were warm and soft, leaving a tantalizing trail on her skin wherever they touched. "So, what are we going to do about this?"

Her breath caught in her throat at the sensations he was causing. It was toe-curlingly good. "Right now, I'll do whatever you want."

Breck laughed, his lips still moving against her throat. "If only you were that easy to control. I'd kidnap you and keep you at home with me."

She liked the sound of that. Or she would if it wasn't for the beach bungalow. That would be too much. "Harper's been talking to real estate agents. There are a few places she thinks might work for us in L.A.."

His mouth stilled against her skin. "Oh yeah?"

It was strange how talking about this was making her

chest feel full. As though her heart was pressing against her ribcage. "Yeah. We talked about it last week. She's been wanting to move to L.A. forever. And now that I've got the contract, it just makes sense." And it would be closer to him. She wondered if he heard the subtext in her words.

He pushed his hand inside her blouse, pressing his palm against her skin. Goosebumps broke out across her flesh. She could feel his excitement pressing against her. "That would make me the happiest man alive," he told her.

"Only a couple of hours from Angel Sands," Caitie said, trying to ignore the desire pulsing inside her. "You could visit me. I could visit you. I'll be free most weekends."

"Fridays have never sounded so sweet," he said, turning her head so he could kiss her lips. "I'll take whatever I can from you, sweetheart. I'll never get enough."

Nor could she. Not now, and not ever. Her need for Breck felt like a piece of her, a part that ran so deep she couldn't avoid it if she tried. She'd move mountains to fulfill it, cross continents, face her biggest fears. Right now it seemed she was doing all these things, and it was as effortless as breathing.

"I love you, Caitie Russell," he whispered against her lips. "More than you'll ever know."

She tasted the sweetness of his words, swallowing them with her kisses.

Only ten more days until the wedding, only a few more mountains to climb. For the first time in her life, she felt as though she would be able to reach the summit, and finally be able to enjoy the view.

Like this man holding her in his strong arms, she knew it would be breathtaking.

## ❦ 23 ❧

"It looks beautiful, darling." Deenie hooked her arm through Caitie's as they walked over to the lit-up Christmas tree. It had pride of place in the ornate hallway of the hotel, towering over everything. Caitie had flown back into California the previous night, and Deenie had driven up first thing in the morning to meet her. With only one day left until the wedding, the hotel was in chaos. Staff were carrying in deliveries of flowers and food, decorations and furniture. Everywhere they walked they had to dodge another piece of wedding décor.

"Well it will be," Caitie said, crossing her fingers behind her back for good luck. "As soon as we have it all in the right place." She was beyond tired after all of her cross country flights. She couldn't wait to be based in one place. Maybe then her muscles would like her again.

"We're so proud of you, and Lucas and Ember are so thankful. I can't believe my little girl managed to do all of this."

It was just the two of them there, mother and daughter. The rest of the crowd would be arriving later to attend the rehearsal dinner, before the craziness started the following morning. Caitie was thankful to have her mom there to help, while Ember and Lucas prepared themselves back in Angel Sands.

This was *finally* happening. Caitie's veins fizzed with anticipation. Could she really pull this off? She couldn't help but feel like everything was finally coming together. Her career, her brother's wedding... and Breck. Her chest felt full of it all.

"Do you think they'll like it?" Caitie asked her mom. It was exactly how she'd want her own wedding, and this hotel was perfect for the theme Ember and Lucas had chosen. The tree was swathed with deep burgundy ribbons and ivory pearls, lights twinkling in the branches. The color was matched wherever they went, with the flowers that spilled out of oversized vases, on the seat covers the staff were already fixing in the ballroom, and the berries on the garlands overhanging every door.

No detail was left out. If Lucas and Ember wanted a Christmas wedding, that was what they were going to get. She only hoped they liked it as much as she did.

"They're going to *love* it. It's so elegant and sophisticated. When Lucas said they wanted a Christmas theme, I imagined waving Santas and stuffed reindeers, but this..." Deenie waved her arm around. "This is magnificent."

"I don't do waving Santas," Caitie said, finally letting a smile curl her lips. "I'm all about glamor."

"Yes you are." They sat down at the table closest to the tree. The staff had brought drinks and pastries out earlier for them. Deenie stirred her green tea, still smiling at Caitie. "So tell me, how's it going? It feels like it's been a long time since we got to have a chat. How are you?"

"I'm fine. Well, I will be when the wedding is over." Caitie took a sip of her coffee, followed by a bite of the pastry. It was warm and full of cinnamon. She couldn't help but smile at the thought of it. She and Breck could finally relax and tell people about their relationship, instead of keeping things on the downlow to avoid drama. It felt stupid, keeping something so important from her mom, but she wasn't going to steal the spotlight from her brother. Not on his big day.

And then there was Lucas's stupid 'bro code.' It was going to take some sweet talking from Breck to show he wasn't taking advantage of Lucas's sister.

"You're glowing. All lit up like that tree." Her mom inclined her head toward the giant fir.

Caitie felt warmth rushing through her. "It's been a good year for me. The contract, the wedding, it's all come together beautifully." And Brecken Miller, the star on top of her own tree.

"I hear you're looking at apartments in L.A.," her mom said, taking another sip of tea. There was a twinkle in her eye.

Caitie tipped her head to the side. "Who told you?"

"Harper, when I tried calling you last week. And I'm sure you can guess what my response was."

"Hell has finally frozen over?"

Deenie laughed. "Yeah, something like that. So what gives? I thought you were New York through and through."

"It feels like the right time. With the new contract, and Harper getting some studio work, it seems like a good plan."

"I don't have to tell you how pleased I am. As much as we love visiting you in New York, it's going to be wonderful having you a few hours down the road."

Caitie looked down, a small spike of shame shooting through her. She never had as much time for her family as she'd wanted. "It's going to be great," she agreed.

Guests began to trickle in throughout the afternoon. Ember and her family and friends arrived at three. Caitie was waiting for her in the lobby, and as the bellhops whisked their luggage straight to their rooms, she walked over to them with a smile, hugging Ember tight.

"How are you feeling?" she asked her.

"Nervous," Ember admitted. Her dark hair was shiny beneath the glow of the chandeliers. "But not as nervous as I'd be if you hadn't swooped in to save us." She lifted her head to look around, taking in the elegantly festive décor, her lips curling into a smile. "It looks amazing," she said, hugging Caitie again. "I can't tell you how grateful I am. I owe you big time."

"It's been a pleasure," Caitie said. Her throat felt thick with emotion. All the craziness and the cross country flights were worth it to see her sister-in-law-to-be's face. "When you get settled, why don't we all meet in the atrium? I'll arrange for some drinks and we can go through the itinerary together, make sure there's nothing we've missed. After that you can start greeting your guests, and I'll make sure everything's ready for the rehearsal dinner."

Half an hour later, Caitie was looking out the glass walls of the atrium when Ember arrived. Next to her was her mom, Laura, and her sister, Chelsea. Brooke and Ally, Ember's close childhood friends, were right behind.

Along with Rachel Foss, Ember's work friend, who'd be walking down the aisle on Breck's arm.

Caitie tried to keep the smile painted on her lips.

"Hi everybody. Who'd like a drink?" She beckoned the waiter over. He took their orders and walked back to the bar.

"This is beautiful," Ember's mom said to Caitie as the waiter served their drinks. "You've done such a wonderful job. Ember and Lucas are so lucky to have you."

"It really is gorgeous," Brooke agreed, smiling at Caitie. "You're so talented. And Ember told me you won the contract you were hoping for. That's great news."

"Thank you." Caitie smiled at her. Ember's friends were lovely. "I just want to make their day special."

"You have," Ember said, smiling softly at her. "You really have."

"So, let me talk you through the plans for today," Caitie said, clearing her throat. "Did you manage to check the seating plan for the rehearsal dinner?"

"Yes we did," Ember said, nodding. "We had to make a couple of adjustments, I hope that's okay. First of all, my Great Uncle Stan called this morning to say he could make it after all. So we've put him at the table with Frank Megassey and Lorne Daniels. He should be happy there, they're all a similar age and know a lot of the same people."

"That's fine." Caitie made a quick note to order an extra meal from the kitchen.

"And we've moved Rachel next to sit with Breck," Ember said, shooting Rachel a smile. "She doesn't know many people here and asked if she could be near him. That's okay, isn't it?"

Caitie ignored the way her chest contracted. "Um, yeah, that's fine." Just one more day. Two at the most, and she wouldn't have to pretend any more.

"Thank you." Rachel smiled at her, and Caitie immediately felt bad. She was nice, all Ember's friends were. Caitie couldn't help but feel like she was lying to her, even though she hadn't said a word.

"I got a text from Aiden," Brooke said. Breck's boss, and the director of Silver Sands was also her boyfriend. "The guys are about five minutes away."

"I should go and meet them," Caitie said, standing up. "I'll point them in this direction once they've checked in. You ladies can stay and finish your drinks."

"Do you need any help?" Ember asked her.

"No, it's all covered. Try to relax as much as you can."

On her way to the lobby, Caitie dropped into the kitchen,

and asked the chef to make an extra meal for Ember's Great Uncle Stan.

"No problem," he said, scribbling on the paper in front of him. "While you're here, can we go through the allergies and special requests for tomorrow's food? I want to make sure nothing goes wrong."

"Of course." Caitie leaned over him, talking through the list, pointing out the gluten-free requirements, the peanut allergies, and the guests who'd requested vegetarian meals. She was so absorbed with the chef, that when two hands grabbed her from behind, she almost jumped out of her skin.

"So this is where you are." Lucas said, his voice warm. "We've been looking all over for you." Behind him were Griff and Jack. At the back of the crowd she spied Breck, leaning on the counter, a half smile on his face. It was directed straight at her. Caitie's body relaxed for the first time in days. Seeing him was like taking a deep breath of fresh, cool air.

Before she could say anything, one of the sous chefs walked into Griff, sending five aluminum trays clattering to the floor. The chef fell to his knees, scrambling around to pick everything up, while the rest of the kitchen staff was laughing.

"Um, we should probably get out of here," Caitie suggested. "If we want to eat this evening we should leave these guys in peace. Have you all checked in and gotten your rooms?"

"All done. We were heading to see Ember and the others," Lucas said, releasing her from his bear hug. "I wanted to see you first and thank you for everything. Are you sure there's nothing you need me to do?"

"No. It's all under control." Caitie smiled at her big brother. "Save your energy for the rehearsal dinner and tomorrow. You'll be exhausted by this evening."

"Not too exhausted I hope," Griff said, winking. "He's got work to do all night."

Caitie rolled her eyes.

"Can it," Lucas said, good naturedly. "Or I'll make you wear that Santa suit down the aisle."

"Oh no, anything but that." Griff pretended to swoon. "Come on, let's go and get ready, leave your sister in peace." He raised an eyebrow. "She's going to need all her energy to dance with me tomorrow."

Over his shoulder she could see Breck watching them, a speculative expression on his face. Was he jealous of Griff? A tiny piece of her hoped he was, at least a little. The same way she felt about Rachel.

She couldn't wait to be in Breck's arms again. They hadn't talked about their holiday plans – she'd been too busy planning the wedding to think any further ahead than the twenty-third, but now that it was getting so close, the only thing on her mind was the aftermath. Finally being able to relax for a few days, after such a frantic fall and winter. If she had her way, she'd spend the rest of her vacation in bed with Breck, laying in his warm embrace. There was absolutely no place she'd rather be.

A loud discussion had broken out at the back of the kitchen, between the sous chef and a waiter who was giving it as good as he got. "I think that's our cue to leave," Caitie said, herding Lucas and the others out into the hallway. "I'll give you a quick tour, then point you in the direction of the atrium."

"Aren't you joining us?" Breck asked. The look he shot her was warm. Enough to make her want to throw herself into his arms.

Only a couple more days and they could be together without having to hide their emotions. That was if the secret didn't kill her first.

Breck only had eyes for Caitie as she led them through the hotel, taking them into the rooms reserved for the wedding the following day. Her face was flushed, and her eyes flashed with happiness as she talked Lucas through the plans. When he congratulated her on the beautiful decorations, thanking her for her efforts, she positively glowed.

Caitie Russell was a beautiful woman. But when she was absorbed in her work, she took on an almost ethereal glow. Such a contrast to the ache in the pit of Breck's stomach as he looked around the rooms. Seeing the reception room in its full glory was like walking into the lion's den for him. A reminder of all he'd lost, of all he'd avoided. Even empty of people, his every nerve was on edge. God only knew how he'd feel tomorrow when the celebrations were in full swing.

This was exactly why he left for Hawaii every December, preferring to spend his time surfing, holed up in a cabin where nobody could disturb him. There was nothing lonelier than being the only unhappy guy surrounded by a joyful crowd.

"So, I've asked the band to play Christmas tunes after dinner," Caitie said, grabbing a list from her pocket. "It's not too cheesy, is it? I can change it if you hate the idea."

Lucas grinned. "Nah, Ember will love it. She wants to go all out. She thinks if people have been willing to give up their Christmas to spend it with us, we should at least bring them a little festive cheer."

Caitie looked relieved. "Okay. I've told them to keep it low and slow, but they'll probably throw in a few modern classics, too. Just kick me or something if it becomes too much."

Breck's chest tightened at the thought of the music. He really needed a drink. Just one. Enough to get a handle on the way he wanted to turn around and get the hell out of there.

"You okay, man?" Jack asked. "You look pale."

Breck's laugh was thin. "I'm good. Just wondering when we're going to get that first beer."

"Amen to that."

Caitie looked at him, concern on her face. He tried to catch her eye, but Griff walked between them, blocking his view.

God, he wanted to touch her. He knew that would make him feel better.

Caitie took a deep breath and turned to Lucas. "The atrium is over there." She pointed to the glass covered room. "And the bar is on the other side of the lobby. I've reserved both areas. And the tab is all set up, you just need to order."

Finally their gazes met. Breck felt the corner of his mouth lift into a half smile. Her eyes were soft as she looked at him, telling him all the things her words couldn't.

He needed to get a grip on himself. It was only a couple of days. He could get through this. Yeah, it was a reminder of everything he'd lost, but Caitie had worked so damn hard to make everything perfect. He wasn't going to let his dislike of Christmas get in the way of that.

She was *his girl*. The one he'd been waiting most of his life for, even if he hadn't realized it. And her job – her passion – was Christmas. There was no way he was going to take any of her accomplishments away from her. She deserved it all. To be loved, to be admired, to have a guy who was proud of her.

"Come on, man," Griff said, grabbing Lucas by the arm. "Time to start celebrating."

"You've got two hours until dinner," Caitie told them. "And when it's over, the bar is all yours. You can do whatever the groom does the night before his wedding."

Griff laughed. "Not when the bride's staying in the same hotel."

Caitie shook her head. "The bride and bridesmaids have

the atrium. The two of you shouldn't have to cross paths unless you want to." She leaned forward. "But if I hear of any problems, you'll have me to get past. I want tomorrow to be perfect."

Lucas gave her a warm smile. "So do I. We'll only have a few drinks and head to bed. I don't want to miss a thing about tomorrow."

Breck could see how much Lucas meant it. His eyes were soft as he talked about his wedding day, and his bride-to-be. They'd done the right thing not burdening him with their relationship until afterward. Tonight and tomorrow were all about Lucas and Ember.

Lucas made to leave, Griff and Jack close behind. Breck lingered there, still looking at Caitie. The way she was staring at him made his mouth turn dry. What wouldn't he give to pick her up right now and drag her to his room?

"Breck, you coming?" Griff asked, turning toward him.

Ah, damn it. One moment wouldn't hurt. He lifted his hand at Griff. "Go on ahead, I'll be right behind you. I have something quick I need to do."

As soon as the door closed behind them, he grabbed Caitie and pulled her into the first room he could find, a closet stocked with mops and brooms. Flicking the light on, he saw her staring up at him, tenderness shining from her eyes.

There was that wobble again. The feeling of not being good enough. Of letting her down every time she talked about her job, her favorite time of year.

Swallowing it down, he cupped her face, kissing her firmly, his lips warm and strong against hers. Her mouth parted and he slid his tongue in, loving the warmth, the fullness of her. By the time they parted they were both breathless.

"I can't stay here long," she whispered. "If I don't get to the dining room before Mom she'll have rearranged the seats, *again*. She seems to think it's a puzzle she can solve." She smiled at him.

Breck could feel his equilibrium slowly seeping back. Away from the decorations, the wedding, all the people, it was him and Caitie, plus a whole closet full of cleaning supplies. "This won't take long," he said, unbuckling his jeans. "Probably a couple of minutes."

Her eyes widened. "Breck, we can't... not here. What if somebody walks in on us?"

He tipped his head back with laughter, slowly buckling his belt back up. "I was kidding, baby. Even I don't get turned on by brooms and mops."

"You were?" She frowned. "Now I feel disappointed."

He ran a finger down her arm. "I hate to disappoint you. You know, I could close my eyes and pretend the mops aren't here."

She smiled. "If I got my hands on you, you'd forget everything, including the goddamn mops. But since I'm trying to organize a wedding practically single handed, you'll have to wait until tonight."

"Tonight?" He lifted a brow.

"Yeah. You're coming to my room, aren't you?"

He cupped her face and kissed her again. "Do you need to ask?" Surely she could feel his need pressed so tightly against her.

"Just wanted to make sure," she murmured. "It's probably the only way I'll get through this evening. It sounds awful, but I can't wait until everything is over and done with tomorrow. I want to lie in bed with you and actually enjoy what's left of Christmas. I barely managed to buy all my gifts."

"Gifts?"

"Yeah, you know, those strange boxes people put under trees. The ones they give out on Christmas morning."

His mouth turned dry. "Ah, yeah, I've heard of them."

"Are you okay?" She frowned. "Jack said something about you being pale earlier. Do you think you're coming down with something?"

He shook his head quickly. "Nothing a beer won't fix. That and a night with my girl."

"Speaking of which, you should probably join the others before they come looking for you. And I have a billion things to do." She stopped talking long enough to press her lips to his. "I can't wait to spend some time with you tonight. I've missed you."

"I've missed you, too, baby. More than you'll ever know."

## ❧ 24 ❧

The rehearsal dinner was running smoothly as planned. Caitie took a sip of her champagne and tried to tell her body to relax, but it wasn't getting the message. She couldn't help but be on high alert, making sure each course came out on time, and the guests with special dietary requirements were given the right dishes. A glance to her left told her that Lucas and Ember were having a good time, and that was what really mattered.

Just before they'd gathered for dinner, the bridal party had done a quick run through of the ceremony in the ballroom which was all ready for the big day tomorrow. Caitie had watched with her heart full of joy as Ember and Lucas stood at the front of the room with the officiant, smiling at each other as they practiced their words. It had been so beautiful to watch. She couldn't wait to see the real thing tomorrow.

It was almost enough to take her attention away from the way Rachel kept grabbing Breck's hand with excitement, and smiling up at him with an adoring expression.

God, that was excruciating.

The wait staff had cleared away the main courses, and

there was a hush for a moment as they walked back into the room carrying a huge cake stand. On top of it was the groom's cake, the traditional dessert at a rehearsal dinner. It was decorated to look like a firefighter's hat, surrounded by a coiled hose, representing Lucas's job.

The men around him cheered when they saw it, and Lucas laughed, looking over at Caitie to mouth a 'thank you'.

She winked back at him, and nodded at the staff to cut it up and distribute it around the room.

In the corner, the band struck up a song. *The Most Wonderful Time of The Year* began to echo across the room, making Ember smile as the violins kicked in.

Deenie leaned in to whisper in Caitie's ear. "That's beautiful. One of my favorite songs."

"Mine too," Caitie said, smiling.

She took a deep breath and scanned the room. How many times had she turned her head to look at Breck that night? Too many for comfort. She was sure somebody would notice sooner or later.

And yet she couldn't help it. She was like a masochist, desperate to see if her worst fears were happening. If Rachel was leaning into him and whispering, the way she had a few times during the meal. Or if Breck was replying, a smile catching his lips.

Caitie's chest felt tight every time she saw it. She knew it meant nothing, but she hated it anyway. Hated the way it made her feel.

But this time when she looked, there was a frown on his lips. He was looking down at the table, as though he was concentrating on something. She stared for a moment too long, aching for him to glance up and see her.

But instead, his frown deepened.

She grabbed her phone and quickly tapped out a message to him, making sure her mom couldn't see the screen.

*Are you okay?*

She watched as he reacted to the buzz of his phone. But he didn't take it out of his pocket.

"The cake is amazing," Deenie said when the staff had handed their slices out. She slid a forkful between her lips. "You're so clever, sweetheart. Of course it had to be a fire-fighter cake. It's so Lucas."

Caitie tried to smile. "Thank you." She looked down at her own slice. The sponge was red velvet – Lucas's favorite. Any other time she'd be devouring it.

The band segued into *Let it Snow*, the lyrical arrangement echoing through the room. Rachel was talking to Breck again, forcing his eyes up from the table where Caitie hadn't been able to. He nodded, but didn't smile.

"Should Daddy do his speech now?" Deenie asked when the music ended. "Don't worry, he's keeping it short. Just a few words to welcome Ember and her family."

Caitie nodded. "That would be a great idea."

As hosts for the rehearsal dinner, her parents stood together and welcomed the guests. They turned to Ember and told her how happy they were to have her in the family, and then to Ember's mom and sister, saying they weren't losing a daughter, but gaining a whole new clan.

"So let us raise our glass to the Kennedy family. Thank you for raising a beautiful daughter, and for letting her be part of our lives," Wallace said, holding his glass up. The guests all stood and repeated his toast, taking a sip of their champagne to close the deal.

Lucas leaned in to kiss his soon-to-be-wife, and walked over to where his father was standing. He whispered something to Wallace and shook his hand, taking the microphone from him.

"This is going to be quick," Lucas said, smiling out at the guests. "Mostly because I plan to spend tomorrow telling you exactly how lucky I am to have a wife like Ember."

That was greeted with a loud cheer from his friends.

"But tonight I want to say thank you to one person. She's responsible for everything you see here in this hotel. The venue, the food, the band, the décor. She arranged everything perfectly." Lucas smiled at Caitie, his eyes soft. "Growing up, I don't think I was always her favorite person. I know I drove her crazy half the time, and ignored her the other half. It's a big brother thing, I guess. But now she's all grown up and I couldn't be prouder of her. Along with Ember and my mom, she's my favorite woman in the world. She's beautiful, she's classy, and she's so talented it makes my heart hurt. I don't deserve to have her as my sister, but I'm glad I do. I give you my sister, Caitlin Russell."

Everybody started to clap their hands and stamp their feet. Caitie bit her lip, trying to ignore the tears filling her eyes.

Lucas leaned into the microphone. "She's also planning to move a little closer to Angel Sands, which I'm over the moon about. And I guess this would be a good time as any to remind all my friends to back off." He turned around, grinning at the group of men behind him. "She might be gorgeous and single, but she's my little sister and she deserves better than you bozos."

The men started to laugh. Caitie swallowed hard, looking over at Breck. But he wouldn't meet her gaze.

"Okay, that's all I gotta say for now. Except thanks to each and every one of you for coming to our Christmas wedding. We can't tell you how happy we are to have you here. Now let's dance, drink, and be merry, for tomorrow I'll be a married man." He lifted his glass. "To Caitie and to everybody. Cheers."

"Cheers!" the crowd echoed back.

The music started up again, this time the band began to play *Winter Wonderland*, and Lucas and Ember walked over to the dancefloor hand in hand, and began to waltz to the beat of the music.

Before long they were joined by Wallace and Deenie, Brooke and Aiden, and Ally and her boyfriend, Nate. From the corner of her eye, Caitie could still see Rachel and Breck talking. She wondered if it would look strange if she walked over there.

"Miss Russell?" A voice whispered in her ear. She turned to see one of the wait staff standing next to her.

"Yes?"

"The chef would like to see you in the kitchen. He wants to discuss timings for tomorrow's meal."

"Sure." Caitie nodded, standing to follow the waitress out of the ballroom. She couldn't help but take a final glance back. Not at the dancefloor, but at the two people talking closely in the corner.

Breck stood, too. Caitie blinked, waiting for him to walk over to her. But instead, he leaned down and said something to Rachel before turning and walking out the door on the far side of the room.

"It's this way," the waitress said when she realized Caitie wasn't following. "Are you ready?"

The door on the far side of the room swung closed. There was no sign of Breck anymore.

"Yes," Caitie said, though she felt anything but. "I'm ready."

---

Breck's hands were shaking as he splashed water onto his face. Even in the men's room he could still hear the music blasting out from the banquet hall. Every note made him feel sick. His heart beat pounded in time to the rhythm, and no matter how hard he tried he couldn't slow it down.

God he hated Christmas music. Hated the way it made him feel, and the memories it always stirred up in his mind. Of the stereo his mom had in her hospital room, tuned to a radio station that played Christmas hits twenty-four hours a day. He'd sit and hold her hand as she tried to sing along, her lips weakly trembling from the exhaustion the cancer had caused.

It made him feel like that kid again. Seventeen-years-old and losing his mom. Not knowing how the hell he was ever going to take care of his eleven-year-old brother.

Slowly, he looked up at himself in the mirror hanging over the sink. His eyes were rimmed red, his skin sallow. He looked as nauseous as he felt.

*Pull it together*, he told the man staring back at him. It's only music. It couldn't hurt him. And yet his chest ached in a way it hadn't for years. This was why he traveled at Christmas. So he couldn't get caught up in the horror of the season.

The door pushed open. Breck swallowed hard as Griff walked in.

"Hey man," Griff said, heading for a stall. "You doing okay?"

"Yeah, fine." Breck nodded.

"Still up for a drink in the bar after the dancing?"

His stomach clenched at the thought of any more alcohol. "Of course," he said, taking a deep breath. "It's Lucas's stag. I'll be there."

Griff washed his hands and put them under the dryer. "It's been a good night so far, hasn't it?" he said, loud enough to be heard over the dryer, oblivious to Breck's unease. "Everything looks amazing. I can't believe what a great job Caitie did. I knew she was talented but..." he shook his head, grinning. "She's even better than I thought."

"It looks great," Breck agreed. His heart was racing so fast he was worried he was having some kind of attack.

"I can't believe she's single." Griff pulled his hands from the dryer and shook them even though all the moisture had gone. "She grew up to be a gorgeous woman. No wonder Lucas is protective of her." Griff grinned. "I guess we're protective, too, right? She's like our little sister. Nobody's good enough for her."

Breck could taste the nausea rising up through his throat. "Nobody," he repeated. He couldn't look at himself in the mirror. There was no way he wanted to see his sickened reflection.

This was supposed to be a celebration. Of Lucas and Ember, and of Caitie, too. And yet all he wanted to do was run as far as he could from the décor and the music and the feeling he'd never be good enough for Lucas Russell's little sister.

He'd never be able to show her the support she needed. Never be able to revel in her achievements in her business. What kind of boyfriend did that make him?

Less than worthless.

"You sure you're okay? You're looking grey around the gills, my friend," Griff said. "Maybe lay off on the beer until we're back in the bar."

"Yeah." Breck nodded. "I'll do that."

"See you in there." Griff lifted his hand in a wave as he walked out of the bathroom, the jaunty sounds of *All I Want For Christmas* filling the air as he made his exit.

Breck pushed himself off the sink and blew out a mouthful of stale air. Twenty-four hours and this would all be over.

But right now, that felt like forever.

## ❦ 25 ❦

Caitie had barely seen Breck all evening. She'd spent most of the time after the rehearsal dinner sorting out last minute problems – rearranging the seating plan for the fifth time to accommodate more out-of-town visitors who had changed their minds about coming, calling the hair-dresser and make-up artist to make sure they arrived an hour earlier than planned, to fit in Deenie and Ember's mom who'd decided they wanted to have their hair professionally styled. Then there were the discussions with the chef, the wedding planner, and the officiant, to make sure they were all on the same page. By the time the music stopped playing in the ball-room, all she wanted to do was slink off to bed.

As she made her way to the atrium, where Ember and her friends were celebrating her last night of freedom, Caitie glanced at her phone. Breck had finally replied to her text from earlier.

*I'm beat. Might sleep in my own room tonight. I don't want to disturb you.*

Her chest tightened at his words. She frowned, trying to think of a way to reply that didn't put any pressure on him.

"What are you doing out here?" Brooke asked, as she opened the door to the atrium. "Come on in, we're ordering another round of cocktails. What would you like?"

She was so happy and friendly, Caitie couldn't say no. Even though all she wanted to do was find Breck and talk to him.

"I'll have a Cosmopolitan," Caitie said. "But only one. I already had a glass of champagne and I don't want my head to get fuzzy."

Brooke slid her arm inside Caitie's and walked with her to the table where they were all sitting down. "You've worked extremely hard, you deserve to relax. Ember's so happy at how well everything's going."

Caitie tried to arrange her lips into a smile. "That's good. I want them to have the perfect day."

"Oh, they will," Brooke said, smiling. "I'm sure of it."

When they reached the table, Brooke gave their orders to the waiter and pulled Caitie out a chair next to her mom. Deenie reached for her hand and squeezed it. "Everything was wonderful tonight, Caitie. I'm so proud of you. And I know for a fact Lucas and Ember are, too."

Wasn't that what it was all about? Making the bride and groom happy?

"Thank you," she said softly. "Are all the guys in the bar now?"

Deenie nodded. "Yes. I told your father to limit his whiskeys. You know what he's like when he's had too many."

"I don't want him looking green around the gills when he walks Ember down the aisle." Ember's own father had died a few years earlier, and she'd asked Wallace to escort her at the wedding.

"Don't worry," Deenie said, winking. "I'll send him a text in half an hour and demand he comes to bed."

Bed. Ah, what she wouldn't do to be there right now.

Preferably in Breck's arms.

From the corner of her eye she could see Rachel talking to Ally, the two of them laughing as their heads almost touched. Caitie's stomach contracted. Why couldn't she feel that carefree?

She couldn't quite put her finger on why she felt so on edge. Everything had been organized to the second. Like Santa, she'd checked her list twice and nothing had been missed. Yet her stomach was churning like it wanted to make butter.

"Mom?" she asked, her voice wavering. "Do you think Breck's okay? He seemed a little out of it earlier."

Deenie tipped her head to the side. "It would be a big surprise if he wasn't. It's almost the anniversary of his mom's death. Even after all these years those anniversaries can be tough. Especially one on Christmas Eve."

The blood drained from Caitie's face. How could she have forgotten that? Her throat tightened as she thought about the way he'd been shifting in his seat all night. Not meeting her gaze. No wonder he'd been looking so sad. All the memories of his mom must have been overwhelming.

And she hadn't given him the support he needed. Too taken up with organizing the wedding to think about the man she loved. She put her cocktail down on the table and stood, her brows knitting together as she looked at her mom.

"There's something I need to do," she said, her voice tight.

"Can I help?" her mom asked. "Is it for the wedding?"

Caitie shook her head. "No, I can do it on my own." She gave her mom a tight smile. "I'll be back in a while."

"Okay, honey. Take it easy."

Caitie's mind was a whirl as she rushed out of the atrium and across the lobby. The bar was on the far side, the double doors closed to keep in the noise of the men as they laughed and talked. She hesitated when she reached the room. Whatever she said, it was going to look suspicious when she walked in to speak with Breck. Her brother wasn't stupid, he'd know something was wrong.

Maybe she could tell him Rachel was looking for him. But the thought of that made her feel even worse. She quickly grabbed her phone and typed out a message. Maybe this way she could avoid walking in the room altogether.

*I'm outside the bar. Can you meet me here?*

She waited for a minute. Then two. He was probably too busy talking with somebody to notice his phone buzzing. And she was beginning to look strange, loitering outside the bar. With him not replying she had no choice but to go in.

Taking a deep breath, she pushed the saloon door open and stepped inside. The room was packed with men. Family, friends, firefighters from Lucas's job. A few of them laughingly told her she was in the wrong room as she pushed through them, scouting the space for Breck's face.

"Caitie?" Lucas said when she reached the far corner. "Are you looking for me? Everything okay?"

Her father was with him, along with Griff and Jack, plus his retired Captain from the service. They all turned to her, smiling and greeting her. Her mouth turned dry at the thought of them all listening.

"I... uh..." She took a mouthful of air. "I'm looking for Breck. I have a quick question for him about tomorrow. Is he here?"

"Breck?" Lucas frowned. "No, he headed up to bed half an hour ago. Said he had a headache."

"He's in his room?" It was getting hard to breathe. "Is he okay?"

"Yeah. He just can't take his drink," Griff said, lifting his own glass. "When I saw him in the bathroom earlier I swear he'd been puking."

Breck wasn't much of a drinker. Caitie knew that. A beer or two as the sun went down was his occasional limit. "I should check on him," she said. "Make sure he's okay. He needs to be well for tomorrow."

"You don't need to do everything," Griff said, putting his arm around her shoulder. "Tell you what, I'll go check on him. You go back to Ember and the girls." He hugged her against him in a brotherly way. "You don't need to clear up after our mess, little sis."

She was starting to panic. There was no way she was going to reveal her relationship with Breck now. Not when everybody was merry and it was her brother's wedding day tomorrow. But she needed to find a way to see him.

"If he's ill I have all the details of the local doctor," she said quickly. "I'll only be a minute. Stay here and enjoy yourself." She lifted her lips into a smile. "And keep an eye on Lucas. I need him sober in the morning."

"Yes, ma'am." Griff released her shoulder and gave her a mock salute. "But give me a shout if you need me, okay?"

She nodded quickly. "Sure."

It took another few minutes to push her way back through the crowd. Everybody she passed wanted to tell her how well things were going, how pretty the hotel looked, how much they were looking forward to the next day. With each conversation she felt her pulse raise. When she managed to exit into the lobby, she took a mouthful of air.

Breck was on the third floor. She'd assigned his room herself. Next to the elevator so he could sneak out and down to the floor below without anybody noticing. She pressed the button and waited for the elevator to arrive, almost running inside when the doors finally opened.

The third floor was quiet. Lucas and his groomsmen took up half the rooms, along with his friends from the service. Ember and her bridal party were on the second, along with her friends, leaving the first floor for both of their families. Caitie had taken great care assigning each room, noting the families who had young children and wouldn't want to be disturbed by rowdiness. She'd learned from experience all these little things counted.

She tapped at Breck's door with the tips of her fingers, not wanting to make too much noise. When there was no answer, she leaned forward, trying to look through the peephole. "Breck? It's me. Are you okay?"

It was at least thirty seconds before he opened the door. Her heartbeat echoed in her ears as she waited silently, worrying about him. Then he was there, his face as grey as Griff had described, his brows pulled close together, making three vertical lines in the skin between them.

"Breck?"

He blinked as though he was trying to work out who she was. He didn't look like himself at all. Not the happy, easygoing Breck she knew so well. There was a wildness to his eyes that made her want to step back.

"Are you okay?" she asked. "Griff said you weren't feeling well."

"I'm fine." He pressed his lips together.

"Can I come in?" She glanced at the hallway behind her to make sure nobody was there. "I only want to talk for a minute."

When she stepped inside there was something strange about his room. It took a moment for her to realize what it was. "Haven't you unpacked?" she asked him, seeing his bag by the door, his suit still in its plastic case.

He shook his head but said nothing.

"Breck?"

"I need to go."

It was her turn to blink. "What? Go where?" she asked. "The bathroom? Are you feeling sick?" She reached for his arm, laying her palm on his bicep. "Is it your mom?" she asked him. "Memories of her?" Caitie licked her lips. "I'm so sorry I didn't remember earlier. You must have been thinking about her all day. I can't imagine how difficult it must be to be here, when all you want to do is—"

"Can you give my apologies to Lucas? I'll call him after the wedding." It was as though he hadn't heard her at all.

"Go where?" she asked again, before realization washed over her like an icy wave. "You're leaving?"

"I need to get home." Breck wouldn't meet her eyes. "I can't stay here. Can you tell Rachel, too. She'll need to walk down the aisle with somebody else."

"Breck. Talk to me." Holding his arm, Caitie took a step forward, raising her face to his. He was still frowning. She reached up to tip his head down, willing him to meet her gaze. "Are you sick? Do you want me to call a doctor?"

He shook his head.

"Is it your mom? Do you want to talk?" Her voice softened. "What's wrong? Let me help you."

He shrugged her off, her hand falling to her side. "I need to get out of here," he muttered. "Please let me go."

---

Breck couldn't remember the last time he'd felt like this. His chest was so tight it was hard to breathe. He sucked in a mouthful of air, but it caught in his throat, making his heart speed up even faster.

The nausea that had been swirling around his stomach all night was still rising. And his head – oh god, his head. It was pounding in a painful rhythm that made him want to scream.

He needed to get out of here. If he could get away from this hotel, he might be able to breathe again. Might be able to get this messy, thick pain out of his head and actually be able to think.

Because right now he couldn't form a single thought. Nothing beyond the need to escape. Every muscle in his body was tense, like an animal faced with the ultimate danger.

"Breck, you need to breathe." He could faintly hear her voice. "Please listen to me."

He shook his head, but the shooting pain in his skull made him wince. Christ, was he going to be sick?

Somewhere in the back of his wooly mind he could hear her voice. Feel her hand as she pressed it against his arm. But it did nothing to soothe away the pain.

Only distance would. He knew that.

"I need to go home," he told her. He reached for his bag, trying not to gasp as the shock of movement made his head protest.

"You can't drive like this. Stay here, let me take care of you. I have some painkillers in my room if you need them." The feeling of her hand stroking his cheek made his spine tense. He couldn't stand it. Couldn't stand being touched. Couldn't stand thinking about his mom and the way she used to touch him.

He really *was* going to be sick.

"Breck?"

He swallowed the nausea down at the last minute. "I'll call the hotel in the morning," he told her. "Pay for my room."

"You can't go like this. You're too sick to drive." She paused, as though she was thinking something through. "I'll come with you. I'll take you home."

"No." His voice was rough. What kind of asshole would ask her to do that? She was in the middle of arranging her brother's wedding for God's sake. He squeezed his eyes shut. He was like some kind of virus. If he didn't get out of here soon, he'd infect them all. "Stay here. I need to be alone."

"But Breck—"

"Leave me alone." It came out louder than he'd planned. Harsher, too. Caitie stepped back, shock on her face as she blinked away the tears. He took another breath, trying to find the right words. But there were none. Because he was an asshole and he needed to stop hurting people to make himself feel better.

Her expression felt like a knife to his heart, adding to the pain in his stomach and head. Everything he touched was turning to ashes. He couldn't stand the way she was looking at him.

He shouldn't have let this happen. Shouldn't have let Caitie think he was fine with Christmas. That he was happy to celebrate with her when the thought of it tore him apart.

This was why he went away every year, keeping his miserable ass away from everybody else. He dealt with it by pretending it wasn't there. It was the only way to survive.

"I'm sorry," he whispered, curling his hands to stop himself from wiping the tears from her cheeks. "I shouldn't have come here." He shook his head. "I never wanted to hurt you..."

"Then stay," she pleaded.

"I can't. I can't do this." His own eyes stung with tears. "I'm sorry."

Her eyes rose up to meet his. "And us?" she whispered. "What about us?"

Even crying, she was beautiful. Her eyes shone, her skin glowed, her lips as pink as berries. Lucas was right, she *was* perfect. The full enchilada. And he was making her cry like he hadn't seen in years.

He was poison. If he wasn't careful, he'd bring them both down.

"I'm sorry," he said, his voice heavy. "There is no us."

## ❧ 26 ❧

Caitie's heart had been hurting all morning, and yet somehow she'd managed to keep it together as she sat with Ember and the other bridesmaids. As she had her hair washed and styled, she kept her facial expression as neutral as she could when the beautician applied her makeup.

Ember and her friends were in high spirits, laughing and teasing each other as they prepared themselves for the ceremony. Even Rachel had managed to shrug off her grumpiness about Breck being gone, and was sipping the champagne Caitie had ordered for them.

"Are you okay?" Ember whispered as the hairdresser sprayed her hair. "You look exhausted."

"I didn't sleep much," Caitie replied, urging her lips to smile. "But I'm fine, I really am."

Lies, all lies. Her stomach was churning, her chest was aching. She needed to get through today, then *maybe* she could breathe again.

Because everything hurt. She wanted to call him, to message him, to see if he was okay. But he'd made it clear he wasn't willing to talk to her. Didn't want to tell her what was wrong. He preferred to leave her alone than open up and say how he really felt.

She might have been in love with him, but she had some pride. Even if she wanted to talk to him, now wasn't the time. If she heard his voice she'd cry, and ruin the beautiful make-up the beautician had applied.

No, she would get through today and worry about every-thing tomorrow. Or maybe after Christmas, because right now her body wanted to sleep for a hundred years.

An hour later, they were standing in the lobby outside the ballroom. Even through her heartache, Caitie couldn't help but smile at Ember, and tell her how pretty she looked.

"My brother is a lucky man," she told her.

"I'm the lucky one," Ember said, smiling. "I can't wait to be his wife." Her love for him was so easy to read; she glowed with it. Caitie tried to ignore the feeling of loneliness threat-ening to suffuse her.

She was going to get through this. She was.

"Are you ready?" her father asked Ember. The bride nodded. The bridal party formed into a line at the front, with Rachel and Caitie paired together in the absence of Breck. The music began as the ushers opened the double doors leading into the ballroom. And as each of them stepped forward, Lucas turned to watch them, smiling as his eyes met Ember's.

For a moment everything seemed to stop. Nobody breathed, nobody walked, because they were all entranced by the emotion in Lucas's eyes. His lips curled into a smile, and the crowd sighed, as the wedding procession began to make their way toward him.

Caitie looked around, her cheeks aching from her struggle to smile. The seat covers matched the bridesmaids' dresses perfectly, the ivory flowers a contrast to the dark burgundy of the fabric. The music was clear, the guests were smiling, and the bride and groom only had eyes for each other.

Everything was perfect. And at least one couple was getting their happy-ever-after today.

---

As soon as he'd made it home in the early hours of the morning, Breck had been full of regret. Once he could breathe again he realized he'd been having a panic attack at the hotel. A massive one that felt like he was dying. He hadn't had one of those in years, thanks to the therapy and work he'd put in after his mother's death.

But now everything felt fresh and painful. And he had no idea how to handle it.

No matter what he did, he couldn't forget the way Caitie had looked when he'd told her he had to leave. The shocked pain on her face had mirrored his own. But this time it had been his fault. He was the one who'd inflicted pain on the woman he loved. And it killed him.

His body was dog tired. His brain, too. But when he'd arrived back in Angel Sands at the early hours of the morning, sleep had been the furthest thing from his mind. Instead, he'd paced the bungalow, the deck, and even the beach, trying to work out what he should do. He'd wanted to talk to her, but it had been three in the morning, and there was no way he was going to wake her up. Making this wedding perfect for her brother was important to her, she'd made that much clear. He'd already caused her enough pain, he wasn't going to make things worse by talking to her all night when she should be resting.

So instead he'd paced his bungalow, his hands clenched into fists as he tried to work out what to do. How to make things right. If this had been a movie he'd drive back to the hotel and interrupt the wedding ceremony to tell the whole wedding party how much he loved her. But he knew Caitie, and he understood she would have hated that. She didn't like grand gestures; she just wanted to be treated kindly.

And he'd failed at that.

As the morning progressed into a temperate December afternoon, Breck glanced at the watch on his tanned wrist. The ceremony would be over by now. They'd all be sitting down to eat; Caitie, Lucas, their family and friends. Laughter and love surrounding a single empty chair.

His chair.

For the past twelve years he'd associated Christmas with loss and pain. With that terrible day when he'd lost his mom and his entire world had fallen apart. But now the wound was fresh and deeper than it had ever been. He didn't know if it would ever heal again.

Each memory of her face and her touch would make it split open a little more.

He could feel his breath becoming labored, the way it had when he'd listened to the Christmas music. His chest was tight, too. He needed to do something to stave off the panic, so he pulled on his running shorts and a shirt, slipping his feet into soft shoes made for jogging on the sand. Maybe a swift five miles would help clear his mind. God knew nothing else was doing the trick.

As he was about to leave the bungalow, his cellphone rang. Reaching out for it, he felt his heart start to race. A hundred possibilities rushed through his mind; it could be Caitie, wanting to kill him, or Lucas wanting to do the same. Then again it could be Griff or Jack, wanting to yell at his stupidity.

Seeing his dad's name on the screen was almost a letdown. He considered ignoring it, but thought better. Even a few minutes of conversation had to be better than the maelstrom in his mind.

"Hey, Dad."

"I caught you. I wasn't sure you'd be able to answer your phone. Maria and I are about to get on our flight to Miami. I wanted to check in with you before we did." A loud speaker interrupted his words, silencing him for a moment. Thirty seconds later, he continued, "Sorry about that. Anyway, how's the wedding?"

A lump the size of an island formed in Breck's throat. Should he lie to put his dad's mind at rest? But in spite of everything he'd done, he was never a good liar. Great at breaking hearts, but a fail when it came to telling untruths. "Yeah, I didn't go."

"Why not?" An edge of concern slipped into his dad's voice. "Are you sick?"

To his core, but that was self-inflicted. "No, it's not that." Breck sat down on the couch. "I, ah... I messed up, Dad. I did something terrible. I hurt somebody I care so deeply about. And I have no idea what to do about it."

"You want me to fly over there?" David asked, his voice full of concern. "I can change my ticket, and be there in an instant."

"No!" Breck was touched at his father's offer, but the thought of ruining yet another person's Christmas made him feel even worse. "Dad, you're about to spend Christmas with your girlfriend. There's no way you can let her down."

"Son, if you need me I'll be on the next flight. Maria will understand. It's what parents do."

His dad's simple offer made Breck want to cry. Thirteen years ago he'd done the exact same thing, flying out to Angel Sands to help his sons at Christmas, and things hadn't really changed much. "Honestly, Dad, I'll be fine. I need to take a couple of days to think about things."

"I hate to think of you all alone on Christmas."

Breck's laugh was short. "I'm on my own every Christmas."

"And I hate it every year. But this year is even worse. I haven't heard you so down in a long, long time."

Thirteen years, probably. But Breck was trying not to think about that. "Yeah, well this is all self-inflicted, so don't feel sorry for me. I pretty much want to punch myself."

"You wanna talk about it?" David asked. "We've got another hour until boarding, and Maria's gone off to window shop."

Breck opened his mouth, determined to say no, but closed it. Keeping things bottled up hadn't worked out so well for him thus far. "I don't even know where to start, Dad. I'm a mess. I can't believe what I did to her."

"Well, you can start by telling me who *she* is."

"Cait," Breck said softly. "Caitlin Russell. You met her at Thanksgiving."

"Little Caitie? Lucas's sister?" David clarified. "Something's going on between the two of you?"

Breck slumped further into the couch cushions, rubbing his neck with the palm of his hand. He had some explaining to do.

Breck carefully filled his father in on how he and Caitie had fallen for each other. As ashamed as he was, he left nothing out, not even the crazy way he'd left the hotel.

"Wow," his dad said, as soon as Breck had finished his story. "You've really gotten yourself in a mess, haven't you?"

"Yeah, you could say that." He squeezed his eyes shut, overwhelmed by how much he'd messed things up.

"I should have known you'd be low at this time of year. I should have checked on you. I'm so used to you going away and avoiding things. I never dreamed you'd walk into a hotel full of Christmas cheer and expect to feel okay about things."

"But I *should* feel okay," Breck said. "It's been years. I'm a grown man. I shouldn't freak out over a few decorations and a fir tree."

"Son, you lost your mom the day before Christmas. It's absolutely normal to feel out of control at this time of year. From what you've said, you're in love with a girl whose life revolves around the holidays. It's like being a vegan and getting married to a butcher."

Breck let out a mouthful of air. "I'm all wrong for her. I didn't even get her a gift. What kind of guy doesn't think about buying a present for the girl he loves? She could do so much better than me."

"She could do a damn sight worse."

"Yeah, well you're biased."

"Damn right I am. I'm also feeling a little bit guilty right now. This isn't all your fault."

"*Guilty?*" Breck was incredulous. What the hell did his father have to feel guilty about? "How'd you figure that?"

"I never forced you to face things. That Christmas when you were eighteen and you asked me to pay for you to travel, I jumped at the chance. I'd seen you at your lowest the December before, and I couldn't stand for you to get so down again. The thought that you'd go and have fun seemed like the best idea ever. But you kept doing it. Going away and avoiding Christmas like it was some kind of poison. And I kept helping you do it. So yes, it's my fault, too. I did it from the best intentions. But we all know those things line the pathway to hell."

"I'm a grown man, Dad. I think I can take responsibility for being a complete mess."

David laughed. "Son, you're *not* a mess. You did something stupid. There's a difference."

Breck squeezed his eyes shut. He could still see Caitie's face behind his lids. The way she'd stared at him, like he was an asshole. Goddamn it, he *was* an asshole.

"She's never going to forgive me," he whispered. "And she shouldn't. I did some messed up, terrible things. I broke her heart the night before her brother's wedding, the one day she needed my support the most."

"Did you ever think of asking for *her* support?" David asked.

"What?" Breck frowned. "Why should she give me support? I'm the one who's supposed to look after her." Yeah, and look how *that* turned out.

"Of course she should support you, exactly the same way you support her. A relationship is supposed to be equal, son. After separating from your mother, I learned that the hard way. If you don't talk to her, how's she supposed to know how you're feeling?"

Breck was silent, thinking about his father's words. Could there be truth in them? The thought of sharing his vulnerability with Caitie, of admitting he was fallible, both thrilled and scared him in equal measure.

"I don't know..." his voice broke. "Dad, I don't know how to make it right."

"Be honest, be open, and tell her how sorry you are. I don't know if that will make it right, but it has to be better than spending your life surrounded by regrets. And again, I'm talking from experience here."

For all his life, Breck had been the strong one. Supporting his mom through her illness, then his brother after her death. Even in adulthood, he worked alongside his father, making sure the company he'd founded went from strength to strength. Was it even possible to change that? He wasn't sure. All he knew was he couldn't stand feeling like this. He'd spoiled the one precious thing in his life, simply because he was afraid to show who he really was.

"She's going to hate me." The truth of his words made him wince. "And she should."

"Yep, almost certainly," his dad agreed. He sounded a little too cheerful for Breck's liking. "But a strong guy like you can take it, can't you?"

Could he? Breck considered the alternative; living life the way he always had. Strong, silent, alone. The thought of it made him want to throw up.

"Yeah, I can take it."

"Good. Because otherwise I'd have to change my flight and come beat you up myself. Now, stop feeling sorry for yourself and figure out a way to talk to that girl before you lose her for good."

As far as Breck was concerned he'd already lost her, and deservedly so. But apart from that, his father was right. He owed her an explanation, and he certainly owed her an apology.

The rest, he'd have to leave up to fate.

---

Somehow Caitie had made it through the rest of the day. She fought her way past the questions about the missing groomsman and held her head high when she explained to the staff they'd need one less place setting. She'd even kept it together as the music played and Lucas and Ember had their first dance, staring into each other's eyes, the love between them palpable. The only person who'd made her stumble was Rachel, and her constant musings about how Breck was feeling. At one point, Rachel talked about going back to Angel Sands after the ceremony to check on him, but luckily Brooke and Ally had persuaded her otherwise.

The dancing was over by midnight, and by that point there were only a trickle of people left in the room. The hotel staff was cleaning around them, stacking chairs and clearing tables. A very-tired looking Lucas and Ember came over to her, smiling in spite of their obvious exhaustion.

"Thank you so much, Caitie," Ember said, grabbing her hand and squeezing it. "Today was so special, and we owe it to you and all your hard work. We couldn't have done this without you."

Caitie's smile was almost genuine. "It was a pleasure. Thank you for including me in your day; I'm honored you let me help."

Lucas hugged her tight. "You're amazing. A real rock. Nothing fazes you, not even having Breck cancel at the last minute. Flu and fever my ass. I bet he was hooking up with some chick."

His words made Caitie's stomach churn. She tried to ignore the way it clenched at the thought. "Yeah, probably," she mumbled.

"Ah, I'll give him hell after the honeymoon."

Grasping at the chance to change the subject, Caitie asked him, "When do you leave again?"

"The day after Christmas," Lucas said. "We'll spend tomorrow night, or I guess it's now *tonight* at our house, then Christmas day with Ember's mom. After that, we're off to LAX and on to Paris."

"It's going to be cold there," Caitie said. "I hope you've got a good coat."

"Ember's bought us a whole new wardrobe. Coats, sweaters, boots. We'll probably never want to come home."

"I don't blame you. I wouldn't want to either." She took a deep breath. "I guess I should head to bed, and let you two go. After all, it *is* your wedding night. You shouldn't really be spending it with your sister."

Ember laughed. "Well, I guess it's past midnight. We really should get some sleep, Mr. Russell."

"I'll be right behind you, Mrs. Russell." Lucas grinned at Caitie. "Good night, sis."

"Good night."

Watching them leave, she tried to ignore the ache in her heart. They were so in love, and they'd declared it in front of all their family and friends. They deserved every bit of the happiness that was glowing from them. Even if it was a painful contrast to the loneliness weighing down on her shoulders.

---

Climbing out of the hot shower, Caitie wrapped a towel around her chest and twisted another onto her head. Her feet throbbed from spending all day in heels, and with each step she took, the pain made her wince. She was too tired to dry her hair, unsure she even had the strength to hold the hairdryer. She'd probably regret it in the morning, but right now going to sleep with it wet seemed like a good idea.

She grabbed her phone from her purse, intending to check her emails before switching it off for the night. That's when she saw the missed calls – four of them – plus a handful of text messages and voicemails. All of them were from the same person.

*Breck.*

Her heart clenched at the sight of his name. She wanted to hear his voice, to feel his arms around her, to make everything okay.

But it wasn't. The way he walked out on her, and on the wedding, without a glance backward still stung. She was sad and tired and everything else that made her body ache.

Breck would have to wait until tomorrow. Maybe everything would be clearer then.

## ❧ 27 ❧

By the time Caitie's parents had driven her back to their house on Christmas Eve, it was almost lunchtime, but her stomach was way too tight to eat any food. Instead, she climbed back into bed, her body weary as hell, and pulled the soft covers over her. Her mind had resisted sleep, still too hyped up with thoughts of Breck and the wedding, not to mention her work. But the tiredness had fought hard, winning out within minutes over the anxieties gnawing at her.

The days from Christmas Eve all the way into the New Year were always the quietest for her professionally. It seemed counter-intuitive at first, that a business which specialized in Christmas should be so quiet at the very time of year she worked toward. Yet by December twenty-fourth everything that could be done, *had* been done. Festive TV shows had aired, Theme Parks were closing, and corporate parties were over and done with for the year. Even her biggest clients – the retail businesses – were wrapping up the decorations, and filling the stores for their New Year sales. She could worry all she wanted, but the fact was there was nothing else for her to do.

Nothing but sleep.

A knock on her door woke her a few hours later. Caitie sat upright in bed, blinking to unstick her eyes. She was wearing a sweatshirt and shorts, her hair sticking out in weird directions. Her eyes were puffy and red from too many late nights and even more tears.

"Caitie?" Deenie stuck her head around the bedroom door. "There's someone to see you."

"Wha?" She was still blinking the dry sleep away. "Who is it?"

"Breck. I think he's come to apologize for being unable to make it yesterday. I have to say he doesn't look much better. I hope he's not contagious. The last thing we need is to come down with something on Christmas Day."

Caitie looked down at her bare legs and her old threadbare sweatshirt. She wasn't exactly dressed for entertaining. "Can you tell him I'll call him later?" she asked.

"Honey, he's come to say sorry. And this is Breck we're talking about. He won't care that you're wearing old clothes, or that your hair's a mess. Oh, or about the red patch on your face from where you've been sleeping."

"Yeah, thanks for noticing that." Caitie rubbed her cheek.

Deenie sighed. "I know you're tired, sweetheart. We all are. Just come out and say hi. He's on his own and I can't help but think about it being the anniversary of his mom's death. Thirteen years might be a long time, but it has to still hurt."

That got her attention. She swung her legs out of bed, her feet hitting the warm rug. "Okay, give me a minute. I'll put on something more appropriate."

It didn't mean anything. Nothing more than a friend caring about a friend. As angry as she was with him, the soft girl inside of her still cared about Breck. About his pain, his grief, about him being all alone.

Grabbing a pair of jeans from her suitcase, she slid them

on and pulled a brush through her matted hair. It got stuck, stubbornly refusing to budge no matter how hard she tugged. In the end, she slid it into a high ponytail. A glance in the mirror told her she looked as bad as she felt. Her face – shiny from no makeup – was also red and blotchy. There were dark shadows beneath her eyes. The lids themselves were puffy from lack of sleep and way too much crying. Even the best tools in her cosmetic bag wouldn't be enough to combat that.

She pulled her shoulders back, straightening her spine. What did it matter anyway? She didn't care what Breck thought of her, or if he saw her at her worst. She was too tired to care about anything at all.

When she walked down the hallway, he was sitting in the kitchen leaning against the counter, his hands wrapped around a mug. A glance inside told her whatever he was drinking was red and warm. No doubt another concoction from her mom.

"Hi," he said as soon as he saw her. He looked as bad as she did. The shadows beneath his eyes were darker than hers. But more than that, he looked drawn and defeated. Like a man who had nothing left to lose.

"How are you feeling?" she asked him.

"A little better." Breck blinked. "I wanted to come by to say sorry." He glanced over at Deenie, who was unashamedly staring at them. "Um, can we go for a walk or something?"

The last thing she wanted was to be alone with him. But the alternative was even worse. The only saving grace from this whole fiasco was that she didn't have to face her family's concern about the end of their brief relationship.

"You can go out on the deck," Deenie suggested. "It's a gorgeous day out there. Daddy's in his study so he won't disturb you."

Shrugging, Caitie stood up, leading Breck out through the glass doors to the wooden deck. The furniture was still out –

no need to put it away for the winter in temperate Angel Sands. They each slid a chair out, sitting a few feet away from each other.

But that distance still wasn't enough. Against her will, Caitie could feel her body warm up at his proximity. It was as if he was imprinted in her DNA; every inch of her yearned for him.

"I'm so sorry." Breck leaned closer, and his scent lifted in the breeze. Sandalwood and Brecken Miller, an intoxicating combination. "I messed up; I hurt you and I can't believe I left like that."

She lifted her eyes to meet his. "I can't believe it either," she whispered. "I only wanted to know that you were okay."

He squeezed his eyes shut for a moment. "I know. And I wasn't. But I shouldn't have pushed you away."

"That hurt. A lot. I knew you were hurting about your mom, and I understood why. I wanted you to let me in."

"And I should have, but I wasn't thinking straight. It felt like everything was closing in on me." He looked down at his feet, biting his bottom lip. "I don't find talking about this stuff easy."

"I get that, I really do. But I can't have a relationship with somebody who won't open up." She sighed. "I tried to talk to you, I really did. And you threw it back in my face." She licked her lips. "I told you everything about my own fears. Do you think that was easy?"

He laced his fingers together and glanced up at her. "I want to open up. I do. I'd like to try and explain. That is, if you'll hear me out."

She picked at a stray thread on her sweater, pulling at the black string until the fabric puckered. "Okay," she said quietly. "I'll listen."

She heard him take in a deep lungful of breath. He leaned

back in his chair, running a hand through his messy hair. "So, I'm not really good at talking about this stuff..."

*No kidding.*

"But I've realized that keeping it all in, well it ends up with me losing it. You either have to break out or break down, I guess. And because I thought I could handle things, I broke down."

Her mouth was dry. She knew how much it took for this strong, proud man to admit to breaking. How hard it was to let himself be vulnerable.

"I talked to my dad yesterday. I told him about everything that had happened. Well, most of it. And he made me realize something. I'm an avoider. If I can't handle something, I do whatever I can to walk away from it. But in the long run, Cait, it means I'm going to lose everything. And I don't want that, not any more. Not now that I know what it feels like to lose you." His voice cracked, and the sound of it broke the dam keeping Caitie's emotions in check. A fat tear rolled down her cheek. "And out of everything in my life, my mom included, losing you hurts the most.

"I grew up thinking that men had to be strong. Showing no emotions. I thought that I had to be a rock. First for my mom, then for Daniel. Even for my dad sometimes. When you came back into my life, it was as if you had a pickaxe, and with every touch, every soft word, you cut away my hard edges. It scared the hell out of me. Because all this stuff I've kept locked up inside, it's threatening to come out." He rubbed his face with the heels of his hands, pulling at the skin.

"You think it's wrong to be vulnerable?"

"I think... I thought... I don't know. I guess I never really thought about it until now. Just wanted to be strong. The knight in shining armor, the one who did the saving. That's how I've always been."

"But I never asked for that," she reminded him quietly.

"I know you didn't. But it's what I want for you. It's what you deserve. Somebody to take care of you, to protect you, to hold you when you're afraid."

"And who holds you?"

"I guess that's the problem; I never thought I had to be held. Not until you." There was a pained expression on his face. As though every word hurt him to say. She didn't underestimate the effort it was taking him to be so open with her. But still, she needed to guard her heart.

"When I sat at the rehearsal dinner and saw everything you'd done, I was more afraid than I've ever been in my whole life. Because, Caitie, everything you'd done was amazingly beautiful. I could see you in every small touch. It made me realize how important Christmas is to you, how much your life revolves around it. And how little I can give you, how wrong I am for you. Even when every inch of me wants me to be right."

"You left me because of Christmas?" She was incredulous. "Because of a few little days?"

"But they're not a few days. They're your job, your life. Lucas told me it's your favorite time of year, and has been since you were a kid."

"Since I was fifteen," she said softly.

"What?"

"It's been my favorite time of the year since I was fifteen. Since the last time I saw you."

He stared at her, his eyes dark and intense. "You like Christmas because of *me*?"

"Not just because of that. But after you and Daniel left, well, it helped me to remember you. And I know it's weird because you guys were so sad that Christmas. But that's what got me started. The reason I specialized my Fine Arts degree."

Breck swallowed. His Adam's apple bobbed beneath the thin skin of his throat. "I hate Christmas. I have since that day... since Mom died. I can't give you what you want. I can't be the guy who dresses up in a Santa outfit and gives out festive cheer. It makes me feel sick to think about it."

"I never asked you to do that."

"But that's what you deserve."

"Don't I get to decide what I deserve?" she asked softly. "You made a decision about my supposed needs without even talking it through with me, and it hurt. I know you were afraid, because I know what fear is like. You were the one who gave me the courage to face mine. And I did it for you, for me; for us, Breck. No matter how awful it made me feel. I'm finally willing to accept I have a problem. Why can't you do the same thing for me?"

That was the crux of the matter. She'd let herself be vulnerable, cut herself open for him. But when asked to do the same, he'd run.

"Because for all my macho bluster and shining armor, it turns out you were stronger than me all along," he said, looking down at the ground. "And it kills me to know how much I let you down. But I'm not done here, Cait, nowhere near. I'm so in love with you it hurts. Losing you is so much worse than facing my fears. In fact, it's my worst fear come true."

There was a part of her that wanted to run into his arms, to cup his anguished face with her warm palms. To soothe and be soothed, to tell him it was all going to be all right.

But the pain of the past two days stopped her. She'd been vulnerable once. Maybe too vulnerable. She wasn't sure she could do it again.

"I'm so sorry," he whispered. "So sorry I hurt you. So sorry I ran out. I'm sorry I ran from the best thing that's ever happened to me. I'm not asking you to say anything. In fact,

I'd prefer if you didn't. I'd like you to think about what I've said. Think about us. Make a decision about whether you can give us another chance or not. But I need to warn you, I'm not going to give up. I'm going to fight for you with every breath I have left. When you finally find love, and realize it's the one thing you've been looking for all your life, you'll do whatever it takes to keep hold of it."

She had to fight to keep her lips clamped shut. The emotions inside of her were rising up, threatening to spill over, in words, in tears, in sighs. At least for a few minutes, she needed to keep it together. Until she was alone.

"Thank you for listening," he said. "I'm going to go now and let you catch up on your sleep. You look exhausted. And if it's okay with you, I'll call you tomorrow. If you don't want to talk, don't pick up."

She nodded.

He stood, towering over her as he always did. "Thank you for listening to me." He swallowed hard. "And Merry Christmas."

He left without another word, taking long strides across the deck. She followed him with her eyes as he retreated, her heart so full it could burst. She wasn't sure, but it felt as though it already had.

## 28

"Is everything okay?" Deenie asked Caitie as she walked back into the kitchen. Her mom was making Eggnog, stirring the milk and cloves together in a pan. She added the yolks and sugar, mixing them all with a wooden spoon. "You were out there for a while after Breck left."

"Yeah." Caitie sank into one of the kitchen stools. After he'd gone, she'd sat on one of the garden chairs and stared aimlessly out at the sky, her mind full of thoughts. "It's been a long day."

"He didn't seem very happy after you spoke." Deenie glanced up from the stove. "Are you still mad at him for missing yesterday? It wasn't his fault. He couldn't help getting sick." Her brow creased as she took in Caitie's sad expression. Realization crossed her face, like the sun coming out from behind a cloud. "Oh, honey, he wasn't sick at all, was he?"

"He was," Caitie said, her voice cracking. "But there's more to it than that."

Deenie clicked the stovetop off, and pulled the pan away, letting it cool. She pulled out the stool next to Caitie, sliding into it. "Want to talk about it?"

Did she? Caitie wasn't sure. But she knew not talking about it was the route to disaster. Breck's confession had shown her that much.

"I'm in love with him."

"Of course you are," Deenie said, matter of factly. "You always were. Even as a kid your face would shine brighter whenever he was around. After he left it was like somebody had snuffed your light out. I worried about you for the longest time." She grabbed Caitie's hand. "Is he in love with you, too?"

"He told me he was."

"So why are you so sad?"

"Because it isn't enough." She felt like she was stabbing herself with an ice pick at her confession. "He couldn't cope with it. He walked away, Mom. He hurt me and I don't know what to do with that."

"Does he regret it?" Deenie asked.

"He says he does. That he loves me and wants to make it up to me."

"One of the hardest lessons we'll ever learn in life is that the people we love are fallible. One of the most painful lessons, too. When you fall in love, you think everything's going to click into place. That it will be like it is in the movies, and somehow you'll spend the rest of your life walking into that mythical sunset. The first time you hit a barrier, it's as though somebody's rewriting all those fairy tales that introduced you to romance and love. And, Caitie, it hurts like hell. No wonder you're knocked down."

Caitie's interest was piqued. "You and Dad had problems?"

"I don't know a couple that hasn't. Nobody's perfect, honey. We all make mistakes. We all hurt the ones we love. The only difference between the couples who succeed and the ones who don't is communication and empathy. Being honest and open. Owning up to our mistakes. Now I don't know what Brecken said to you out there, but whatever it was I can see how much it affected you. Opening up their hearts isn't an easy thing for men to do. I know how scared you are of being hurt, and I can't promise you never will be, but I can tell you that unless you allow yourself to be vulnerable, you'll never experience the beauty love can bring."

Her mother's words – as heartfelt and wise as they were – knocked Caitie back. Her mind flitted to the way he'd looked on the deck, the softness of his expression, the sadness in his eyes. She'd never seen him so defenseless before.

Breck exposed himself to her – faults and all. He showed her all he had been hiding behind. Everything he had struggled with. That's when it hit her. She was doing the exact same thing as he'd been doing. Hiding her feelings and pain from her mom as Breck had hid his from her. A wave of shame washed over her.

"I'm not perfect either," she confessed.

"I've known that since I tried to potty train you." Deenie flashed her a reassuring smile. "I love you the way you are. You never have to be anything other than real to me."

"After the accident... the one on the beach... I, uh, I never really recovered." Caitie found herself stuttering out the words. "I haven't been able to stand the sight of water since I nearly drowned. I get panic attacks whenever I'm near the beach. I've started working on it, Mom. I've found a behavioral therapist."

Deenie squeezed her hand tighter. "Oh honey. I wish you'd told me about it. I knew there was something that upset you, something that kept you away all these years. I should have said something about it. I could have helped you."

Caitie shook her head. "I was the best liar. Even if you'd asked I would have denied there was anything wrong."

"What made you decide to do something about it?"

"Breck did." Those two simple words made her insides ache. The memory of his tenderness as she tried to face her fears took her breath away. She could almost feel his soft hands on her, soothing her body, making her ache for him from the inside out.

"He's a good man."

"He is." So good he made her heart hurt.

"You should go back to bed. You look beat. Try to get some sleep. Tomorrow's another day. You can worry about all of this then. I have the distinct impression we'll be having a visitor, even though he hates Christmas."

"He said he would call." For the first time in days, she thought she might even answer. She wanted to hear what he had to say. "You're right. I'll head off now. See you in the morning, Mom."

"Merry Christmas, sweetheart."

For the first time in more than a day, Caitie thought maybe it could be.

---

"I told you I'd kill you if you broke her heart." Daniel's voice held a hint of amusement as he talked to Breck through the phone. "What the hell did you do, bro? I can't believe you're forcing me to commit fratricide. Do you think '*my brother's an idiot*' will stand up in court?"

Breck rolled his eyes. "I guess Dad's been talking to you."

"Yeah, he called when he landed. He's worried about you. He asked if we should fly over to give you some support."

"I hope you told him not to," Breck said. "He deserves to enjoy Christmas with Maria. And I'm okay. Not great, but okay. I don't need babysitting."

"You never did. You were always the one doing the

babysitting," Daniel pointed out. "But you know I'm here if you want to talk. Or if you want me to shout at you or something."

Breck's voice softened. "Thanks, Daniel. I appreciate that, I really do. But I made this mess and I'm going to clean it up."

"So you're not running away any more?"

"Wasn't planning on it. I've run away enough. It's time to make up for what I've done. I love her, bro. I'm completely and stupidly in love with that girl. If I thought it would help, I'd hit myself for being so stupid."

"Ah, it can't do any harm."

"You should probably shut up now."

Daniel laughed. "So, is she talking to you yet?"

"Sort of," Breck replied. "She listened when I went over to talk to her. That's more than I expected after walking out on her."

"It's a start, that's for sure."

"I'm not giving up. Not until she tells me there's not a chance in hell she'll take me back. Until then I'll keep trying, keep showing her how sorry I am. It's the only thing I can do."

"So what's your plan?" Daniel asked.

"I'm going to her house tomorrow. I'm not invited, but I can't go another day without talking to her." The need to be by her was eating away at him. Seeing her tonight and not touching her was almost too painful to bear.

"You're going to the Russells' house on Christmas day? Wow." Daniel whistled. "That's brave."

Of course Daniel would understand. It was where it had all started, the trauma, the pain, the knowledge their mom had died and was never coming back. The last time he'd even acknowledged Christmas was thirteen years ago in that house.

"It's what I need to do."

"Are you taking her a gift?" Daniel asked. "You can't really show up without one. Not at Christmas." *Not again.* Daniel may not have said it, but Breck heard it anyway.

"Yeah, I need to figure that out." And figure out how the hell he was going to find something this late on Christmas Eve.

"I've got an idea," Daniel said. "It's gonna take all the time you've got, a bit of effort, and you'll probably need to go on Craigslist and beg, but it might work."

As Daniel outlined his plan, Breck listened, a smile forming on his lips. His brother may have been a pain in the ass growing up, and a real know-it-all now that he's an adult, but there was no denying he was always full of good ideas.

And maybe, just maybe, this one might actually work out.

## ✤ 29 ✤

There was a cool breeze dancing in from the Pacific Ocean as Breck drove through Angel Sands on Christmas morning. It lifted his hair and caressed his skin through his car's open window, carrying the sound of singing from the Baptist Church on the corner, next to Megassey's Hardware store. But this time he didn't wince. Didn't even blink. Somehow the pain of the past few days had taken away the potency of it all. Christmas wasn't responsible for him losing his mother all those years ago. Cancer was. And that sucked, but he still had a life to live.

As far as he was concerned, that life started today.

From the corner of his eye he could see the gift wrapped box he'd placed on the passenger seat. It had taken him all night to prepare it – he'd had to call Daniel three times to make sure he had it completely right. It was almost midnight by the time he'd realized he had no Christmas gift wrap, and had to dash to the convenience store in the next town along to pay the extortionate price for a single sheet.

But it was worth it, because *she* was worth it.

He was aching to see her. Even though she was angry with

him, she still managed to touch him like nobody else could. And her anger was deserved after what he'd done. He'd make it up to her for as long as it took.

If it took forever? Well, he was a patient man.

He pulled his car into an empty spot next to the little cottage facing the beach and climbed out, closing his eyes against the grains of sand lifted by the wind. He took a deep breath in, enough to fill up his lungs and push out his chest, then walked to the back door and wrapped his knuckles against the wood.

"Breck?" Lucas's brows dipped as he saw his friend standing on the porch. "I wasn't expecting to see you. Are you feeling any better?"

Breck had forgotten all about his excuse for missing the wedding. He'd forgotten about almost everything except Caitlin Russell. "I'm good." He nodded firmly. "And congratulations. I'm sorry I missed your wedding."

Lucas gave him an easy smile. "No harm no foul. It's better than throwing up over the bridesmaids, right?" He inclined his head into the living room. "You want to come in? Ember's just cooking some breakfast."

Breck shook his head. "No, I don't want to impose. I just needed to talk to you about something."

"You do?" Two tiny lines formed on Lucas's brow. "What is it?" He paused then continued, "Oh man, it's Christmas. Is it something to do with your mom? I'm sorry. I know it's been a while but you never really get over something like that."

There was a look of sympathy in Lucas's eyes that cut Breck to the core. He'd lied to his friend, done things behind his back that no friend should do. And yet he couldn't bring himself to regret any of it – not a single touch, a single whisper, a single kiss. Every moment with Caitie was worth it.

"I didn't leave your wedding because I was sick," Breck said, his voice low. "I left because I was an asshole."

"You were?" Lucas's voice was full of confusion. "How?"

Where to begin? Breck frowned, trying to work out how to tell his best friend about his feelings for Caitie. But somewhere in the middle of his brainstorm, he found his lips moving without even thinking it through.

"I've been sleeping with your sister."

*Wham!*

Lucas's fist barely glanced Breck's cheek before it hit the hard wood of the door, but it was enough to make him lose his balance and fall to the left. Breck reached out to try and stop his fall, but his head hit the doorjamb, the edge of it slamming into the corner of his eye before he could brace himself against the impact.

"Shit!" Lucas jumped back, cupping his fist in his hand. "Damn that hurts."

Breck steadied himself, his left eye throbbing with pain. "Sure does." He lifted his hand to his cheek and touched himself gingerly, wincing at the tenderness of his skin.

"What the heck is going on?" Ember asked, walking into the living room with a spatula in her hand. "Lucas, did you just hit Breck?"

Breck took a deep breath and tried to open his left eye, but he could already feel it swelling. "It wasn't his fault, I just told him I've been sleeping with Caitie. But what I should have said is that I'm in love with her. I can't remember a time I wasn't in love with her." He pressed his lips together and looked Lucas straight in the eye. "I'm sorry," he said, his voice soft, "that I didn't tell you before. I should have. And I know you want better for her than a loser like me, but I love her, man. And I want to spend the rest of my life with her."

Ember had reached the doorway. She lifted Lucas's hand

up and sighed as she inspected the rawness of his knuckles. "I can't believe you hit your best friend."

"I can't believe he's been sleeping with my sister."

Breck winced. He could barely believe it himself.

Ember turned her head to look at Breck. "Did you force her to sleep with you?"

He winced. "Hell no."

"And you said you love her?"

He nodded. "Love doesn't seem like enough of a word. I adore her. I worship the ground she walks on. And then I broke her heart the night before your wedding."

"Can I hit him again?" Lucas muttered.

"Stop it," Ember told him. "Listen to him. He's in love with Caitie, and she loves him back."

"I don't know about that..." Breck mumbled.

"Well I do." Ember smiled. "No wonder she looked so upset on our wedding day. I kept wondering why that was. Every time she thought nobody was looking tears would fill her eyes."

"I was an asshole," Breck said again. "I'd do anything to take it back."

"Of course you would. But people do stupid things sometimes. Like hit their best friends." She raised her eyebrows at Lucas. "Doesn't mean that they wanted to hurt the other person."

"I really am sorry," Breck told them both. "For causing you problems at the wedding, and for upsetting your sister. I know how angry you must be at me, because I'm angry at myself. But I'm going to make it up to her."

Lucas looked him in the eye. "You'd better," he growled.

"Stop it." Ember rolled her eyes. "It's Christmas, be nice. Breck's your friend, and he's come over here to apologize." She rubbed his knuckles and smiled at him, the corner of her eyes crinkling.

Lucas sighed then held out his injured hand. "She's right, I'm sorry. I don't know what I was thinking."

"You were thinking about Caitie. The same way I am." Breck offered him a smile. "I can't blame you for taking care of your sister." He took Lucas's hand and shook it gently, being careful not to injure him further. "And for what it's worth, I promise you don't have to worry about her. Not with me. I meant what I said, I love her. I'm as protective of her as you are."

Lucas nodded. "I know. You're a good guy, Breck. Just take care of her heart, okay? It's precious."

"I will."

"Good." Ember grinned at them both. "I'm glad you've made up. Now who wants some breakfast?"

"I thought you'd never ask," Lucas said. "I'm starving."

"Not for me, thanks." Breck shook his head. "There's somebody I need to see."

Ember's eyes sparkled as she raised her brows. "Then what are you waiting for? Go get your girl."

---

The whole house smelled like Christmas when Caitie woke up on Christmas morning. The aroma of a ham baking in the oven, combined with the yeasty goodness of the freshly cooked rolls, made her mouth water. She felt as though she'd eaten nothing for days, and her stomach was contracting with the need to be fed. Grabbing a banana from the fruit bowl, she unpeeled it and practically stuffed it in her mouth whole. Once she swallowed, she took a hot roll from the cooling rack and stuffed it in her mouth. When her hunger was finally appeased, she glanced at her phone expectantly, checking to see if he had called.

Of course, he hadn't.

If Harper were here, she'd tell Caitie to call him instead. Maybe she would if he didn't contact her soon. But something inside her told her to wait it out, to let him take the lead. He'd opened himself up to her yesterday, finally showing his vulnerability. Now she needed to let him show his masculinity, too. Another thing she'd learned from her talk with her mom.

"There's an envelope with your name on it over there," her mom said, inclining her head to the white-painted cabinet. Like everything else in the kitchen it screamed shabby chic. "It was on the doormat when we got up this morning. Somebody must have put it through the letter box late last night."

Intrigued, Caitie grabbed the white rectangular envelope, staring at it with her brows pulled down. There was no indication of who it was from, just her name written in all capitals with black ink. She slid her thumb into the corner opening, sliding it across.

Inside was a white card with red and gold glossy print.

*All I want for Christmas is You.*

Caitie bit down her smile, opening it up to see the handwriting within.

*Dear Cait,*

*It's cheesy but true. You make me want to celebrate the one day I've been avoiding for most of my life.*

*Wait for me. I'll be there soon.*

*Breck*

She tried to picture him pushing the card through the door in the middle of the night. Had he ever sent a Christmas card to anyone before now? She couldn't imagine him writing any out as a teenager, and ever since he'd been avoiding the festive season like the plague.

"Is it from him?" Deenie asked.

"Yeah, it is." Caitie slid her fingers over his words, reading them again. This time a smile broke out, curling her lips up, whether she liked it or not. The fact was she did like it, very much.

"He must have been up early. Or late. Either way it was nice of him."

"Yes, yes it was." She hugged the card close to her chest.

Her dad chose that moment to walk in, stopping to give his wife a kiss on her cheek before ruffling Caitie's hair. "Merry Christmas, ladies. Caitie, I'm so glad you're here with us this year."

She looked around the old familiar kitchen, warmth coiling inside her. "So am I."

---

It was almost lunch time when the doorbell rang, making Caitie jump as she set the table, only three places now that Lucas was a married man. She looked up, her fingers still wrapped around a fork handle, her heart hammering in her chest.

"Brecken, Merry Chri... oh my, where did you get that?" Her mom's voice echoed from the hallway. Caitie frowned. What on Earth did he have that made her mom falter? It took her less than a minute to find out, as her mom led him down the hallway and into the dining room.

The sight of him made Caitie's mouth drop open. Where he'd only had tired lines and shadows before, was now a fresh, shining black eye.

"Ouch." She winced. "That looks painful."

He walked toward her, stopping a few feet short of where she stood. In spite of the black eye, he was smiling, his wide grin making his eyes crinkle. "Nothing more than I deserved."

"Where'd you get it?" She was a little breathless. The way he was looking at her – bruises not withstanding – was making her heart speed up.

"At Walmart. They were selling two for one. I thought I'd save the other for later," he joked.

"A bargain." She grinned and shook her head. "Now seriously, who hit you?"

"Lucas."

That shut her up. Her eyes widened as she took in his words. "My brother hit you? Why?"

"I told him about us. And I told him how I left you the night before the wedding. Then he tried to hit me and I stumbled into the door jamb. It wasn't either of our finest hours." He grinned sheepishly.

"You guys are crazy." She reached up, her fingers gentle as she stroked the edge of the blackness. "We need to put something on your eye before it gets any worse."

Breck shrugged. "I kind of like it. A badge of war or something. Anyway, it was worth it to come clean to your brother and make our peace. He's my closest friend, I owed him the truth." He tipped his head to the side, staring at her. "You don't mind me telling him, do you?"

"I..." She blew out a mouthful of air. "I don't think I mind."

"You don't sound too sure."

"I'm not sure of anything right now."

Deenie walked in, carrying their old medical kit. Though she hadn't seen it for years, Caitie recognized the red box right away. She'd seen it enough as a kid.

"I thought you might need this, young man." Deenie said.

"I've got some ointment in there somewhere. And I made you an icepack. Now sit down. Honestly, I thought you were thirty, not thirteen. What the hell are you doing getting into fights at your age?"

Breck sat there patiently while Deenie cleaned him up, all the while huffing and puffing about him having more muscles than sense. By the time he was all bandaged up, Caitie was smiling in spite of herself.

"So, I guess I should leave you two alone," Deenie said, looking from left to right at them. "Dinner's going to be another hour. You'll be joining us, won't you, Brecken?"

He glanced at the decorations hanging from the tree in the corner, his face turning pale. "Um, yeah. That would be great."

"Just a simple dinner," Deenie continued. "Ham and potatoes. It's only the four of us so no party here." She didn't have to tell him they wouldn't make it too festive, they all heard her subtext. Breck gave her a relieved smile.

"That sounds great, Mrs. Russell."

"Maybe you should take Breck to your room, Caitie. I'll be in and out of here as I finish getting dinner ready. I don't want to disturb you."

Two red spots formed on Caitie's cheeks. The thought of taking Breck to her room made her feel like she was fifteen years old again. "Oh, yeah, okay."

When they got there, Breck leaned on her old desk, still looking at her with those hot, dark eyes. "This room looks exactly how I remember it."

"That's because it hasn't changed in years. I've hardly been here over the last decade. I guess Mom didn't want to empty it out without me here to guide her."

"I feel seventeen years old again." Breck shifted on his feet. "Like I'm up to no good."

"You're always up to no good."

His grin was so sexy it made her want to run at him. "That's a true story."

"I got your card this morning. Thank you." She pointed at the windowsill, where she'd propped it up. "You must have been up late last night."

"I got you a present, too." He took a small rectangular package from his pocket. It was wrapped in the gaudiest, cheesiest paper she could imagine. Reindeers and Santas playing in the snow. "I hope you like it."

Her hand shook as she took it from his grasp. His fingers lingered on hers, as though he was as reluctant as she was to break the connection. Finally, he pulled back. "Open it," he said, his voice thick and deep.

She pulled at the clear tape, tearing it loose from the paper. Whatever it was inside, was small and light. No bigger than a cellphone. Unwrapping the paper, she watched it fall to the floor, revealing a thick white iPod. The old kind she hadn't seen in years.

"You got me this?" she asked, feeling confused. "Where did you find it?"

"Craigslist," he said. "It's not exactly the same as the one you gave Daniel, but it's close enough."

She touched the wheel on the front, making the screen flicker to life. That's when she saw the playlist. Song for song, it was the exact same as the one she'd made all those years ago. Starting with Jeff Buckley's *Hallelujah*.

Her eyes shone as she looked at him. "Should I play it?" she asked. "I've got some speakers here."

Breck nodded. A moment later she plugged it in and cued up the music. The first notes rang out of the speakers, soft and melancholy. That's when Breck touched her for the first time, taking her hands in his and pulling her flush against him. Curling the fingers of one hand around her palm and sliding the other onto her waist, he began to move her in time to the music.

Caitie closed her eyes, resting her face against his shoulder. She could feel his lips against her head, soft and gentle. Everything about him made her heart ache.

"I missed dancing with you at the wedding," he whispered, as he pulled her closer still. "I missed doing everything with you. I can't be without you anymore."

"What did you do that day?"

"I paced the bungalow, a lot. Shouted at my reflection. I even thought about going for a run. But nothing helped. It didn't mean a thing without you, Cait. Please let me in. Give me another chance. You're all I can think about."

They were moving in circles around her bedroom, their bodies tight against each other as they swayed. Everything about the moment felt perfect, from the painfully sweet song to the way he was touching her.

It was then Caitie knew. It wasn't about fear, it was about overcoming it. About laughing in the face of the things that kept her awake at night. About trusting the person her heart yearned for.

"I missed you, too," she whispered into his shirt.

Breck tipped her head up, pressing his lips to hers. His breath was soft and warm. She slid her arms around his neck, her fingers brushing against his hair. He kissed her hard, his tongue sliding against hers, his hands digging into her hips until she could feel exactly how excited she made him.

Everything in her world revolved around that kiss. As he slid his hands down further, pulling her in, her mouth dissolved into his. The sensation of him against her was making her needy. She was a moment away from dragging him onto her bed.

"Cait," he moaned, her kisses swallowing his words. "Cait, you're driving me crazy."

"The feeling's mutual."

"If you don't stop grinding against me, I'm gonna do something we'll both regret."

She laughed, releasing her hold on him. "Good point. I'll stop."

"It's the worst point ever," he said, grimacing as he adjusted himself. "It's going to be a long day."

She swallowed, though her mouth was dry. "I'll come back to your place tonight."

"You'd come to my house? *Seriously?* Even though it's so close to the beach?" He shook his head. "Let's take it easy. Maybe get a hotel room instead."

"I'm determined to beat it, you know. I'm sick of being held back by fear. If I'm moving back to California, it's time to get back to the beach."

"You don't have to do it for me," he told her. "I'll move from the water. Move out of town. I'll go anywhere that makes you comfortable."

"You'd do that?" From the expression on his face, she knew he would.

"Cait, I love you. I want to be with you. If that means moving, or giving up surfing, that's what I'll do. Hell, I'll even celebrate Christmas every day of the year if you want me to."

"Let's not go too far," she said. "One thing at a time. Plus, from what I've read, exposing myself to my triggers bit by bit is definitely the best way to overcome things. And in the meantime, I want to spend the night with you."

He grinned from ear to ear. "I guess that's settled." He glanced at his watch. "Can we leave right after dinner?"

"We'll have to help with the dishes."

"I can wash really fast."

"I bet you can."

He winked. "I'm going to spend the whole meal thinking

about what I'm going to do to you tonight. And tomorrow. And for the rest of our lives."

The song came to an end, segueing into the next one. It was like listening to the soundtrack of her fifteen-year-old life. And here she was, in the arms of the boy she'd fallen in love with all those years ago, her heart hammering in time to his.

"You were my first kiss, did you know that?" she whispered.

"What?" Breck frowned. "You've never kissed a guy before me? How did you get to twenty-eight without kissing anybody?"

She couldn't help but laugh. "I'm not talking about this year. I mean when we were kids. I'd kissed you that Christmas when I was fifteen. I crept into your room while you were asleep and held you as you cried. You never woke up, but I needed to be there with you."

He stopped dancing and looked at her, shock written all over his face. His throat bobbed as he swallowed hard. "You kissed me?"

"Yes," she whispered.

He closed his eyes for a moment. "I wish I could remember. Out of all the crap that happened that holiday, there was one beautiful moment. And I'd slept through it."

"I can remember enough for the two of us," she told him, tracing her finger along his jaw. "It was short and it was sweet, but it was beautiful. You ruined me forever, Brecken Miller, and you weren't even awake for it."

"You'll need to show me what you did when I get you home tonight. Maybe we can reenact it again and again."

She smiled softly. "Sounds like a great idea."

"Your first kiss, and your last kiss," he whispered, pressing his mouth against hers again. "There's a certain symmetry to it."

"Both on Christmas day, too."

"Your first kiss was, but your last kiss won't be. I intend on kissing you a lot, Caitie Russell. Every chance I get. Until you can't breathe, and you can't talk, and all you can do is drag me to bed."

"Sounds delicious," she said.

"Sounds perfect," he agreed.

"Sounds like we should go and wolf down some dinner before my mom hunts us down."

Breck took her hand, kissed her palm, and folded her fingers around his. "And after that, we can leave and I'll show you exactly how much I've missed you."

"I can't think of a better way to spend Christmas," she said, reluctantly pulling him into the hallway.

The smile he gave her was dazzling. "Nor can I, my darling. Nor can I."

EPILOGUE

"Are you okay?" Breck asked as he carried a taped-up box into their new apartment. Caitie was standing at the window, staring out at the view. He put the box down by the door, next to the others, and walked over to her, sliding his arms around her waist. She leaned back against him, her silken hair brushing against his jaw.

"I'm more than okay," she said, a smile in her voice. "I was thinking about how far we've come."

He followed her gaze across the rooftops of Angel Sands, past Main Street and the boardwalk, to the beach below. Though they were half a mile away from the coastline, Breck still held her close, wanting to protect her from her fears.

"You sure you're okay with this?" he asked, nodding at the window. "There are apartments without ocean views in this building. We could trade."

She shook her head. "We're not trading. And I'm good with the view." She turned her head to look at him. "It's pretty."

God, he loved every part of her. Her vulnerabilities and

her strengths, her optimism and her determination. For the past six months, while she'd been living in L.A. and he'd been here in Angel Sands, he'd watched as she battled her demons.

And won.

Now here they were, moving in together, and though this apartment was new, it felt like coming home. There was a warmth in his body that had nothing to do with the sun beating down outside, but everything to do with this woman in his arms.

She completed him. And wasn't that a crazy thing? He hadn't known there was a hole in his heart until she'd filled it. Hadn't realized what he was missing until the moment he'd laid eyes on her in the Beach Club.

And now here they were, moving in together. Blending their lives the same way they'd already blended their hearts. He dipped his head to press his lips against hers, marveling at how sweet she always tasted.

"This is the last one," Lucas called out. When he spotted them embracing by the window his voice lowered. "Guys, can you get a room? Caitie's still my sister."

"They got an apartment," Ember said, following close behind him. "And you're going to have to get over the ick. Look how in love they are." She grinned at Breck and Caitie as they pulled apart. "They make my heart melt."

Breck grinned at Caitie as he stepped away. "Beer?" he asked Lucas.

"Yeah. That would be good." Lucas followed him into the spacious kitchen, where every surface was covered with boxes. They'd already unpacked their emergency supplies – coffee, milk, sodas, and beer, along with a few glasses and mugs. Breck grabbed two beers from the refrigerator and popped the caps, passing one to Lucas.

"You doing okay?" he asked, eyeing Lucas warily. He knew

how hard this was for him. His protective streak was strong when it came to his sister, and it had taken him a while to warm up to their relationship.

Lucas took a long mouthful of beer. "I am now," he said when he'd swallowed it down. "I've been thinking about this all day."

"Thanks for helping us move. It means a lot to us both." Breck lifted his own beer to his lips and swallowed it down. "And you know I'm never going to hurt her. Not again. I promise you that."

"I know you won't," Lucas said, his voice thick. He tapped his brow with his fingers. "At least I do up here." He moved his hands down to his chest. "But in here, she's still my kid sister, you know? It's taking some time for me to accept she's all grown up."

Through the kitchen door, Breck could see Harper walking into the hallway, carrying an armful of curtains. He lifted a hand to wave at her and she grinned back. Another person who was still getting used to Breck and Caitie moving in together.

"Cait's my life," he told Lucas. "I feel as protective of her as you do. Whatever it takes to make her happy, that's what I'll do. You don't have to worry about us."

Lucas nodded and put his bottle down on the countertop. "That's good to know," he said, pressing his lips together. "Because there's somebody else I'm going to need to worry about soon."

Breck tipped his head to the side, a smile playing around his lips. "Who?"

Lucas gave a little laugh, leaning back on the counter. "I'm gonna be a dad. Another seven months and everything changes."

There was a huge squeal from the living room. A moment

later, Caitie ran into the kitchen and tackle-hugged Lucas, the biggest grin on her face, Ember and Harper following behind. "Oh my god!" she said, almost jumping with delight. "I can't believe my big brother's going to be a daddy. That's the best news ever."

Lucas turned to him with a raised brow. "You need to watch yourself, my friend. She has the hearing of an elephant. Nothing gets past my sister."

Breck lifted his bottle, his mouth splitting into a grin. "Congratulations, man," he said, and turned to Ember, kissing her on the cheek. "You guys are going to make the best parents."

Ember grinned. "Thank you."

Lucas caught his eye, and Breck realized that his friend was nervous. Afraid. And no wonder. Becoming a parent wasn't something you took lightly. It was both a blessing and a burden, Breck realized. It changed you completely from the inside out. It pushed you down the priority list, below the partner you loved and the child you made together.

Weird how he couldn't wait for that to happen for him and Caitie.

"We should open that champagne," Caitie said, sliding her arm around Breck's waist. "There's so much to celebrate."

There really was. And as she leaned into him, her eyes soft, her smile softer, he knew that everything he'd ever wanted was right here. His heart felt full with the knowledge of it. He didn't care about Christmas, didn't care about the ocean, they were just hills they had to climb. And now that they'd reached the peak – together – it was time to breathe and enjoy what they had.

And the view from here was beautiful.

---

"Are you sure these are okay?" Harper asked, as she hooked the final curtain to the rail. She'd made every single one of them by hand – buying the fabric from a market in L.A., matching them to Caitie's décor plans, measuring up each window to ensure the perfect fit. Though Caitie had tried to pay her friend for them, Harper had refused, reminding her they were a moving in gift.

"They're wonderful," Caitie said, hugging her friend. "Thank you so much. They make the room look so much better than those blinds. I can't believe how talented you are." She bit her lip. "I'm going to miss you."

Harper's eyes filled with tears, making Caitie's heart ache. One of the reasons it had taken her six months to move in with Breck was the thought of leaving her best friend and roommate in L.A. They'd lived together since college, longer than some marriages lasted.

"Not as much as I'm going to miss you," Harper said, her voice wobbling. She wiped the back of her hand across her cheek, ridding herself of her tears. "And I'm so happy for you. You deserve this, all of it. The guy, the apartment, the future together."

"I'll be coming to L.A. all the time for work," Caitie said quickly. "We can meet up whenever I do, if you can spare the time."

"Of course I can spare the time, dummy." Harper made a silly face. "I've always got time for you."

"Come with me, I have something to show you," Caitie said, taking her friend's hand, and leading her into the hallway. On the other side from Caitie's bedroom was a doorway. She pushed it open, and light flooded out.

There was a bed and a desk in there, along with a huge box. Caitie knelt down and opened it, beckoning Harper over. "This is for you," she said, her voice full of emotion.

"What is it?" Harper asked, a confused smile on her face. She knelt next to Caitie and stared into the box. "A sewing machine?" she asked, turning her face to look at Caitie. "Is that for me?"

Caitie nodded. "It's like a reverse moving in gift from Breck and me. We thought that whenever you get tired of L.A. you can come here and design things. Take a break from the big city and soak up the ocean air. Let it refill your creative tank." She smiled at Harper's wide eyes. "This is your room. Come and visit whenever you like."

"Won't Breck mind?" Harper asked, biting her lip.

"It was his idea." Caitie grinned. "He loves you almost as much as I do. You're like his sister." She lowered her voice. "And I know that because I heard him telling Jack that you're off limits. It's the bro code." Caitie rolled her eyes so hard it hurt.

Harper laughed. "Look where that stupid code got him." She reached into the box and ran the tip of her finger along the sewing machine, her eyes still shiny with tears. "This is beautiful," she said softly. "Thank you."

"I meant it. There's no way I can go long without seeing you, not after all these years. So if you don't come here, I'll be hunting you down in L.A. and dragging you back for some well earned rest."

"That doesn't sound like a hardship," Harper confessed. "I love this place. The town, the people, the lifestyle." She sighed. "I can see why you've decided to come back."

Caitie looked around the room and sighed. It was strange, coming home after so long. Especially to a town she'd hated spending time in. But she saw it differently now, thanks to Breck and her therapist. This town was never the problem, it was *her*. Her fears, her avoidance, her unwillingness to show her vulnerabilities. It had taken an act of will to finally face them. To let herself be pulled apart, so she could rebuild all over again.

"I think I might have fallen for it, too," she told Harper.

Her friend grinned. "I think it's a certain Angel Sands guy you've fallen for. And I can see why." She took Caitie's hand in her own. "Are you happy?"

"Yes, I am," Caitie said, her chest tight with emotion. "So happy. I almost can't believe it's real." And as she smiled, she could feel the truth of her words. Once she'd wondered if it was possible to have it all.

Now she knew it was.

<hr />

It was evening by the time everybody left the apartment, and Caitie and Breck were alone in their new home. She was sliding the last plate into the dishwasher when Breck walked into the kitchen, grabbed her by the waist, and spun her around.

He kissed her hard, one hand splayed against the small of her back, the other cupping the back of her head to angle her face to his. His lips were warm, demanding, sending pulses of electricity through her veins.

"I can't believe we can do this every day," he said, his voice thick when they breathlessly pulled apart. "No more Skyping, no more calling just to hear your voice. I get to wake up to you every morning."

"You'll be sick of me within a week," Caitie said, grinning.

His expression was serious. "I will never get sick of you, Caitlin Russell."

The way he was staring made her skin heat up with desire. "I can never get enough of you, either," she told him, a shiver snaking down her spine.

"Let's go to bed." He took her hand, folding it in his own. "The cleaning up can wait."

An hour later, after he'd loved her warm and hard the way she liked, Breck took her in his arms, spooning her so her body fit against his. She closed her eyes and breathed him in, thinking about all those nights when she'd fallen asleep to his voice on her phone and longed for his touch.

"Harper liked her gift," she said sleepily, as he pressed his lips to her cheek. "It was so lovely of you to think of it."

"I'm glad she did." He kissed her again. "And I meant what I said, she's always welcome. She's part of you, and I love her for it. Plus she took care of you when I couldn't."

"It's been a good day," Caitie said with a smile, her eyes drifting closed. "Can you believe I'm going to be an auntie?"

She felt him smile against her skin. "You'll be an amazing auntie," he told her, running his lips down the side of her neck. "The same way you'll be a fantastic mother one day."

Caitie couldn't help but grin. They'd talked about children – Breck wanted four, she wanted two and the occasional chance at sleep – and they'd agreed that sometime in the next couple of years they'd try. Once she'd recruited enough consultants that the business could live with her taking a step back, and when Breck had built up the team he needed to make Miller Construction a success on the West Coast.

She loved that they were in agreement about everything. Their friends, their family, their future together. After all the heartache she'd been through, being with Breck felt like the final piece of the jigsaw, slotting in so easily, making everything complete.

"I love you," she said, her voice heavy with sleep. It had been a long day, and her body was ready to give up for the night.

"Not as much as I love you," he told her, pulling her

tightly against him. Her spine curved into his chest and stomach, their legs tangling together.

Her eyes fluttered closed. As she drifted off there was a smile curling her lips. Because she knew, even in slumber, that in the morning she'd wake up in his arms, where she'd always belonged.

He was her safe haven and she was his. Together, they finally had it all.

# DEAR READER

Thank you so much for reading Breck and Caitie's story. If you enjoyed it and you get a chance, I'd be so grateful if you can leave a review. And don't forget to keep an eye out for **BABY I'M YOURS**, the fifth book in the series, releasing on Feb 12, 2020.

To learn more, you can sign up for my newsletter here: http://www.subscribepage.com/e4u8i8

I can't wait to share more stories with you.

Yours,

Carrie xx

# ABOUT THE AUTHOR

Carrie Elks writes contemporary romance with a sizzling edge. Her first book, *Fix You*, has been translated into eight languages and made a surprise appearance on *Big Brother* in Brazil. Luckily for her, it wasn't voted out.

Carrie lives with her husband, two lovely children and a larger-than-life black pug called Plato. When she isn't writing or reading, she can be found baking, drinking an occasional (!) glass of wine, or chatting on social media.

*You can find Carrie in all these places*
www.carrieelks.com
carrie.elks@mail.com

## ALSO BY CARRIE ELKS

### STANDALONE

Fix You

### ANGEL SANDS SERIES

Let Me Burn

She's Like the Wind

Sweet Little Lies

Just A Kiss

Baby I'm Yours

### THE SHAKESPEARE SISTERS SERIES

Summer's Lease (The Shakespeare Sisters #1)

A Winter's Tale (The Shakespeare Sisters #2)

Absent in the Spring (The Shakespeare Sisters #3)

By Virtue Fall (The Shakespeare Sisters #4)

### THE LOVE IN LONDON SERIES

Coming Down (Love in London #1)

Broken Chords (Love in London #2)

Canada Square (Love in London #3)

**If you'd like to get an email when I release a new book, please sign up here:**

**CARRIE ELKS' NEWSLETTER**

CPSIA information can be obtained
at www.ICGtesting.com
Printed in the USA
FSHW022058191119
64307FS